Elsie Dinsmore

The Original Elsie Classics

Elsie Dinsmore

Elsie's Holidays at Roselands

Elsie's Girlhood

Elsie's Womanhood

Elsie's Motherhood

Elsie's Children

Elsie's Widowhood

Grandmother Elsie

Elsie's New Relations

Elsie at Nantucket

The Two Elsies

Elsie's Kith and Kin

Elsie's Friends at Woodburn

Christmas with Grandma Elsie

Elsie and the Raymonds

Elsie Yachting with the Raymonds

Elsie's Vacation

Elsie at Viamede

Elsie at Ion

Elsie at the World's Fair

Elsie's Journey on Inland Waters

Elsie at Home

Elsie on the Hudson

Elsie in the South

Elsie's Young Folks

Elsie's Winter Trip

Elsie and Her Loved Ones

Elsie and Her Namesakes

Elsie Dinsmore

Book One of
The Original Elsie Classics

Martha Finley

Elsie Dinsmore
by Martha Finley

Any unique characteristics of this edition:
Copyright © 2000 by Cumberland House Publishing, Inc.

PUBLISHED BY
CUMBERLAND HOUSE PUBLISHING, INC.
431 Harding Industrial Drive
Nashville, Tennessee 37211

Cover design by Gore Studio, Inc.
Photography by Dean Dixon Photography
Hair and Makeup by Calene Radar
Text design by Heather Armstrong

Printed in Canada
4 5 6 7 8 9 10 — 07 06 05 04 03

Hope's precious pearl, in sorrow's cup,
Unmelted at the bottom lay,
To shine again, when, all drunk up,
The bitterness should pass away.

—Moore's Loves of the Angels

CHAPTER FIRST

I never saw an eye so bright,
And yet so soft as hers;
It sometimes swam in liquid light,
And sometimes swam in tears;
It seemed a beauty set apart
For softness and for sighs.

—*Mrs. Welby*

THE SCHOOLROOM AT ROSELANDS was a very pleasant apartment. The ceiling, it is true, was somewhat lower than in the more modern portion of the building. The wing in which it was situated dated back to the old-fashioned days prior to the Revolution, while the larger part of the mansion had not stood more than twenty or thirty years. The effect was relieved by windows reaching from floor to ceiling and opening on a veranda which overlooked a lovely flower-garden, beyond which were fields and woods and hills. The view from the veranda was very beautiful, and the room itself looked most inviting with its neat matting, its windows draped with snow-white muslin, its comfortable chairs, and pretty rosewood desks.

Within this pleasant apartment sat Miss Day with her pupils, six in number. She was giving a lesson to Enna, the youngest, the spoiled darling of the family, the favorite of both father and mother.

It was always a trying task to both teacher and scholar, for Enna was very willful, and her teacher's patience by no means inexhaustible.

"There!" exclaimed Miss Day, shutting the book and giving it an impatient toss on to the desk. "Go, for I might as well try to teach old Bruno. I presume he would learn about as fast."

And Enna walked away with a pout on her pretty face, muttering that she would "tell mamma."

"Young ladies and gentlemen," said Miss Day, looking at her watch, "I shall leave you to your studies for an hour, at the end of which time I shall return to hear your recitations. Those who have attended properly to their duties will be permitted to ride out with me to visit the fair."

"Oh, that will be jolly!" exclaimed Arthur, a bright-eyed, mischief-loving boy of ten.

"Hush!" said Miss Day sternly. "Let me hear no more such exclamations, and remember that you will not go unless your lessons are thoroughly learned. Louise and Lora," addressing two young girls of the respective ages of twelve and fourteen, "that French exercise must be perfect, and your English lessons as well." To a little girl of eight, sitting alone at a desk near one of the windows, and bending over a slate with an appearance of great industry, she said, "Elsie, every figure of that example must be correct, your geography lesson recited perfectly, and a page in your copybook written without a blot."

"Yes, ma'am," said the child meekly, raising a pair of large soft eyes of the darkest hazel for an instant to her teacher's face, and then dropping them again upon her slate.

"And see that none of you leave the room until I return," continued the governess. "Walter, if you miss one word of that spelling, you will have to stay at home and learn it over."

"Unless mamma interferes, as she will be pretty sure to do," muttered Arthur, as the door closed on Miss Day, and her retreating footsteps were heard passing down the hall.

For about ten minutes after her departure, all was quiet in the schoolroom, each seemingly completely absorbed in study. But at the end of that time Arthur sprang up, and, flinging his book across the room, exclaimed, "There! I know my lesson, and if I didn't, I shouldn't study another bit for old Day, nor Night either."

"Do be quiet, Arthur," said his sister Louise. "I can't study in such a racket."

Arthur stole on tiptoe across the room, and coming up behind Elsie, tickled the back of her neck with a feather.

She started, saying in a pleading tone, "Please, Arthur, don't."

"It pleases me to do so," he said, repeating the experiment.

Elsie changed her position, saying in the same gentle, persuasive tone, "Oh, Arthur! Please let me alone, or I never shall be able to do this example."

"What! All this time on one example! You ought to be ashamed. Why, I could have done it half a dozen times over."

"I have been over and over it," replied the little girl in a tone of despondency, "and still there are two figures that will not come out right."

"How do you know they are not right, little puss?" shaking her curls as he spoke.

"Oh, please, Arthur, don't pull my hair! I have the answer—that's the way, I know."

"Well, then, why don't you just set the figures down. I would."

"Oh, no, indeed! That would not be honest."

"Pooh! Nonsense! Nobody would be the wiser, nor the poorer."

"No, but it would be just like telling a lie. But I can never get it right while you are bothering me so," said Elsie, laying aside her slate in despair. Then taking out her geography, she began studying most diligently. But Arthur continued his persecutions—tickling her, pulling her hair, twitching the book out of her hand, and talking almost incessantly, making remarks, and asking questions, till at last Elsie said, as if just ready to cry, "Indeed, Arthur, if you don't let me alone, I shall never be able to get my lessons."

"Go away then. Take your book out on the veranda, and learn your lessons there," said Louise. "I'll call when Miss Day comes."

"Oh, no, Louise! I cannot do that, because it would be disobedience," replied Elsie, taking out her writing materials.

Arthur stood over her criticizing every letter she made, and finally jogged her elbow in such a way as to cause her to drop all the ink in her pen upon the paper, making quite a large blot.

"Oh!" cried the little girl, bursting into tears. "Now I shall lose my ride, for Miss Day will not let me go, and I was so anxious to see all those beautiful flowers."

Arthur, who was really not very vicious, felt some compunctions when he saw the mischief he had done. "Never mind, Elsie," said he, "I can fix it yet. Just let me tear out this page, and you can begin again on the next, and I'll not bother you. I'll make these two figures come out right too," he added, taking up her slate.

"Thank you, Arthur," said the little girl, smiling through her tears. "You are very kind, but it would not be honest to do either, and I would rather stay at home than be deceitful."

"Very well, miss," said he, tossing his head, and walking away, "since you won't let me help you, it is all your own fault if you have to stay home."

"Elsie," exclaimed Louise, "I have no patience with you! Such ridiculous scruples as you are always raising. I shall not pity you one bit, if you are obliged to stay at home."

Elsie made no reply, but, brushing away a tear, bent over her writing, taking great pains with every letter, though saying sadly to herself all the time, "It's no use, for that great ugly blot will spoil it all."

She finished her page, and, excepting the unfortunate blot, it all looked very neat indeed, showing plainly that it had been written with great care. She then took up her slate and patiently went over and over every figure of the troublesome example, trying to discover where her mistake had been. But much time had been lost through Arthur's teasing, and her mind was so disturbed by the accident to her writing that she tried in vain to fix it upon the business at hand. Before the two troublesome figures had been made right, the hour was past and Miss Day returned.

"Oh," thought Elsie, "if she will only hear the others first, I may be able to get this and the geography ready yet; and perhaps, if Arthur will be generous enough to tell her about the blot, she may excuse me for it."

But it was a vain hope. Miss Day had no sooner seated herself at her desk, than she called, "Elsie, come here and say that lesson, and bring your copybook and slate, that I may examine your work."

Elsie tremblingly obeyed.

The lesson, though a difficult one, was very tolerably recited, for Elsie, knowing Arthur's propensity for teasing, had studied it in her own room before school hours. But Miss Day handed back the book with a frown, saying, "I told you the recitation must be perfect, and it was not."

She was always more severe with Elsie than with any other of her pupils.

"There are two incorrect figures in this example," said she, laying down the slate, after glancing over its contents. Then taking up the copybook, she exclaimed, "Careless, disobedient child! Did I not caution you to be careful not to blot your book! There will be no ride for you this morning. You have failed in everything. Go to your seat. Make that example right, and do the next. Learn your geography lesson over, and write another page in your copybook—and mind, if there is a blot on it, you will get no dinner."

Weeping and sobbing, Elsie took up her books and obeyed.

During this scene Arthur stood at his desk pretending to study, but glancing every now and then at Elsie, with a conscience evidently ill at ease. She cast an imploring glance at him, as she returned to her seat, but he turned away his head, muttering,

"It's all her own fault, for she wouldn't let me help her."

As he looked up again, he caught his sister Lora's eyes fixed on him with an expression of scorn and contempt. He colored violently, and dropped his gaze upon his book.

"Miss Day," said Lora indignantly, "I see Arthur does not mean to speak, and as I cannot bear to see such injustice, I must tell you that it is all his fault that Elsie has failed in her lessons. She tried her best, but he teased her incessantly, and also jogged her elbow and made her spill the ink on her book. To her credit she was too honorable to tear out the leaf from her copy book, or to let him make her example right—both of which he very generously proposed doing after causing all the mischief."

"Is this so, Arthur?" asked Miss Day angrily.

The boy hung his head, but made no reply.

"Very well, then," said Miss Day, "you too must stay at home."

"Surely," said Lora, in surprise, "you will not keep Elsie, since I have shown you that she was not to blame."

"Miss Lora," replied her teacher, haughtily, "I wish you to understand that I am not to be dictated to by my pupils."

Lora bit her lip, but said nothing, and Miss Day went on hearing the lessons without further remark.

In the meantime, little Elsie sat at her desk, striving to conquer the feelings of anger and indignation that were swelling in her heart. Elsie, though she possessed much of "the ornament of a meek and quiet spirit," was not yet perfect, and often had a fierce contest with her naturally quick temper.

Yet it was seldom, very seldom, that word or tone or look betrayed the existence of such feelings, and it was a common remark in the family that Elsie had no spirit.

The recitations were scarcely finished when the door opened and a lady entered dressed for a ride.

"Not through yet, Miss Day?" she asked.

"Yes, madam, we are just done," replied the teacher, closing the French grammar and handing it to Louise.

"Well, I hope your pupils have all done their duty this morning, and are ready to accompany us to the fair," said Mrs. Dinsmore. "But what is the matter with Elsie?"

"She has failed in all her exercises, and therefore has been told that she must remain at home," replied Miss Day with heightened color and in a tone of anger. "As Miss Lora tells me that Master Arthur was partly the cause, I have forbidden him also to accompany us."

"Excuse me, Miss Day, for correcting you," said Lora, a little indignantly, "but I did not say partly for I am sure that it was entirely his fault."

"Hush, hush, Lora," said her mother, a little impatiently. "How can you be sure of any such thing? Miss Day, I must beg of you to excuse Arthur this once, for I have quite set my heart on taking him along. He is fond of mischief, I know, but he is only a child, and you must not be too hard upon him."

"Very well, madam," replied the governess stiffly. "You have, of course, the best right to control your own children."

Mrs. Dinsmore turned to leave the room.

"Mamma," asked Lora, "is not Elsie to be allowed to go too?"

"Elsie is not my child, and I have nothing to say about it. Miss Day, who knows all the circumstances, is much better able than I to judge whether or not she is deserving of punishment," replied Mrs. Dinsmore, sailing out of the room.

"You will let her go, Miss Day?" said Lora, inquiringly.

"Miss Lora," replied Miss Day, angrily, "I have already told you I was not to be dictated to. I have said Elsie must remain at home, and I shall not break my word."

"Such injustice!" muttered Lora, turning away.

"Lora," said Louise, impatiently, "why need you concern yourself with Elsie's affairs? For my part, I have no pity for her, so full as she is of nonsensical scruples."

Miss Day crossed the room to where Elsie was sitting leaning her head upon the desk, struggling hard to keep down the feelings of anger and indignation aroused by the unjust treatment she had received.

"Did I not order you to learn that lesson over?" said the governess. "And why are you sitting here idling?"

Elsie dared not speak lest her anger should show itself in words, so she merely raised her head, and hastily brushing away her tears, opened the book. But Miss Day, who was irritated by Mrs. Dinsmore's interference, and also by the consciousness that she was acting unjustly, seemed determined to vent her displeasure upon her innocent victim.

"Why do you not speak?" she exclaimed, seizing Elsie by the arm and shaking her violently. "Answer me this instant. Why have you been idling all the morning?"

"I have not," replied the child hastily, stung to the quick by her unjust violence. "I have tried hard to do my duty, and you are punishing me when I don't deserve it at all."

"How dare you? There! Take that for your impertinence," said Miss Day, giving her a box on the ear.

Elsie was about to make a still more angry reply, but she restrained herself, and turning to her book, tried to study, though the hot, blinding tears came so thick and fast that she could not see a letter.

"De carriage am waiting, ladies, an' missus in a hurry," said a servant, opening the door, and Miss Day hastily left the room, followed by Louise, Lora, and the others, and Elsie was left alone.

She laid down the geography, and opening her desk, she took out a small pocket Bible, which bore the marks of frequent use. She turned over the leaves as though seeking for some particular passage. At length she found it, and wiping away the blinding tears, she read these words in a low, murmuring tone:

"For this is thankworthy, if a man for conscience toward God endure grief, suffering wrongfully. For what glory is it if, when ye be buffeted for your faults, ye shall take it patiently? But if when ye do well, and suffer for it, ye take it patiently, this is acceptable with God. For even hereunto were ye called; because Christ also suffered for us, leaving us an example that ye should follow His steps."

"Oh! I have not done it. I did not take it patiently. I am afraid I am not following in His steps," she cried, bursting into an agony of tears and sobs.

"My dear little girl, what is the matter?" asked a kind voice, and a soft hand was gently laid on her shoulder.

The child looked up hastily. "Oh, Miss Allison!" she said. "Is it you? I thought I was quite alone."

"And so you were, my dear, until this moment," replied the lady, drawing up a chair, and sitting down close beside her. "I was on the veranda, and hearing sobs, came in to see if I could be of any assistance. You look very much distressed. Will you not tell me the cause of your sorrow?"

Elsie answered only by a fresh burst of tears.

"They have all gone to the fair and left you at home alone—perhaps to learn a lesson you have failed in reciting?" said the lady, inquiringly.

"Yes, ma'am," said the child, "but that is not the worst." And her tears fell faster, as she laid the little Bible on the desk, and pointed with her finger to the words she had been reading. "Oh!" she sobbed. "I—I did not do it. I did not bear it patiently. I was treated unjustly, and punished when I was not to blame, and I grew angry. Oh, I'm afraid I shall never be like Jesus! Never, never."

The child's distress seemed very great, and Miss Allison was extremely surprised. She was a visitor who had been in the house only a few days, and, herself a devoted Christian, had been greatly pained by the utter disregard of the family in which she was sojourning for the teachings of God's word. Rose Allison was from the North, and Mr. Dinsmore, the proprietor of Roselands, was an old friend of her father, to whom he had been paying a visit. Finding Rose in delicate health, he had prevailed upon her parents to allow her to spend the winter months with his family in the more congenial clime of their Southern home.

"My poor child," she said, passing her arm around the little one's waist, "my poor little Elsie! That is your name, is it not?

"Yes ma'am. Elsie Dinsmore," replied the little girl.

"Well, Elsie, let me read you another verse from this blessed Book. Here it is: 'The blood of Jesus Christ, His Son, cleanseth us from all sin.' And here again: 'If any man sin, we have an advocate with the Father, Jesus Christ the righteous.' Dear Elsie, if we confess our sins, He is faithful and just to forgive us our sins."

"Yes, ma'am," said the child. "I have asked Him to forgive me, and I know He has, but I am so sorry, oh, so sorry that I have grieved and displeased Him. For, oh Miss Allison, I do love Jesus, and want to be like Him always!"

"Yes, dear child, we must grieve for our sins when we remember that they helped to slay the Lord. But I am very, very glad to learn that you love Jesus, and are striving to do His will. I love Him, too, and we will love one another, for you know He says, 'By this shall all men know that ye are my disciples, if ye have love one to another,'" said Miss Allison, stroking the little girl's hair, and kissing her tenderly.

"Will you love me? Oh, how glad I am!" exclaimed the child joyfully. "I have nobody to love me but my poor old mammy."

"And who is mammy?" asked the lady.

"My dear old nurse, who has always taken care of me. Have you not seen her, ma'am?"

"Perhaps I may. I have seen a number of nice old colored women about here since I came. But, Elsie, will you tell me who taught you about Jesus, and how long you have loved Him?"

"Ever since I can remember," replied the little girl earnestly, "and it was dear old mammy who first told me how He suffered and died on the cross for us." Her eyes filled with tears and her voice quivered with emotion. "She used to talk to me about it just as soon as I could understand anything," she continued. "And then she would tell me that my own dear mamma loved Jesus, and had gone to be with Him in heaven. She would tell how, when she was dying, she put me—a little, wee baby, I was then not quite a week old—into her arms, and said, 'Mammy, take my dear little baby and love her, and take care of her just as you did of me. And, oh, mammy, be sure that you teach her to love God!' Would you like to see my mamma, Miss Allison?"

As she spoke she drew from her bosom a miniature set in gold and diamonds, which she wore suspended by a gold chain around her neck, and put it in Rose's hand.

It was the likeness of a young and blooming girl, not more than fifteen or sixteen years of age. She was very beautiful, with a sweet, gentle, winning countenance, the same soft hazel eyes and golden brown curls that the little Elsie possessed, the same regular features, pure complexion, and sweet smile.

Miss Allison gazed at it a moment in silent admiration. Then turning from it to the child with a puzzled expression, she said, "But Elsie, I do not understand. You are not sister to Enna and the rest, and is not Mrs. Dinsmore mother to them all?"

"Yes, ma'am, to all of them, but not to me nor my papa. Their brother Horace is my papa, and so they are all my aunts and uncles."

"Indeed," said the lady, musingly. "I thought you looked very unlike the rest. And your papa is away, is he not, Elsie?"

"Yes, ma'am. He is in Europe. He has been away almost ever since I was born, and I have never seen him. Oh, how I do wish he would come home! How I long to see him! Do you think he would love me, Miss Allison? Do you think he would take me on his knee and hug me, as grandpa does Enna?"

"I should think he would, dear. I don't know how he could help but love his own dear little girl," said the lady, again kissing the rosy little cheek. "But now," she added, rising, "I must go away and let you learn your lesson."

Then taking up the little Bible, and turning over the leaves, she asked, "Would you like to come to my room sometimes in the mornings and evenings, and read this Book with me, Elsie?"

"Oh, yes, ma'am, dearly!" exclaimed the child, her eyes sparkling with pleasure.

"Come then this evening, if you like. And now goodbye for the present." And pressing another kiss on the child's cheek, she left her and went back to her room, where she found her friend Adelaide Dinsmore, a young lady near her own age, and the eldest daughter of the family. Adelaide was seated on a sofa, busily employed with some fancywork.

"You see I am making myself quite at home," she said, looking up as Rose entered. "I cannot imagine where you have been all this time."

"Can you not? In the schoolroom, talking with little Elsie. Do you know, Adelaide, I thought she was your sister, but she tells me not."

"No, she is Horace's child. I supposed you knew, but if you do not, I may just as well tell you the whole story. Horace was a wild boy, pampered and spoiled, and always used to having his own way, and when he was about seventeen—quite a forward youth he was too—he insisted upon going to New Orleans to spend some months with a schoolmate. And there he met, and fell desperately in love with, a very beautiful girl a year or two younger than himself, an orphan and very wealthy. Fearing that objections would be made on the score of their youth, he persuaded her to consent to a private marriage, and they had been man and wife for some months before her friends or his suspected it.

"Well, when it came at last to papa's ears, he was very angry, both on account of their extreme youth, and because, as Elsie Grayson's father had made all his money by trade, he did not consider her quite my brother's equal. So he called Horace home and sent him North to college. Then he studied law, and since that he has been traveling in foreign lands. To return to his wife: it seems that her guardian was quite as much opposed to the match as papa, and the poor girl was made to believe that she should never see her husband again. All their letters were intercepted, and finally she was told that he was dead. So, as Aunt Chloe says, 'she grew thin and pale, and weak and melancholy,' and when the little Elsie was not yet quite a week old, she died. We never saw her. She died in her guardian's house. There the little Elsie stayed in charge of Aunt Chloe, who was an old servant of the family and had nursed her mother before her. There was also a housekeeper, Mrs. Murray, a pious old Scotch woman, until about four years ago, when her guardian's death broke up her family. Then they came to us. Horace never comes home, and does not seem to care for his child, for he never mentions her in his letters, except when it is necessary in the way of business."

"She is a dear little thing," said Rose. "I am sure he could not help loving her, if he could only see her."

"Oh, yes! She is well enough, and I often feel sorry for the lonely little thing, but the truth is, I believe we are a little jealous of her—she is so extremely beautiful, and heiress to such an immense fortune. Mamma often frets, and says that one of these days she will quite eclipse her younger daughters."

"But then," said Rose, "she is almost as near—her own granddaughter."

"No, she is not so very near," replied Adelaide, "for Horace is not mamma's son. He was seven or eight years old when she married papa, and I think she was never particularly fond of him."

"Ah, yes," thought Rose, "that explains it. Poor little Elsie! No wonder you pine for your father's love, and grieve over the loss of the mother you never knew."

"She is an odd child," said Adelaide. "I don't understand her. She is so meek and patient she will fairly let you trample upon her. It provokes papa.

He says she is no Dinsmore, or she would know how to stand up for her own rights. And yet she has a temper. I know, for once in a great while it shows itself for an instant—only an instant though, and at very long intervals. And then she grieves over it for days, as though she had committed some great crime, while the rest of us think nothing of getting angry half a dozen times in a day. And then she is forever poring over that little Bible of hers. What she sees so attractive in it I'm sure I cannot tell, for I must say I find it the dullest of books."

"Do you?" said Rose. "How strange! I had rather give up all other books than that one. 'Thy testimonies have I taken as a heritage forever, for they are the rejoicing of my heart.' 'How sweet are Thy words unto my taste! Yea, sweeter than honey to my mouth!'"

"Do you really love it so, Rose?" asked Adelaide, lifting her eyes to her friend's face with an expression of astonishment. "Do tell me why?"

"For its exceeding great and precious promises, Adelaide; for its holy teachings; for its offers of peace and pardon and eternal life. I am a sinner, Adelaide—lost, ruined, helpless, hopeless—and the Bible brings me the glad news of salvation offered as a free, unmerited gift. It tells me that Jesus died to save sinners—just such sinners as I. I find that I have a heart deceitful above all things and desperately wicked. And the blessed Bible tells me how that heart can be renewed, and where I can obtain that holiness without which no man shall see the Lord. I find myself utterly unable to keep God's holy law, and it tells me of One who has kept it for me. I find that I deserve the wrath and curse of a justly offended God, and it tells me of Him who was made a curse for me. I find that all my righteousnesses are as filthy rags, and it offers me the beautiful, spotless robe of Christ's perfect righteousness. Yes, it tells me that God can be just, and the justifier of him who believes in Jesus."

Rose spoke these words with deep emotion, then suddenly clasping her hands and raising her eyes, she exclaimed, "'Thanks be unto God for His unspeakable gift!'"

For a moment there was silence. Then Adelaide spoke:

"Rose," said she, "you talk as if you were a great sinner, but I don't believe it. It is only your humility that makes you think so. Why, what have you ever done? Had you been a thief, a murderer, or guilty of any other great crime, I could see the propriety of your using such language with regard to yourself. But for a refined, intelligent, amiable young lady — excuse me for saying it, dear Rose, but such language seems to me simply absurd."

"'Man looketh upon the outward appearance, but the Lord pondereth the heart,'" said Rose, gently. "No, dear Adelaide, you are mistaken, for I can truly say mine iniquities have gone over my head as a cloud, and my transgressions as a thick cloud. Every duty has been stained with sin, every motive impure, every thought unholy. From my earliest existence, God has required the undivided love of my whole heart, soul, strength, and mind, and so far from yielding it, I lived at enmity with Him, and rebellion against His government, until within the last two years. For seventeen years he has showered blessings upon me, giving me life, health, strength, friends, and all that was necessary for my happiness, and for fifteen of those years I returned

Him nothing but ingratitude and rebellion. For fifteen years I rejected His offers of pardon and reconciliation, turned my back upon the Saviour of sinners, and resisted all the strivings of God's Holy Spirit—and will you say I am not a great sinner?" Her voice quivered, and her eyes were full of tears.

"Dear Rose," said Adelaide, putting her arm around her friend and kissing her cheek affectionately, "don't think of these things. Religion is too gloomy for one so young as you."

"Gloomy, dear Adelaide!" replied Rose, returning the embrace. "I never knew what true happiness was until I found Jesus. My sins often make me sad, but religion, never.

> *Oft I walk beneath the cloud,*
> *Dark as midnight's gloomy shroud*
> *But when fear is at the height,*
> *Jesus comes, and all is light.*"

CHAPTER SECOND

Thy injuries would teach patience to blaspheme,
Yet thou art a dove.

—Beaumont's Double Marriage

When forced to part from those we love,
Though sure to meet to-morrow;
We yet a kind of anguish prove
And feel a touch of sorrow.
But oh! what words can paint the fears
When from these friends we sever,
Perhaps to part for months — for years
Perhaps to part forever.

—Anon

WHEN MISS ALLISON HAD GONE, Elsie found herself once more quite alone. She rose from her chair, and kneeling down with the open Bible before her, she poured out her story of sins and sorrows, in simple, child-like words, into the ear of the dear Saviour whom she loved so well. She confessed that when she had done well and suffered for it, she had not taken it patiently, and earnestly pleaded that she might be made like unto the meek and lowly Jesus. Low sobs burst from her burdened heart, and the tears of penitence fell upon the pages of the Holy Book. But when she rose from her knees, her load of sin and sorrow was all gone, and her heart made light and happy with a sweet sense of peace and pardon. Once again, as often before, the little Elsie was made to experience the blessedness of "the man whose transgression is forgiven, whose sin is covered."

She now set to work diligently at her studies, and ere the party returned was quite prepared to meet Miss Day, having attended faithfully to all she had required of her. The lesson was recited without the smallest mistake, every figure of the examples worked out correctly, and the page of the copybook neatly and carefully written.

Miss Day had been in a very captious mood all day, and seemed really provoked that Elsie had not given her the smallest excuse for faultfinding. Handing the book back to her, she said, very coldly, "I see you can do your duties well enough when you choose."

Elsie felt keenly the injustice of the remark, and longed to say that she had tried quite earnestly in the morning. But she resolutely crushed down the indignant feeling, and calling to mind the rash words that had cost her so many repentant tears, she replied meekly, "I am sorry I did not succeed better this morning, Miss Day, though I did really try. And I am still more sorry for the saucy answer I gave you, and I ask your pardon for it."

"You ought to be sorry," replied Miss Day, severely, "and I hope you are, for it was a very impertinent speech indeed, and deserving of a much more severe punishment than you received. Now go, and never let me hear anything of the kind from you again."

Poor little Elsie's eyes filled with tears at those ungracious words accompanied by a still more ungracious manner, but she turned away without a word, and placing her books and slate carefully in her desk, left the room.

Rose Allison was sitting alone in her room that evening, thinking of her far-distant home, when hearing a gentle rap at her door, she rose and opened it to find Elsie standing there with her little Bible in her hand.

"Come in, darling," she said, stopping to give the little one a kiss. "I am very glad to see you."

"I may stay with you for half an hour, Miss Allison, if you like," said the child, seating herself on the low ottoman pointed out by Rose, "and then mammy is coming to put me to bed."

They read a chapter together—Rose now and then pausing to make a few explanations—and then kneeling down, she offered up a prayer for the teachings of the Spirit, and for God's blessing on themselves and all their dear ones.

"Dear little Elsie," she said, folding the child in her arms, when they had risen from their knees, "how I love you already, and how very glad I am to find that there is one in this house beside myself who loves Jesus, and loves to study His word, and to call upon His name."

"Yes, dear Miss Allison, and there is more than one, for mammy loves Him, too, very dearly," replied the little girl earnestly.

"Does she, darling? Then I must love her, too, for I cannot help loving all who love my Saviour."

Then Rose sat down, and drawing the little girl to a seat on her knee, they talked sweetly together of the race they were running, and the prize they hoped to obtain at the end of it. They talked of the battle they were fighting, and the invisible foes with whom they were called to struggle — the armor that had been provided, and of Him who had promised to be the Captain of their salvation, and to bring them off more than conquerors. They were pilgrims in the same straight and narrow way, and it was very pleasant thus to walk together. "Then they that feared the Lord spake often one to another; and the Lord hearkened and heard it; and a book of remembrance was written before Him for them that feared the Lord, and that thought upon His name. And they shall be mine, saith the Lord of hosts, in that day when I make up my jewels; and I will spare them, as a man spareth his own son that serveth him."

"That is mammy coming for me," said Elsie, as a low knock was heard at the door.

"Come in," said Rose, and the door opened, and a very nice colored woman of middle age, looking beautifully neat in her snow-white apron and turban, entered with a low curtsy, asking, "Is my little missus ready for bed now?"

"Yes," said Elsie, jumping off Rose's lap. "But come here, mammy. I want to introduce you to Miss Allison."

"How do you do, Aunt Chloe? I am very glad to know you, since Elsie tells me you are a servant of the same blessed Master whom I love and try to serve," said Rose, putting her small white hand cordially into Chloe's dusky one.

"'Deed I hope I is, missus," replied Chloe, pressing it fervently in both of hers. "I'se only a poor ole black sinner, but de good Lord Jesus,

He loves me jes de same as if I was white, an' I love Him an' all His chillen with all my heart."

"Yes, Aunt Chloe," said Rose. "He is our peace, and hath made both one, and hath broken down the middle wall of partition between us, so that we are no more strangers and foreigners, but fellow-citizens with the saints and of the household of God, and are built upon the foundation of the apostles and prophets, Jesus Christ Himself being the chief cornerstone."

"Yes, missus, dat's it for sure. Ole Chloe knows dat's in de Bible, an if we be built on dat bressed cornerstone, we's safe ebery one. I'se heard it many's de time, an it fills dis ole heart with joy an' peace in believing," she exclaimed, raising her tearful eyes and clasping her hands. "But good night, missus. I must put my chile to bed," she added, taking Elsie's hand.

"Good night, Aunt Chloe; come in again," said Rose. "And good night to you too, dear little Elsie," folding the little girl again in her arms.

"Ain't dat a bressed young lady, darlin'?" exclaimed Chloe, earnestly, as she began the business of preparing her young charge for bed.

"O mammy, I love her so much! She's so good and kind," replied the child, "and she loves Jesus and loves to talk about Him."

"She reminds me of your dear mamma, Miss Elsie, but she's not so handsome," replied the nurse, with a tear in her eye. "Ole Chloe tinks dere's nebber any lady so beautiful as her dear young missus was."

Elsie drew out the miniature and kissed it, murmuring, "Dear, darling mamma," then put it back in her bosom again, for she always wore it day and night. She was standing in her white nightdress, the tiny white feet just peeping from under it, while Chloe brushed back her curls and put on her nightcap.

"Dere now, darlin', you's ready for bed," she exclaimed, giving the child a hug and a kiss.

"No, mammy, not quite," replied the little girl, and gliding away to the side of the bed, she knelt down and offered up her evening prayer. Then coming back to the dressing table, she opened her little Bible, saying, "Now, mammy, I will read you a chapter while you are getting ready for bed."

The room was large and airy, and Aunt Chloe, who was never willing to leave her nursling, but watched over her night and day with the most devoted affection, slept in a cot bed in one corner.

"Tank you, my dear young missus, you's berry good," said she, beginning the preparations for the night by taking off her turban and replacing it by a thick nightcap.

When the chapter was finished Elsie got into bed, saying, "Now, mammy, you may put out the light as soon as you please, and be sure to call me early in the morning, for I have a lesson to learn before breakfast."

"That I will, darlin'," replied the old woman, spreading the cover carefully over her. "Good night, my love, your ole mammy hopes her chile will have pleasant dreams."

Rose Allison was an early riser, and as the breakfast hour at Roselands was eight o'clock, she always had an hour or two for reading before it was time to join the family circle. She had asked Elsie to come to her at half-past seven, and punctually at the hour the little girl's gentle rap was heard at her door.

"Come in," said Rose, and Elsie entered, looking as bright and fresh and rosy as the morning. She had her little Bible under her arm and a bouquet of fresh flowers in her hand. "Good morning, dear Miss Allison," she said, dropping a graceful curtsy as she presented it. "I have come to read, and I have just been out to gather these for you, because I know you love flowers."

"Thank you, darling, they are very lovely," said Rose, accepting the gift and bestowing a caress upon the giver. "You are quite punctual," she added, "and now we can have our half hour together before breakfast."

The time was spent profitably and pleasantly, and passed so quickly that both were surprised when the breakfast bell rang.

Miss Allison spent the whole fall and winter at Roselands, and it was very seldom during all that time that she and Elsie failed to have their morning and evening reading and prayer together. Rose was often made to wonder at the depth of the little girl's piety and the knowledge of divine things she possessed. But Elsie had had the best of teaching. Chloe, though entirely uneducated, was a simple-minded, earnest Christian, and with a heart full of love to Jesus, had early endeavored to lead the little one to Him. And Mrs. Murray—the housekeeper whom Adelaide had mentioned, and who had assisted Chloe in the care of the child from the time of her birth until a few months before Rose's coming, when she had suddenly been summoned home to Scotland—had proved a very faithful friend. She was an intelligent woman and devotedly pious. She had carefully instructed this lonely little one, for whom she felt almost a parent's affection, and her efforts to bring her to a saving knowledge of Christ had been signally owned and blessed of God. In answer to her earnest prayers, the Holy Spirit had vouchsafed His teachings, without which all human instructions must ever be in vain. And young as Elsie was, she had already a very lovely and well-developed Christian character. Though not a remarkably precocious child in other respects, she seemed to have very clear and correct views on almost every subject connected with her duty to God and her neighbor. She was very truthful, both in word and deed, very strict in her observance of the Sabbath—though the rest of the family were by no means particular in that respect—very diligent in her studies, respectful to superiors, and kind to inferiors and equals. She was gentle, sweet tempered, patient, and forgiving to a remarkable degree. Rose became strongly attached to her and the little girl fully returned her affection.

Elsie was very sensitive and affectionate, and felt keenly the want of sympathy and love, for which, at the time of Rose's coming, she had no one to look to but poor old Chloe, who loved her with all her heart.

It is true, Adelaide sometimes treated her almost affectionately, and Lora, who had a very strong sense of justice, occasionally interfered and took her part when she was very unjustly accused, but no one seemed really to care for her, and she often felt sad and lonely. Mr. Dinsmore, though her own grandfather, treated her with entire neglect, seemed to have not the slightest affection for her, and usually spoke to her as "old Grayson's grandchild." Mrs. Dinsmore really disliked her, because she looked upon her as the child of a stepson for whom she had never felt any affection, and also as the future rival of her own children. The governess and the younger members of the family, following the example of the elders, treated her with neglect, and occasionally even with abuse. Miss Day, knowing that she was in no danger of incurring the displeasure of her superiors by so doing, vented upon her all the spite she dared not show to her other pupils. Continually, Elsie was made to give up her toys and pleasures to Enna, and even sometimes to Arthur and Walter. It often cost her a struggle, and had she possessed less of the ornament of a meek and quiet spirit, her life may have seemed wretched indeed.

But in spite of all her trials and vexations, little Elsie was the happiest person in the family, for she had in her heart that peace which the world can neither give nor take away, that joy which the Saviour gives to His own, and no man taketh from them. She constantly carried all her troubles and sorrows to Him. The coldness and neglect of others seemed but to drive her nearer to that Heavenly Friend, until she felt that while possessed of His love, she could not be unhappy, though treated with scorn and abuse by all the world.

The good are better made by ill,
As odors crushed are sweeter still . . .

And even so it seemed to be with little Elsie. Her trials seemed to have only the effect of purifying and making more lovely her naturally amiable character.

Elsie talked much and thought more of her absent and unknown father, and longed with an intensity of desire for his return home. It was her dream, by day and by night, that he had come, that he had taken her to his heart, calling her his "own darling child," his "precious little Elsie," for such were the loving epithets she often heard lavished upon Enna, and which she longed to hear addressed to herself. But from month to month, and year to year, that longed-for return had been delayed until the little heart had grown sick with hope deferred, and was often weary with its almost hopeless waiting.

"Elsie," said Adelaide, as Miss Allison and the little girl entered the breakfast room on the morning after Elsie's disappointment, "the fair is not over yet, and Miss Allison and I are going to ride out there this afternoon. So, if you are a good girl in school, you may go with us."

"Oh, thank you, dear Aunt Adelaide!" exclaimed the little girl, clapping her hands with delight. "How kind you are! And I shall be so glad."

Miss Day frowned, and looked as if she wanted to reprove her for her noisy demonstrations of delight, but standing somewhat in awe of Adelaide, said nothing.

But Elsie suddenly relapsed into silence. At that moment Mrs. Dinsmore entered the room, and it was seldom that she could utter a word in her presence without being reproved and told that "children should be seen and not heard," though her own were allowed to talk as much as they pleased.

Miss Day seemed cross, Mrs. Dinsmore was moody and taciturn, complaining of a headache, and Mr. Dinsmore occupied with the morning paper, and so the meal passed off in almost unbroken silence. Elsie was glad when it was over, and hastening to the schoolroom, she began her tasks without waiting for the arrival of the regular hour for study.

She had the room entirely to herself, and had been busily engaged for half an hour in working out her examples, when the opening of the door caused her to look up, and, to her dismay, Arthur entered. He did not, however, as she feared, begin his customary course of teasing and tormenting, but seated himself at his desk, leaning his head upon his hand in an attitude of dejection.

Elsie wondered what ailed him, his conduct was so unusual, and she could not help every now and then sending an inquiring glance toward him. And at length she asked, "What is the matter, Arthur?"

"Nothing much," said he, gruffly, turning his back to her.

Thus repulsed, she said no more, but gave her undivided attention to her employment, and so diligent was she, that Miss Day had no excuse whatever for faultfinding this morning. Her tasks were all completed within the required time, and she enjoyed her promised ride with her aunt and Miss Allison and her visit to the fair, very much indeed.

It was still early when they returned, and finding that she had nearly an hour to dispose of before teatime, Elsie thought she would finish a drawing which she had left in her desk in the schoolroom. While searching for it and her pencil, she heard Lora's and Arthur's voices on the veranda.

She did not notice what they were saying, until her own name struck her ear.

"Elsie is the only person," Lora was saying, "who can, and probably will, help you, for she has plenty of money, and she is so kind and generous. But, if I were you, I should be ashamed to ask her, after the way you have acted toward her."

"I wish I hadn't teased her so yesterday," replied Arthur, disconsolately. "But it's such fun—I can't help it sometimes."

"Well I know I wouldn't ask a favor of anybody I had treated so," said Lora, walking away.

Elsie sat still a few moments, working at her drawing and wondering all the time what it was Arthur wanted, and thinking how glad she would be of an opportunity of returning him good for evil. She did not like, though, to seek his confidence, but presently hearing him heave a deep sigh, she rose and went out to the veranda.

He was leaning on the railing in an attitude of dejection, his head bent down and his eyes fixed on the floor. She went up to him, and laying her hand softly on his shoulder, said, in the sweet, gentle tones natural to her, "What ails you, Arthur? Can I do anything for you? I will be very glad if I can."

"No—yes—" he answered hesitatingly. "I wouldn't like to ask you after—after—"

"Oh, never mind!" said Elsie, quickly. "I do not care anything about that now. I had the ride today, and that was better still, because I went with Aunt Adelaide and Miss Allison. Tell me what you want."

Thus encouraged, Arthur replied, "I saw a beautiful little ship yesterday when I was in the city. It was only five dollars, and I've set my heart on having it, but my pocket money's all gone, and papa won't give me a cent until next month's allowance is due, and by that time the ship will be gone, for it's such a beauty somebody'll be sure to buy it."

"Won't your mamma buy it for you?" asked Elsie.

"No, she says she hasn't the money to spare just now. You know it's near the end of the month, and they've all spent their allowance except Louise, and she says she'll not lend her money to such a spendthrift as I am."

Elsie drew out her purse, and seemed just about to put it into his hand, but, apparently changing her mind, she hesitated a moment, and then returning it to her pocket, said, with a half smile, "I don't know, Arthur. Five dollars is a good deal for a little girl like me to lay out at once. I must think about it a little."

"I don't ask you to give it," he replied scornfully. "I'll pay it back in two weeks."

"Well, I will see by tomorrow morning," she said, darting away, while he sent an angry glance after her, muttering the word "stingy" between his teeth.

Elsie ran down to the kitchen, asking of one and another of the servants as she passed, "Where's Pompey?" The last time she put the question to Phoebe the cook, but was answered by Pompey himself. "Here am Pomp, Miss Elsie. What does little missy want wid dis chile?"

"Are you going to the city tonight, Pompey?"

"Yes, Miss Elsie, I'se got some arrants to do for missus an' de family in ginral, an' I ben gwine start in 'bout ten minutes. Little missy wants sumpin, eh?"

Elsie motioned to him to come close to her, and then putting her purse into his hands, she told him in a whisper of Arthur's wish, and directed him to purchase the coveted toy, and bring it to her, if possible, without letting anyone else know anything about it. "And keep half a dollar for yourself, Pompey, to pay you for your trouble," she added in conclusion.

"Tank you, little missy," he replied, with a broad grin of satisfaction. "Dat be berry good pay, and Pomp am de man to do dis business up for you 'bout right."

The tea bell rang, and Elsie hastened away to answer the summons. She looked across the table at Arthur with a pleasant smile on her countenance, but he averted his eyes with an angry scowl, and with a slight sigh she turned away her head, and did not look at him again during the meal.

Pompey executed his commission faithfully, and when Elsie returned to her own room, after her evening hour with Miss Rose, Chloe pointed out the little ship standing on the mantel.

"Oh, it's a little beauty!" cried Elsie, clapping her hands and dancing up and down with delight. "How Arthur will be pleased! Now mammy, can you take it to the schoolroom, and put it on Master Arthur's desk, without anybody seeing you?"

"Ole Chloe'll try, darlin," she said, taking it in her hands.

"Oh, wait one moment!" exclaimed Elsie. And taking a card, she wrote on it, "A present to Arthur, from his niece Elsie." Then laying it on the deck of the little vessel, "There, mammy," she said, "I think that will do, but please look out first to see whether anyone is in the hall."

"Coast all clear, darlin'," replied Chloe, after a careful survey. "All de chillens am in bed before dis time, I spec." And taking a candle in the one hand

and the little ship in the other, she started for the schoolroom. She soon returned with a broad grin of satisfaction on her black face, saying, "All right, darlin', I put him on Massa Arthur's desk, an' nobody de wiser."

So Elsie went to bed very happy in the thought of the pleasure Arthur would have in receiving her present.

She was hurrying down to the breakfast room the next morning, a little in advance of Miss Rose, who had stopped to speak to Adelaide, when Arthur came running up behind her. He had just come in by a side door from the garden, and seizing her round the waist, he said, "Thank you, Elsie! You're a real good girl! She sails beautifully. I've been trying her on the pond. But it mustn't be a present; you must let me pay you back when I get my allowance."

"Oh, no, Arthur! That would spoil it all," she answered quickly. "You are entirely welcome, and you know my allowance is so large that half the time I have more money than I know how to spend."

"I should like to see the time when that would be the case with me," said he, laughing. Then in a lower tone, "Elsie, I'm sorry I teased you so. I'll not do it again soon."

Elsie answered him with a grateful look, as she stepped past him and quietly took her place at the table.

Arthur kept his word, and for many weeks entirely refrained from teasing Elsie. While freed from that annoyance, she was always able to have her tasks thoroughly prepared. Her governess was often unreasonable and exacting, and there was scarcely a day in which she was not called upon to yield her own wishes or pleasures, or in some way to inconvenience herself to please Walter or Enna, or occasionally the older members of the family. Yet it was an unusually happy winter to her, for Rose Allison's love and uniform kindness shed sunshine on her path. She had learned to yield readily to others, and when fretted or saddened by unjust or unkind treatment, a few moments alone with her precious Bible and her loved Saviour made all right again, and she would come from those sweet communings looking as serenely happy as if she had never known an annoyance. She was a wonder to all the family. Her grandfather would sometimes look at her as, without a frown or a pout, she would give up her own wishes to Enna, and shaking his head, say, "She's no Dinsmore, or she would know how to stand up for her own rights better than that. I don't like such tame-spirited people. She's not Horace's child: it never was an easy matter to impose upon or conquer him. He was a boy of spirit."

"What a strange child Elsie is!" Adelaide remarked to her friend one day. "I am often surprised to see how sweetly she gives up to all of us; really she has a lovely temper. I quite envy her. It was always hard for me to give up my own way."

"I do not believe it was easy for her at first," said Rose. "I think her sweet disposition is the fruit of grace in her heart. It is the ornament of a meek and quiet spirit, which God alone can bestow."

"I wish I had it, then," said Adelaide, sighing.

"You have only to go to the right source to obtain it, dear Adelaide," replied her friend, gently.

"And, yet," said Adelaide, "I must say I sometimes think that, as papa says, there is something mean-spirited and cowardly in always giving up to other people."

"It would indeed be cowardly and wrong to give up principle," replied Rose, "but surely it is noble and generous to give up our own wishes to another where no principle is involved."

"Certainly, you are right," said Adelaide, musingly. "And now I recollect that, readily as Elsie gives up her own wishes to others on ordinary occasions, I have never known her to sacrifice principle. But, on the contrary, she has several times made mamma excessively angry by refusing to romp and play with Enna on the Sabbath, or to deceive papa when questioned with regard to some of Arthur's misdeeds, yet she has often borne the blame of his faults, when she might have escaped by telling of him. Elsie is certainly very different from any of the rest of us, and if it is piety that makes her what she is, I think piety is a very lovely thing."

Elsie's mornings were spent in the schoolroom. In the afternoon she walked, or rode out, sometimes in company with her young uncles and aunts, and sometimes alone, a Negro boy following at a respectful distance, as a protector. In the evening there was almost always company in the parlor, and she found it more pleasant to sit beside the bright wood-fire in her room, with her fond old nurse for a companion, than to stay there, or with the younger ones in the sitting room or nursery. If she had no lesson to learn, she usually read aloud to Chloe, as she sat knitting by the fire, and the

Bible was the book generally preferred by both. And then when she grew weary of reading, she would often take a stool, and sitting down close to Chloe, put her hand in her lap, saying, "Now, mammy, tell me about mamma."

And then for the hundredth time or more the old woman would go over the story of the life and death of her "dear young missus," as she always called her, telling of her beauty, her goodness, and of her sorrows and sufferings during the last year of her short life.

It was a story that never lost its charm for Elsie—a story which the one never wearied of telling, nor the other of hearing. Elsie would sit listening, with her mother's miniature in her hand, gazing at it with tearful eyes, then press it to her lips, murmuring, "My own mamma. Poor, dear mamma." And when Chloe had finished that she would usually say, "Now, mammy, tell me all about papa."

But upon this subject Chloe had very little information to give. She knew him only as a merry, handsome young stranger, whom she had seen occasionally during a few months, and who had stolen all the sunshine from her beloved young mistress's life, and left her to die alone. Yet she did not blame him when speaking to his child, for the young wife had told her that he had not forsaken her of his own free choice. Though she could not quite banish from her own mind the idea that he had not been altogether innocent in the matter, she breathed no hint of it to Elsie. Chloe was a sensible woman, and knew that to lead the little one to think ill of her only remaining parent would but tend to make her unhappy.

Sometimes Elsie would ask very earnestly, "Do you think papa loves Jesus, mammy?" And Chloe would reply with a doubtful shake of the head, "Dunno, darlin', but ole Chloe prays for him every day."

"And so do I," Elsie would answer. "Dear, dear papa, how I wish he would come home!"

And so the winter glided away, and spring came, and Miss Allison must soon return home. It was now the last day of March, and her departure had been fixed for the second of April. For a number of weeks Elsie had been engaged, during all her spare moments, in knitting a purse for Rose, wishing to give her something which was the work of her own hands, knowing that as such it would be more prized by her friend than a costlier gift. She had just returned from her afternoon ride, and taking out her work she sat down to finish it. She was in her own room, with no companion but Chloe, who sat beside her, knitting as usual.

Elsie worked on silently for some time, then suddenly holding up her purse, she exclaimed, "See, mammy, it is all done but putting on the tassel! Isn't it pretty? And won't dear Miss Allison be pleased with it?"

It really was very pretty indeed, of crimson and gold, and beautifully knit, and Chloe, looking at it with admiring eyes, said, "I spec she will, darlin'. I tink it's berry handsome."

At this moment Enna opened the door and came in.

Elsie hastily attempted to conceal the purse by thrusting it into her pocket, but it was too late, for Enna had seen it, and running toward her cried out, "Now, Elsie, just give that to me!"

"No, Enna," replied Elsie, mildly. "I cannot let you have it, because it is for Miss Rose."

"I will have it," exclaimed the child, resolutely, "and if you don't give it to me at once I shall just go and tell mamma."

"I will let you take it in your hand a few moments to look at it, if you will be careful not to soil it, Enna," said Elsie, in the same gentle tone. "And if you wish, I will get some more silk and beads, and make you one just like it. But I cannot give you this, because I will not have time to make another for Miss Rose."

"No, I shall just have that one, and I shall have it to keep," said Enna, attempting to snatch it out of Elsie's hand.

But Elsie held it up out of her reach, and after trying several times in vain to get it, Enna left the room, crying and screaming with passion.

Chloe locked the door, saying "Great pity, darlin', we forgot to do dat' fore Miss Enna came. I'se afraid she gwine bring missus for make you gib um up."

Elsie sat down to work again, but she was very pale, and the little hands trembled with agitation, and her soft eyes were full of tears.

Chloe's fears were but too well founded, for the next moment hasty steps were heard in the passage, and the handle of the door was laid hold of with no very gentle grasp. And then, as it refused to yield to her touch, Mrs. Dinsmore's voice was heard in an angry tone giving the command, "Open this door instantly."

Chloe looked at her young mistress.

"You will have to," said Elsie, tearfully, slipping her work into her pocket again, and lifting up her heart in prayer for patience and meekness, for she well knew she would have need of both.

Mrs. Dinsmore entered, leading the sobbing Enna by the hand. Her face was flushed with passion, and addressing Elsie in tones of violent anger, she asked, "What is the meaning of all this, you good-for-nothing hussy? Why are you always tormenting this poor child? Where is that paltry trifle that all this fuss is about? Let me see it this instant."

Elsie drew the purse from her pocket, saying in tearful, trembling tones, "It is a purse I was making for Miss Rose, ma'am, and I offered to make another just like it for Enna, but I cannot give her this one, because there would be no time to make another before Miss Rose goes away."

"You can not give it to her, indeed? You will not, you mean. But I say you shall; and I'll see if I'm not mistress in my own house. Give it to the child this instant. I'll not have her crying her eyes out that you may be humored in all your whims. There are plenty of handsomer ones to be had in the city, and if you are too mean to make her a present of it, I'll buy you another tomorrow."

"But that would not be my work, and this is," replied Elsie, still retaining the purse, loath to let it go.

"Nonsense! What difference will that make to Miss Rose?" said Mrs. Dinsmore, and snatching it out of her hand, she gave it to Enna, saying, "There, my dear, you shall have it. Elsie is a naughty, mean, stingy girl, but she sha'n't plague you while your mamma's about."

Enna cast a look of triumph at Elsie, and ran off with her prize, followed by her mother, while poor Elsie hid her face in Chloe's lap, and cried bitterly.

It required all Chloe's religion to keep down her anger and indignation at this unjust and cruel treatment of her darling. For a few moments she allowed her to sob and cry without a word, only soothing her with caresses, not daring to trust her voice, lest her anger should find vent in words. But at length, when her feelings had grown somewhat calmer, she said soothingly, "Nebber mind it, my poor darlin' chile. Just go to de city and buy de prettiest purse you can find, for Miss Rose."

But Elsie shook her head sadly. "I wanted it to be my own work," she sobbed, "and now there is no time."

"Oh! I'll tell you what, my love," exclaimed Chloe suddenly. "Dere's de purse you was aknittin' for your papa, an' dey wouldn't send it for you. You can get dat done for de lady, and knit another for your papa, 'fore he comes home."

Elsie raised her head with a look of relief, but her face clouded again, as she replied, "But it is not quite done, and I haven't the beads to finish it with, and Miss Rose goes day after tomorrow."

"Nebber mind dat, darlin'," said Chloe, jumping up. "Pomp he been gwine to de city dis berry afternoon, an' we'll tell him to buy de beads, an' den you can get de purse finished 'fore tomorrow night, an' de lady don' go till de next day, an' so it gwine all come right yet."

"Oh, yes, that will do! Dear old mammy, I'm so glad you thought of it," said Elsie, joyfully. And rising, she went to her bureau, and unlocking a drawer, took from it a bead purse of blue and gold, quite as handsome as the one of which she had been so ruthlessly despoiled. And rolling it up in a piece of paper, she handed it to Chloe, saying, "There, mammy, please give it to Pomp, and tell him to match the beads and the silk exactly."

Chloe hastened in search of Pomp, but when she found him, he insisted that he should not have time to attend to Miss Elsie's commission and do his other errands. Chloe, knowing that he, in common with all the other servants, was very fond of the little girl, felt satisfied that it was not merely an excuse, and therefore did not urge her request. She stood a moment in great perplexity, then suddenly exclaimed, "I'll go myself. Miss Elsie will spare me an I'll go right along wid you, Pomp."

Chloe was entirely Elsie's servant, having no other business than to wait upon her and take care of her clothing and her room, and the little girl, of course, readily gave her permission to accompany Pomp and do the errand.

But it was quite late ere Chloe returned, and the little girl spent the evening alone in her room. She was sadly disappointed that she could not even have her hour with Miss Rose, who was detained in the parlor with company whom she could not leave. And so the evening seemed very long and wore away very slowly.

But at last Chloe came, and in answer to her eager inquiries displayed her purchases with great satisfaction, saying, "Yes, darlin', I'se got de berry tings you wanted."

"Oh, yes!" said Elsie, examining them with delight. "They are just right. And now I can finish it in a couple of hours."

"Time to get ready for bed now, ain't it, love?" asked Chloe, but before the little girl had time to answer, a servant knocked at the door, and handed in a note for her. It was from Miss Allison, and, hastily tearing it open, she read:

"Dear Elsie—I am very sorry that we cannot have our reading together this evening, but be sure, darling, to come to me early in the morning. It will be our last opportunity, for, dear child, I have another disappointment for you. I had not expected to leave before day after tomorrow, but I have learned this evening that the vessel sails a day sooner than I had supposed, and therefore I shall be obliged to start on my journey tomorrow.

"Your friend, Rose."

Elsie dropped the note on the floor and burst into tears.

"What de matter, darlin'?" asked Chloe, anxiously.

"Oh! Miss Rose, dear, dear Miss Rose is going tomorrow," she sobbed. Then hastily drying her eyes, she said, "But I have no time for crying. I must sit up and finish the purse tonight, because there will be no time tomorrow."

It was long past her usual time for retiring when at last her task, or rather her labor of love, was completed. Yet she was up betimes, and at the usual hour her gentle rap was heard at Miss Allison's door.

Rose clasped her in her arms and kissed her tenderly.

"Oh, Miss Rose! Dear, dear Miss Rose, what shall I do without you?" sobbed the little girl. "I shall have nobody to love me now but mammy."

"You have another and a better Friend, dear Elsie, Who has said, 'I will never leave thee, nor forsake thee,'" whispered Rose, with another tender caress.

"Yes," said Elsie, wiping away her tears, "and He is your friend, too. And don't you think, Miss Rose, He will bring us together again someday?"

"I hope so indeed, darling. We must keep very close to Him, dear Elsie. We must often commune with Him in secret, often study His Word, and try always to do His will. Ah, dear child! If we can only have the assurance that that dear Friend is with us—that we have His presence and His love, we shall be supremely happy, though separated from all earthly friends. I know, dear little one, that you have peculiar trials, and that you often feel the want of sympathy and love, but you may always find them in Jesus. And now we will have our reading and prayer as usual."

She took the little girl in her lap, and opening the Bible, read aloud the fourteenth chapter of John, a touching part of the farewell of our Saviour to His sorrowing disciples, and then they knelt to pray. Elsie was only a listener, for her little heart was too full to allow her to be anything more.

"My poor darling!" Rose said, again taking her in her arms. "We will hope to meet again before very long. Who knows but your papa may come home, and someday bring you to see me. It seems not unlikely, as he is so fond of traveling."

Elsie looked up, smiling through her tears, "Oh, how delightful that would be," she said. "But it seems as though my papa would never come," she added, with a deep-drawn sigh.

"Well darling, we can hope," Rose answered cheerfully. "And, dear child, though we must be separated in body for a time, we can still meet in spirit at the mercy-seat. Shall we not do so at this hour every morning?"

Elsie gave a joyful assent.

"And I shall write to you, darling," Rose said. "I will write on my journey, if I can, so that you will get the letter in a week from the time I leave, and then you must write to me. Will you?"

"If you won't care for the mistakes, Miss Rose. But you know I am a very little girl, and I wouldn't like to let Miss Day read my letter to you, to correct it. But I shall be so very glad to get yours. I never had a letter in my life."

"I sha'n't care for the mistakes at all, dear, and no one shall see your letters but myself," said Rose, kissing her. "I should be as sorry as you to have Miss Day look at them."

Elsie drew out the purse and put it in her friend's hand saying, "It is all my own work, dear Miss Rose. I thought you would value it more for that."

"And indeed I shall, darling," replied Rose, with tears of pleasure in her eyes. "It is beautiful in itself, but I shall value it ten times more because it is a gift, and the work of your own dear little hands."

But the breakfast bell now summoned them to join the rest of the family, and, in a few moments after they left the table, the carriage which was to take Rose to the city was at the door. Rose had endeared herself to all, old and young, and they were loath to part with her. One after another bade her an affectionate farewell. Elsie was the last. Rose pressed her tenderly to her bosom, and kissed her again and again, saying, in a voice half choked with grief, "God bless and keep you, my poor little darling! My dear, dear little Elsie!"

Elsie could not speak, and the moment the carriage had rolled away with her friend, she went to her own room, and locking herself in, cried long and bitterly. She had learned to love Rose very dearly, and to lean upon her very much, and now the parting from her, with no certainty of ever meeting her again in this world, was the severest trial the poor child had ever known.

CHAPTER THIRD

The morning blush was lighted up by hope—
The hope of meeting him.

—Miss Landon

Unkindness, do thy office; poor heart, break.

A WEEK HAD NOW PASSED AWAY since Miss Allison's departure, and Elsie, to whom it had been a sad and lonely one, was beginning to look eagerly for her first letter.

"It is just a week today since Rose left," remarked Adelaide at the breakfast table, "and I think we ought to hear from her soon. She promised to write on her journey. Ah! Here comes Pomp with the letters now," she added, as the servant man entered the room bearing in his hand the bag in which he always brought the letters of the family from the office in the neighboring city, whither he was sent every morning.

"Pomp, you are late this morning," said Mrs. Dinsmore.

"Yes, missus," replied the Negro, scratching his head. "De horses am berry lazy. Spec dey's got de spring fever."

"Do make haste, papa, and see if there is not one from Rose," said Adelaide coaxingly, as her father took the bag, and very deliberately adjusted his spectacles before opening it.

"Have patience, young lady," said he. "Yes, here is a letter for you, and one for Elsie," tossing them across the table as he spoke.

Elsie eagerly seized hers and ran away to her own room to read it. It was a feast to her, this first letter, and from such a dear friend too. It gave her almost as much pleasure for the moment as Miss Rose's presence could have afforded.

She had just finished its perusal and was beginning it again, when she heard Adelaide's voice calling her by name, and the next moment she entered the room, saying, "Well, Elsie, I suppose you have read your letter, and now I have another piece of news for you. Can you guess what it is?" she asked, looking at her with a strange smile.

"Oh, no, Aunt Adelaide! Please tell me. Is dear Miss Rose coming back?"

"Oh, nonsense! What a guess!" said Adelaide. "No, stranger than that. My brother Horace—your papa—has actually sailed for America, and is coming directly home."

Elsie sprang up, her cheeks flushed, and her little heart beating wildly.

"Oh, Aunt Adelaide!" she cried. "Is it really true? Is he coming? And will he be here soon?"

"He has really started at last, but how soon he will be here, I don't know," replied her aunt, turning to leave the room. "I have told you all I know about it."

Elsie clasped her hands together, and sank down upon a sofa, Miss Rose's letter, prized so highly a moment before, lying unheeded at her feet. Her thoughts were far away, following that unknown parent as he crossed the ocean, trying to imagine how he would look, how he would speak, what would be his feelings toward her.

"Oh!" she asked, with a beating heart. "Will he love me? My own papa! Will he let me love him? Will he take me in his arms and call me his own darling child?"

But who could answer the anxious inquiry? She must just wait until the slow wheels of time should bring the much longed-for, yet sometimes half-dreaded arrival.

Elsie's lessons were but indifferently recited that morning. Miss Day frowned, and said in a tone of severity that it did not agree with her to receive letters, and that, unless she wished her papa to be much displeased with her on his expected arrival, she must do a great deal better than that.

She had touched the right chord then, for Elsie, intensely anxious to please that unknown father, and, if possible, gain his approbation and affection, gave her whole mind to her studies with such a determined purpose that the governess could find no more cause for complaint.

But while the child is looking forward to the expected meeting with such longing affection for him, how is it with the father?

Horace Dinsmore was, like his father, an upright, moral man, who paid an outward respect to the forms of religion, but cared nothing for the vital power of godliness, trusted entirely to his morality, and looked upon Christians as hypocrites and deceivers. He had been told that his daughter Elsie was one of these, and, though he would not have acknowledged it even to himself, it had prejudiced him against her. Then, too, in common with all the

Dinsmores, he had a great deal of family pride. Though old Mr. Grayson had been a man of sterling worth, intelligent, honest, and pious, and had died very wealthy, yet because he was known to have begun life as a poor boy, the whole family was accustomed to speaking as though Horace had stooped very much in marrying his heiress.

And Horace himself had come to look upon his early marriage as a piece of boyish folly, of which he was rather ashamed. And so constantly had Mr. Dinsmore spoken in his letters of Elsie as "old Grayson's grandchild," that he had got into the habit of looking upon her as a kind of disgrace to him, especially as she had always been described as a disagreeable, troublesome child.

He had loved his wife with all the warmth of his passionate nature, and had mourned bitterly over her untimely death, but years of study and travel and worldly pleasures had almost banished her image from his mind. He seldom thought of her except in connection with the child for whom he felt a secret dislike.

Scarcely anything but the expected arrival was now spoken or thought of at Roselands, and Elsie was not the only one to whom old Time seemed to move with an unusually laggard pace.

But at length a letter came telling them that they might look upon it as being but one day in advance of its writer, and now all was bustle and preparation.

"O mammy, mammy!" exclaimed Elsie, jumping up and down, clapping her hands for joy, as she came in from her afternoon ride. "Just think—papa, dear papa will be here tomorrow morning."

She seemed wild with delight, but suddenly sobered down, and a look of care stole over the little face, as the torturing question recurred to her mind, "Will he love me?"

She stood quite still, with her eyes fixed thoughtfully, and almost sadly, upon the floor, while Chloe took off her riding dress and cap and smoothed her hair. As she finished arranging her dress she clasped the little form in her arms, and pressed a fond kiss on the fair brow, thinking to herself that it was the sweetest and loveliest little face she had ever looked upon.

Just at that moment an unusual bustle was heard in the house.

Elsie started, changed color, and stood listening with a throbbing heart.

Presently little feet were heard running rapidly down the hall, and Walter, throwing open the door, called out, "Elsie, he's come!" and catching her hand, hurried her along to the parlor door.

"Stop, stop, Walter," she gasped as they reached it. And she leaned against the wall, her heart throbbing so wildly she could scarcely breathe.

"What is the matter?" said he. "Are you ill? Come along," and pushing the door open, he rushed in, dragging her after him.

So over-wrought were the child's feelings that she nearly fainted. Everything in the room seemed to be turning round, and for an instant she scarcely knew where she was.

But a strange voice asked, "And who is this?" And looking up as her grandfather pronounced her name, she saw a stranger standing before her — very handsome and very youthful-looking in spite of a heavy dark beard and mustache—who exclaimed hastily, "What! This big girl my child? Really enough to make a man feel old."

Then taking her hand, he stooped and coldly kissed her lips.

She was trembling violently, and the very depth of her feelings kept her silent and still. Her hand lay still in his, cold and clammy.

He held it an instant, at the same time gazing searchingly into her face, then dropped it, saying in a tone of displeasure, "I am not an ogre, that you need be so afraid of me, but there, you may go. I will not keep you in terror any longer."

She rushed away to her own room, and there throwing herself upon the bed wept long and wildly. It was the disappointment of a lifelong hope. Since her earliest recollection she had looked and longed for this hour, and it seemed as though the little heart would break with its weight of bitter anguish.

She was all alone, for Chloe had gone down to the kitchen to talk over the arrival, not doubting that her darling was supremely happy in the possession of her long looked-for parent.

And so the little girl lay there with her crushed and bleeding heart, sobbing, mourning, weeping as though she would weep her very life away, without an earthly friend to speak one word of comfort.

"Oh, papa, papa!" she sobbed. "My own papa, you do not love me—me, your own little girl. Oh, my heart will break! Oh, mamma, mamma! If I could only go to you, for there is no one here to love me, and I am so lonely, oh, so lonely and desolate!"

And thus Chloe found her, when she came in an hour later, weeping and sobbing out such broken exclamations of grief and anguish.

She was much surprised, but comprehending at once how her child was suffering, she raised her up in her strong arms, and laying the little head lovingly against her bosom, she smoothed the tangled hair, kissed the tear-swollen eyes, and bathed the throbbing temples. She said, "My precious love, my darlin' chile, your ole mammy loves you better dan life, an' did my darlin' forget de almighty Friend dat says, 'I have loved thee with an everlasting love,' an' 'I will never leave thee, nor forsake thee.' He sticks closer dan a brudder, precious chile, and says, 'though a woman forget her sucking child, He will not forget His chillen.' Mothers loves dere chillens better dan fathers, darlin', and so you see Jesus' love is better dan all other love, an' I knows you hes got dat."

"Oh, mammy! Ask Him to take me to Himself, and to mamma—for oh, I am very lonely, and I want to die."

"Hush, hush, darlin'. Ole Chloe nebber could ask dat. Dis ole heart would break for sure. You's all de world to your ole mammy, darlin', an' you know we must all wait de Lord's time."

"Then ask Him to help me to be patient," she said, in a weary tone. "And, oh, mammy!" she added, with a burst of bitter tears, "ask Him to make my father love me."

"I will, darlin', I will," sobbed Chloe, pressing the little form closer to her heart. "An' don't you go for to be discouraged right away, for I'se sure Massa Horace must love you 'fore long."

The tea bell rang, and the family gathered about the table, but one chair remained unoccupied.

"Where is Miss Elsie?" asked Adelaide of one of the servants.

"Dunno, missus," was the reply.

"Well, then, go and see," said Adelaide. "Perhaps she did not hear the bell."

The servant returned in a moment, saying that Miss Elsie had a bad headache and did not want any supper.

Mr. Horace Dinsmore paused in the conversation he was carrying on with his father, to listen to the servant's announcement. "I hope she is not a sickly child," said he, addressing Adelaide. "Is she subject to such attacks?"

"Not very," replied his sister, dryly, for she had seen the meeting, and felt really sorry for Elsie's evident disappointment. "I imagine crying has brought this on."

He colored violently, and said in a tone of great displeasure, "Truly, the return of a parent is a cause for grief, yet I hardly expected my presence to be quite so distressing to my only child. I had no idea that she had already learned to dislike me so thoroughly."

"She doesn't," said Adelaide. "She has been looking and longing for your return ever since I have known her."

"Then she has certainly been disappointed in me. Her grief is not at all complimentary, explain it as you will."

Adelaide made no reply, for she saw that he was determined to put an unfavorable construction upon Elsie's conduct, and feared that any defense she could offer would only increase his displeasure.

It was a weary, aching head the little girl laid upon her pillow that night, and the little heart was sad and sore. Yet she was not altogether comfortless, for she had turned in her sorrow to Him who has said, "Suffer the little children to come unto me, and forbid them not," and she had the sweet assurance of His love and favor.

It was with a trembling heart, hoping yet fearing, longing and yet dreading to see her father, that Elsie descended to the breakfast room the next morning. She glanced timidly around, but he was not there.

"Where is papa, Aunt Adelaide?" she asked.

"He is not coming down to breakfast, as he feels quite fatigued with his journey," replied her aunt. "So you will not see him this morning, and perhaps not at all today, for there will be a good deal of company here this afternoon and evening."

Elsie sighed, and looked sadly disappointed. She found it very difficult to attend to her lessons that morning, and every time the door opened she started and looked up, half hoping it might be her papa.

But he did not come, and when the dinner hour arrived, the children were told that they were to dine in the nursery, on account of the large number of guests to be entertained in the dining room. The company remained until bedtime, and she was not called down to the parlor. And so she saw nothing of her father that day.

But the next morning Chloe told her the children were to breakfast with the family, as all the visitors had left excepting one or two gentlemen. So Elsie went down to the breakfast room, where, to her surprise, she found her papa sitting alone, reading his morning paper.

He looked up as she entered.

"Good morning, papa," she said, in half-trembling tones.

He started a little—for it was the first time he had ever been addressed by that title, and it sounded strange to his ears—gave her a glance of mingled curiosity and interest, half held out his hand, but drawing it back again, simply said, "Good morning, Elsie," and returned to his paper.

Elsie stood irresolutely in the middle of the floor, wanting, yet not daring to go to him.

But just at that instant the door opened, and Enna, looking rosy and happy, came running in, and rushing up to her brother, climbed upon his knee, and put her arms around his neck, saying, "Good morning, brother Horace. I want a kiss."

"You shall have it, little one," said he, throwing down his paper.

Then, kissing her several times and hugging her in his arms, he said, "You are not afraid of me, are you? Nor sorry that I have come home?"

"No indeed," said Enna.

He glanced at Elsie as she stood looking at them, her large soft eyes full of tears. She could not help feeling that Enna had her place, and was receiving the caresses that should have been lavished upon herself.

"Jealous," thought her father. "I cannot bear jealous people," and he gave her a look of displeasure that cut her to the heart, and she turned quickly away and left the room to hide the tears she could no longer keep back.

"I am envious," she thought, "jealous of Enna. Oh, how wicked!" And she prayed silently, "Dear Saviour, help me! Take away these sinful feelings."

Young as she was, she was learning to have some control over her feelings. In a few moments she had so far recovered her composure as to be able to return to the breakfast room and take her place at the table. The rest were already seated there. Her sweet little face was sad indeed and bearing the traces of tears, but quite calm and peaceful.

Her father took no further notice of her, and she did not dare trust herself to look at him. The servants filled her plate, and she ate in silence, feeling it a great relief that all were too busily engaged in talking and eating to pay any attention to her. She scarcely raised her eyes from her plate, and did not know how often a strange gentleman, who sat nearly opposite, fixed his upon her.

As she left the room at the conclusion of the meal, he asked, while following her with his eyes, "Is that one of your sisters, Dinsmore?"

"No," said he, coloring slightly. "She is my daughter."

"Ah, indeed!" said his friend. "I remember to have heard that you had a child, but had forgotten it. Well, you have no reason to be ashamed of her. She is lovely, perfectly lovely! Has the sweetest little face I ever saw."

"Will you ride, Travilla?" asked Mr. Dinsmore hastily, as though anxious to change the subject.

"I don't care if I do," was the reply, and they went out together.

Some hours later in the day Elsie was at the piano in the music-room practicing, when a sudden feeling that someone was in the room caused her to turn and look behind her.

Mr. Travilla was standing there.

"Excuse me," said he, bowing politely, "but I heard the sound of the instrument, and, being very fond of music, I ventured to walk in."

Elsie was very modest, and rather timid too, but also very polite, so she said, "No excuse is necessary. But will you not take a seat, sir? Though I fear my music will not afford you any pleasure, for you know I am only a little girl, and cannot play very well yet."

"Thank you," said he, taking a seat by her side. "And now will you do me the favor to repeat the song I heard you singing a few moments since?"

Elsie immediately complied, though her cheeks burned, and her voice trembled at first from embarrassment. But it grew stronger as she proceeded, and in the last verse was quite steady and full. She had a very fine voice for a child of her age; its sweetness was remarkable both in singing and speaking, and she had also a good deal of musical talent, which had been well cultivated, for she had had good teachers, and had practiced with great patience and perseverance. Her music was simple, as suited her years, but her performance of it was very good indeed.

Mr. Travilla thanked her very heartily, and complimented her singing, then asked for another and another song, another piece and another piece, chatting with her about each, until they grew quite familiar, and Elsie lost all feeling of embarrassment.

"Elsie, I think, is your name, is it not?" he asked after a little.

"Yes, sir," said she. "Elsie Dinsmore."

"And you are the daughter of my friend, Mr. Horace Dinsmore?"

"Yes, sir."

"Your papa has been absent a long time, and I suppose you must have quite forgotten him."

"No, sir, not forgotten, for I never had seen him."

"Indeed!" said he, in a tone of surprise. "Then, since he is an entire stranger to you, I suppose you cannot have much affection for him?"

Elsie raised her large, dark eyes to his face, with an expression of astonishment. "Not love papa, my own dear papa, who has no child but me? Oh, sir! How could you think that?"

"Ah! I see I was mistaken," said he, smiling. "I thought you could hardly care for him at all. But do you think that he loves you?"

Elsie dropped her face into her hands, and burst into an agony of tears.

The young gentleman looked extremely vexed with himself.

"My poor little girl, my poor, dear little girl," he said, stroking her hair, "forgive me. I am very, very sorry for my thoughtless question. Do be comforted, my poor child, for whether your papa loves you now or not, I am quite sure he soon will."

Elsie dried her tears, arose, and closed the instrument. He assisted her, and then asked if she would not take a little walk with him in the garden. She complied. Feeling really very sorry for the wound he had so thoughtlessly inflicted, as well as interest in his little companion, he exerted all his powers to entertain her. He talked with her about the plants and flowers, described those he had seen in foreign lands, and related incidents of travel, usually choosing those in which her father had borne a part, because he perceived that they were doubly interesting to her.

Elsie, having been thrown very much upon her own resources for amusement, and having a natural love for books, and constant access to her grandfather's well-stocked library, had read many more, and with much more thought, than most children of her age, so that Mr. Travilla found her a not uninteresting companion, and was often surprised at the intelligence shown by her questions and replies.

When the dinner bell rang he led her in, and seated her by himself, and never was any lady more carefully waited upon than little Elsie at this meal. Two or three other gentlemen guests were present, giving their attention to the older ladies of the company, and thus Mr. Travilla seemed to feel quite at liberty to devote himself entirely to her, attending to all her wants, talking with her, and making her talk.

Elsie now and then stole a glance at Mrs. Dinsmore, fearing her displeasure, but to her great relief, the lady seemed too much occupied to notice her. Once she looked timidly at her father, and her eyes met his. He was looking at her with an expression half-curious, half-amused. She was at a loss to understand the look, but, satisfied that there was no displeasure in it, her heart grew light, and her cheeks flushed with happiness.

"Really, Dinsmore," said Mr. Travilla, as they stood together near one of the windows of the drawing room soon after dinner, "your little girl is remarkably intelligent, as well as remarkably pretty, and I have discovered that she has quite a good deal of musical talent."

"Indeed! I think it is quite a pity that she does not belong to you, Travilla, instead of me, since you seem to appreciate her so much more highly," replied the father, laughing.

"I wish she did," said his friend. "But seriously, Dinsmore, you ought to love that child, for she certainly loves you devotedly."

He looked surprised. "How do you know?" he asked.

"It was evident enough from what I saw and heard this morning. Dinsmore, she would value a caress from you more than the richest jewel."

"Doubtful," replied Horace, hastily leaving the room, for Elsie had come out on to the portico in her riding suit, and Jim, her casual attendant, was bringing up the horse.

"Are you going to ride, Elsie?" asked her father, coming up to her.

"Yes, papa," she said, raising her eyes to his face.

He lifted her in his arms and placed her on the horse, saying to the servant as he did so, "Now, Jim, you must take good care of my little girl."

Tears of happiness rose in Elsie's eyes as she turned her horse's head and rode down the avenue. "He called me his little girl," she murmured to herself, "and bade Jim take good care of me. Oh! He will love me soon, as good, kind Mr. Travilla said he would."

Her father was still standing on the portico, looking after her.

"How well she sits her horse!" remarked Travilla, who had stepped out and stood close by his side.

"Yes, I think she does," was the reply, in an absent tone. He was thinking of a time, some eight or nine years before, when he had assisted another Elsie to mount her horse, and had ridden for hours at her side.

All the afternoon memories of the past came crowding thickly on his mind, and an emotion of tenderness began to spring up in his heart toward the child of her who had once been so dear to him. As he saw the little girl ride up to the house on her return, he again went out, and lifting her from her horse, asked kindly, "Had you a pleasant ride, my dear?"

"Oh, yes, papa! Very pleasant," she said, looking up at him with a face beaming with delight. He stooped and kissed her, saying, "I think I shall ride with you one of these days. Should you like it?"

"Oh, so very, very much, papa!" she answered, eagerly.

He smiled at her earnestly, and she hastened away to her room to change her dress and tell Chloe of her happiness.

Alas! It was but a transient gleam of sunshine that darted across her path, to be lost again almost instantly behind the gathering clouds.

More company came, so that the drawing room was quite full in the evening, and, though Elsie was there, her father seemed too much occupied with the guests to give her even a glance. She sat alone and unnoticed in a corner, her eyes following him wherever he moved, her ear strained to catch every tone of his voice, until Mr. Travilla, disengaging himself from a group of ladies and gentlemen on the opposite side of the room, came up to her, and taking her by the hand, led her to a pleasant-looking elderly lady, who sat at the center-table examining some choice engravings which Mr. Dinsmore had brought with him from Europe.

"Mother," said Mr. Travilla, "this is my little friend, Elsie."

"Ah!" said she, giving the little girl a kiss. "I am glad to see you, my dear."

Mr. Travilla set a chair for her close to his mother, and then sat down on her other side, and taking on the engravings one after another, he explained them to her in a most entertaining manner, generally having some anecdote to tell in connection with each.

Elsie was so much amused and delighted with what he was saying that she at last quite forgot her father, and did not notice where he was.

Suddenly, Mr. Travilla laid down the engraving he had in his hand, saying, "Come, Miss Elsie, I want my mother to hear you play and sing. Will you not do me the favor to repeat that song I admired so much this morning?"

"Oh, Mr. Travilla!" exclaimed the little girl, blushing and trembling. "I could not play nor sing before so many people. Please excuse me."

"Elsie," said her father's voice just at her side, "go immediately, and do so as the gentleman requests."

His tone was very stern, and as she lifted her eyes to his face, she saw that his look was still more so; and trembling and tearfully she rose to obey.

"Stay," said Mr. Travilla kindly, pitying her distress, "I withdraw my request."

"But I do not withdraw my command," said her father in the same stern tone. "Go at once, Elsie, and do as I bid you."

She obeyed instantly, struggling hard to overcome her emotion.

Mr. Travilla, scolding himself inwardly all the time for having brought her into such trouble, selected her music, and placing it before her as she took her seat at the instrument, whispered encouragingly, "Now, Miss Elsie, only have confidence in yourself. That is all that is necessary to your success."

But Elsie was not only embarrassed, but her heart well nigh broken by her father's sternness, and the tears would fill her eyes so that she could see neither notes nor words. She attempted to play the prelude, but blundered sadly, her embarrassment increasing every moment.

"Never mind," said Mr. Travilla, "never mind the prelude, but just begin the song."

She made the attempt, but fairly broke down, and burst into tears before she had got through the first verse. Her father had come up behind her, and was standing there, looking much mortified.

"Elsie," he said, leaning down and speaking in a low, stern tone, close to her ear, "I am ashamed of you. Go to your room and to your bed immediately."

With a heart almost bursting with grief and mortification she obeyed him, and her pillow was wet with many bitter tears ere the weary eyes closed in slumber.

When she came the next morning she learned to her great grief that Mr. Travilla and his mother had returned to their own home. She was very sorry she had not been permitted to say goodbye to her friend, and for several days felt very sad and lonely. All her father's coldness of manner had returned, and he scarcely ever spoke to her, while the younger members of the family ridiculed her for her failure in attempting to play for company, and Miss Day, who seemed unusually cross and exacting often taunted her with it also.

These were sad, dark days for the little girl. She tried most earnestly to attend to all her duties, but so depressed were her spirits, so troubled was her mind, that she failed repeatedly in her lessons, and so was in continual disgrace with Miss Day, who threatened more than once to tell her papa.

It was a threat which Elsie dreaded extremely to have put in execution, and Miss Day, seeing that it distressed her, used it the more frequently, and thus kept the poor child in constant terror.

How to gain her father's love was the constant subject of her thoughts, and she tried in many ways to win his affection. She always yielded a ready and cheerful obedience to his commands, and strove to anticipate and fulfill all his wishes. But he seldom noticed her, unless to give a command or administer a rebuke, while he lavished many a caress upon his little sister, Enna. Often Elsie would watch him with her, until, unable any longer to control her feelings, she would rush away to her own room to weep and mourn in secret, and pray that her father might someday learn to love her. She never complained even to poor old Aunt Chloe, but the anxious nurse watched all things with the jealous eye of affection. She saw that her child—as she delighted to call her—was very unhappy, and was growing pale and melancholy, and her heart ached for her, and many were the tears she shed in secret over the sorrow of her nursling.

"Don't 'pear so sorrowful, darlin'," she sometimes said to her. "Try to be merry, like Miss

Enna, and run and jump on Massa Horace's knee, and den I tink he will like you better."

"O mammy! I can't," Elsie would say. "I don't dare to do it."

And Chloe would sigh and shake her head sorrowfully.

CHAPTER FOURTH

With more capacity for love than earth
Bestows on most of mortal mould and birth.

—*Byron*

What are the hopes?
Like garlands, on affections forehead worn,
Kissed in the morning, and at evening torn.

—*Davenport's King John and Matilda.*

SUCH HAD BEEN THE STATE OF AFFAIRS for about a week, when one morning Elsie and her father met at the breakfast room door.

"Good morning, papa," she said timidly.

"Good morning, Elsie," her father replied in an unusually pleasant tone.

Then taking her by the hand, he led her in and seated her beside himself at the table.

Elsie's cheek glowed and her eyes sparkled with pleasure.

There were several guests present, and she waited patiently while they and the older members of the family were being helped. At length it was her turn.

"Elsie, will you have some meat?" asked her grandfather.

"No," said her father, answering for her. "Once a day is as often as a child of her age ought to eat meat. She may have it at dinner, but never for breakfast nor tea."

The elder Mr. Dinsmore laughed, saying, "Really, Horace, I had no idea you were so opinionated. I always allowed you to eat whatever you pleased, and I never saw that it hurt you. But of course you must manage your own child in your own way."

"If you please, papa, I would rather have some of those hot cakes," said Elsie, timidly, as her father laid a slice of bread upon her plate.

"No," said he decidedly. "I don't approve of hot bread for children. You must eat the cold." Then to a servant who was setting down a cup of coffee beside the little girl's plate, "Take that away, Pomp, and bring Miss Elsie a tumbler of milk. Or would you prefer water, Elsie?"

"Milk, if you please, papa," she replied with a little sigh, for she was extremely fond of coffee, and it was something of a trial to give it up.

Her father put a spoonful of stewed fruit upon her plate, and as Pompey set down a tumbler of rich milk beside it, said, "Now you have your breakfast before you, Elsie. Children in England are not allowed to eat butter until they are ten or eleven years of age, and I think it an excellent plan, to make them grow up rosy and healthy. I have neglected my little girl too long, but I intend to begin to take good care of her now," he added with a smile, and laying his hand for an instant upon her head.

The slight caress and the few kind words were quite enough to reconcile Elsie to the rather meager fare, and she ate it with a happy heart. But the meager fare became a constant thing, while the caresses and kind words were not, and though she submitted without a murmur, she could not help sometimes looking with longing eyes at the coffee and hot buttered rolls, of which she was very fond. But she tried to be contented, saying to herself, "Papa knows best, and I ought to be satisfied with whatever he gives me."

"Isn't it delightful to have your papa at home, Elsie?" Mr. Dinsmore one morning overheard Arthur saying to his little girl in a mocking tone. "It's very pleasant to live on bread and water, isn't it, eh?"

"I don't live on bread and water," Elsie replied, a little indignantly. "Papa always allows me to have as much good, rich, milk, and cream, and fruit as I want, or I can have eggs, or cheese, or honey, or anything else, except meat, and hot cakes, and butter, and coffee. And who wouldn't rather do without such things all their lives than not have a papa to love them? And besides, you know, Arthur, that I can have all the meat I want at dinner."

"Pooh! That's nothing. And I wouldn't give much for all the love you get from him," said Arthur, scornfully.

There was something like a sob from Elsie, and as her father rose and went to the window, he just caught a glimpse of her white dress disappearing down the garden walk.

"What do you mean, sir, by teasing Elsie in that manner?" he exclaimed angrily to Arthur, who still stood where the little girl had left him, leaning against one of the pillars of the portico.

"I only wanted to have a little fun," returned the boy doggedly.

"Well, sir, I don't approve of such fun, and you will please to let the child alone in the future," replied his brother as he returned to his newspaper again.

But somehow the paper had lost its interest. He seemed constantly to hear that little sob, and to see a little face all wet with tears of wounded feeling.

Just then the school bell rang, and suddenly throwing down his paper, he took a card from his pocket, wrote a few words upon it, and calling a servant, said, "Take this to Miss Day."

Elsie was seated at her desk, beginning her morning's work, when the servant entered and handed the card to the governess.

Miss Day glanced at it and said, "Elsie, your father wants you. You may go."

Elsie rose in some trepidation and left the room, wondering what her papa could want with her.

"Where is papa, Fanny?" she asked of the servant.

"In de drawin'-room, Miss Elsie," was the reply, and she hastened to seek him there.

He held out his hands as she entered, saying with a smile, "Come here, daughter."

It was the first time he had called her that, and it sent a thrill of joy to her heart.

She sprang to his side, and, taking her hand in one of his, and laying the other gently on her head, and bending it back a little, he looked keenly into her face. It was bright enough now, yet the traces of tears were very evident.

"You have been crying," he said, in a slightly reproving tone. "I am afraid you do a great deal more of that than is good for you. It is a very baby-ish habit, and you must try to break yourself of it."

The little face flushed painfully, and the eyes filled again.

"There," he said, stroking her hair, "don't begin it again. I am going to drive over to Ion, where your friend Mr. Travilla lives, to spend the day. Would my little daughter like to go with me?"

"Oh, so very much, papa!" she answered eagerly.

"There are no little folks there," he said smiling, "nobody to see but Mr. Travilla and his mother. But I see you want to go, so run and ask Aunt Chloe to get you ready. Tell her I want you nicely dressed, and the carriage will be at the door in half an hour."

Elsie bounded away to his bidding, her face radiant with happiness, and at the specified time came down again, looking so very lovely that her father gazed at her with proud delight. He could not refrain from giving her a kiss as he lifted her up to place her in the carriage.

Then seating himself beside her, he took her hand in his, and, closing the door with the other, bade the coachman drive on.

"I suppose you have never been to Ion, Elsie?" he said, inquiringly.

"No, sir, but I have heard Aunt Adelaide say she thought it a very pretty place," replied the little girl.

"So it is—almost as pretty as Roselands," said her father. "Travilla and I have known each other from boyhood, and I spent many a happy day at Ion, and we had many a boyish frolic together, before I ever thought of you."

He smiled, and patted her cheek as he spoke.

Elsie's eyes sparkled. "Oh, papa!" she said eagerly. "Won't you tell me about those times? It seems so strange that you were ever a little boy and I was nowhere."

He laughed, then said, musingly, "It seems but a very little while to me, Elsie, since I was no older than you are now."

He heaved a sigh, and relapsed into silence.

Elsie wished very much that he would grant her request, but did not dare to disturb him by speaking a word, and they rode on quietly for some time, until a squirrel darting up a tree caught her eye, and she uttered an exclamation. "Oh, papa! Did you see that squirrel? Look at him now, perched up on that branch. There, we have passed the tree, and now he is out of sight."

This reminded Mr. Dinsmore of a day he had spent in those woods hunting squirrels, when quite a boy, and he gave Elsie an animated account of it. One of the incidents of the day had been the accidental discharge of the fowling piece of one of his young companions, close at Horace Dinsmore's side, missing him by but a hair's breadth.

"I felt faint and sick when I knew how near I had been to death," he said, as he finished his narrative.

Elsie had been listening with breathless interest.

"Dear papa," she murmured, laying her little cheek against his hand, "how good God was to spare your life! If you had been killed I could never have had you for my papa."

"Perhaps you might have had a much better one, Elsie," he said gravely.

"Oh, no, papa! I wouldn't want any other," she replied earnestly, pressing his hand to her lips.

"Ah, here we are!" exclaimed her father, as at that instant the carriage turned into a broad avenue, up which they drove quite rapidly. The next moment they had stopped, the coachman had thrown open the carriage door, and Mr. Dinsmore, springing out, lifted his little girl in his arms and set her down on the steps of the veranda.

"Ah, Dinsmore! How do you do? Glad to see you and my little friend, Elsie, too. Why this is really kind," cried Mr. Travilla, in his cheerful, hearty way, as, hurrying out to welcome them, he shook Mr. Dinsmore cordially by the hand, and kissed Elsie's cheek.

"Walk in, walk in," he continued, leading the way into the house. "My mother will be delighted to see you both, Miss Elsie especially, for she seems to have taken a very great fancy to her."

If Mrs. Travilla's greeting was less boisterous, it certainly was not lacking in cordiality, and she made Elsie feel at home at once, taking off her bonnet, smoothing her hair, and kissing her affectionately.

The gentlemen soon went out together, and Elsie spent the morning in Mrs. Travilla's room, chatting with her and assisting her with some coarse garments she was making for her servants.

Mrs. Travilla was an earnest Christian, and the lady and the little girl were not long in discovering the tie which existed between them.

Mrs. Travilla, being also a woman of great discernment, and having known Horace Dinsmore nearly all his life, had conceived a very correct idea of the trials and difficulties of Elsie's situation, and without alluding to them at all, gave her some most excellent advice, which the little girl received very thankfully.

They were still chatting together when Mr. Travilla came in, saying, "Come, Elsie, I want to take you out to see my garden and hot-house. We will just have time before dinner. Will you go along, mother?"

"No, I have some little matters to attend to before dinner, and will leave you to do the honors," replied the lady, and taking the little girl's hand he led her out.

"Where is papa?" asked Elsie.

"Oh, he's in the library, looking over some new books," replied Mr. Travilla. "He always cared more for books than anything else. But what do you think of my flowers?"

"Oh, they are lovely! What a variety you have. What a splendid cape-jessamine that is! And there is a variety of cactus I never saw before! Oh, you have a great many more, and handsomer, I think, than we have at Roselands!" exclaimed Elsie, as she passed admiringly from one to another.

Mr. Travilla was much pleased with the admiration she expressed, for he was very fond of his flowers, and took great pride in showing them.

But they were soon called into dinner, where Elsie was seated by her father.

"I hope this little girl has not given you any trouble, Mrs. Travilla," said he, looking gravely at her.

"Oh, no," the lady hastened to say, "I have enjoyed her company very much indeed, and hope you will bring her to see me again very soon."

After dinner, as the day was very warm, they adjourned to the veranda, which was the coolest place to be found, it being on the shady side of the house, and also protected by thick trees, underneath which a beautiful fountain was playing.

But the conversation was upon some subject which did not interest Elsie, and she presently stole away to the library. Seating herself in a corner of the sofa, she was soon lost to everything around her in the intense interest with which she was reading a book she had taken from the table.

"Ah, that is what you are about, Miss Elsie! A bookworm, just like your father, I see. I had been wondering what had become of you for the last two hours," exclaimed Mr. Travilla's pleasant voice. And sitting down beside her, he took the book from her hand, and putting it behind him, said, "Put it away now. You will have time enough to finish it, and I want you to talk to me."

"Oh, please let me have it," she pleaded. "I shall not have much time, for papa will soon be calling me to go home."

"No, no, he is not to take you away. I have made a bargain with him to let me keep you," said Mr. Travilla, very gravely. "We both think that there are children enough at Roselands without you, and so your papa has given you to me, and you are to be my little girl, and call me papa in the future."

Elsie gazed earnestly in his face for an instant, saying in a half-frightened tone, "You are only joking, Mr. Travilla."

"Not a bit of it," said he. "Can't you see that I'm in earnest?"

His tone and look were both so serious that for an instant Elsie believed that he meant all that he was saying, and springing to her feet with a little cry of alarm, she hastily withdrew her hand which he had taken. Rushing out to the veranda, where her father still sat conversing with Mrs. Travilla, she flung herself into his arms, and clinging to him, hid her face on his chest, sobbing, "Oh, papa, dear papa! Don't give me away, please don't—I will be so good—will do everything you bid me—I—"

"Why, Elsie, what does all this mean?" exclaimed Mr. Dinsmore in great surprise and perplexity, while Mr. Travilla stood in the doorway looking half amused, half sorry for what he had done.

"Oh, papa!" sobbed the little girl, still clinging to him as though fearing she should be torn from his arms. "Mr. Travilla says you have given me to him. Oh, papa, don't give me away!"

"Pooh! Nonsense, Elsie! I am ashamed of you! How can you be so very silly as to believe for one moment anything so perfectly absurd as that I should think of giving you away? Why I would as soon think of parting with my eyes."

Elsie raised her head and gazed searchingly into his face, then with a deep-drawn sigh of relief, dropped it again, saying, "Oh, I am so glad."

"Really, Miss Elsie," said Travilla, coming up and patting her on the shoulder, "I can't say that I feel much complimented. Indeed, I don't see why you need have been so much distressed at the prospect before you, for I must say I have vanity enough to imagine that I should make the better—or at least the more indulgent—father of the two. Come now, wouldn't you be willing to try me for a month, if your papa will give consent?"

Elsie shook her head.

"I will let you have your own way in everything," urged Travilla, coaxingly, " and I know that is more than he does."

"I don't want my own way, Mr. Travilla. I know it wouldn't always be a good way," replied Elsie, decidedly.

Her father laughed and passed his hand caressingly over the curls.

"I thought you liked me, little Elsie," said Travilla, in a tone of disappointment.

"So I do, Mr. Travilla. I like you very much," she replied.

"Well, don't you think I would make a good father?"

"I am sure you would be very kind, and that I should love you very much, but not so much as I love my own papa, because, you know, you are not my papa, and never can be, even if he should give me to you."

Mr. Dinsmore laughed heartily, saying, "I think you may as well give it up, Travilla. It seems I'll have to keep her whether or no, for she clings to me like a leech."

"Well, Elsie, you will at least come to the piano and play a little for me, will you not?" asked Travilla, smiling.

But Elsie still clung to her father, seeming loath to leave him, until he said, in his grave, decided way, "Go Elsie. Go at once, and do as you are requested."

Then she rose instantly to obey.

Travilla looked somewhat vexed. "I wish," he afterward remarked to his mother, "that Dinsmore was not quite so ready to second my requests with his commands. I want Elsie's compliance to be voluntary—else I think it worth very little."

Elsie played and sang until they were called to tea, after which she sat quietly by her father's side, listening to the conversation of her elders until the carriage was announced.

"Well, my daughter," said Mr. Dinsmore, when they were fairly upon their way to Roselands, "have you had a pleasant day?"

"Oh, very pleasant, papa, excepting—" She paused, looking a little embarrassed.

"Well, excepting what?" he asked, smiling down at her.

"Excepting when Mr. Travilla frightened me so, papa," she replied, moving closer to his side, blushing and casting down her eyes.

"And you do love your own papa best and don't want to exchange him for another?" he said inquiringly, as he passed his arm affectionately around her waist.

"Oh, no, dear papa! Not for anybody else in all the world," she said earnestly.

He made no reply in words, but, looking highly gratified, bent down and kissed her cheek.

He did not speak again during their ride, but when the carriage stopped he lifted her out, and setting her gently down, bade her a kind goodnight, saying it was time for mammy to put her to bed.

She ran lightly upstairs, and springing into her nurse's arms, exclaimed, "Oh, mammy, mammy! What a pleasant, pleasant day I have had! Papa has been so kind, and so were Mr. Travilla and his mother."

"I'se berry glad, darlin', an' I hope you gwine hab many more such days," replied Chloe, embracing her fondly. Then proceeding to take off her bonnet and prepare her for bed, Elsie gave her a minute account of the occurrences of the day, not omitting the fright Mr. Travilla had given her, and how happily her fears had been relieved.

"You look berry happy, my darlin' love," said Chloe, clasping her nursling again in her arms when her task was finished.

"Yes, mammy, I am happy, oh so happy, because I do believe that papa is beginning to love me a little, and I hope that perhaps, after a while, he will love me very much."

The tears gathered in her eyes as she spoke.

The next afternoon, as Elsie was returning home from her walk, she met her father.

"Elsie," said he, in a reproving tone, "I have forbidden you to walk out alone. Are you disobeying me?"

"No, papa," she replied meekly, raising her eyes to his face. "I was not alone until about five minutes ago when Aunt Adelaide and Louise left me. They said it did not matter, as I was so near home; and they were going to make a call, and did not want me along."

"Very well," he said, taking hold of her hand and making her walk by his side. "How far have you been?"

"We went down the river bank to the big spring, papa. I believe it is a little more than a mile that way, but when we came home, we made it shorter by coming across some of the fields and through the meadow."

"Through the meadow?" said Mr. Dinsmore. "Don't you go there again Elsie, unless I give you express permission."

"Why, papa?" she asked, looking up at him in some surprise.

"Because I forbid it," he replied sternly. "That is quite enough for you to know. All you have to do is to obey, and you need never ask me why when I give you an order."

"I did not mean to be naughty, papa," she said, struggling to keep down a sob, "and I will try never to ask why again."

"There is another thing," said he. "You cry quite too easily. It is entirely too babyish for a girl of your age. You must quit it."

"I will try, papa," said the little girl, wiping her eyes, and making a great effort to control her feelings.

They had entered the avenue while this conversation was going on, and were now drawing near the house; and just at this moment a little girl about Elsie's age came running to meet them, exclaiming, "Oh, Elsie! I'm glad you've come at last. We've been here a whole hour—mamma, and Herbert, and I—and I've been looking for you all this time."

"How do you do, Miss Lucy Carrington? I see you can talk as fast as ever," said Mr. Dinsmore laughing, and holding out his hand.

Lucy took it, saying, with a little pout, "To be sure Mr. Dinsmore, it isn't more than two or three weeks since you were at our house, and I wouldn't forget how to talk in that time." Then looking at Elsie, she went on, "We've come to stay a week. Won't we have a fine time?" and, catching her friend round the waist, she gave her a hearty squeeze.

"I hope so," said Elsie, returning the embrace. "I am glad you have come."

"Is your papa here, Miss Lucy?" asked Mr. Dinsmore.

"Yes, sir, but he's going home again tonight, and then he'll come back for us next week."

"I must go in and speak to him," said Mr. Dinsmore. "Elsie, you entertain Lucy."

"Yes, sir, I will," said Elsie. "Come with me to my room, won't you, Lucy?"

"Yes, but won't you speak to mamma first? And Herbert too, you are such a favorite with both of them, and they still are in the dressing-room, for mamma is not very well, and was quite fatigued with her ride."

Lucy led the way to her mamma's room, as she spoke, Elsie following.

"Ah, Elsie dear! How do you do? I'm delighted to see you," said Mrs. Carrington, rising from the sofa as they entered.

Then, drawing the little girl closer to her, she passed her arm affectionately around her waist, and kissed her several times.

"I suppose you are very happy now that your papa has come home at last?" she said, looking searchingly into Elsie's face. "I remember you used to be looking forward to his return, constantly talking of it and longing for it."

Poor Elsie, conscious that her father's presence had not brought with it the happiness she had anticipated, and yet unwilling either to acknowledge that fact or tell an untruth, was at a loss for what to say.

But she was relieved from the necessity of replying by Herbert, Lucy's twin brother, a pale, sickly-looking boy, who had for several years been a sufferer from hip complaint.

"Oh, Elsie!" he exclaimed, catching hold of her hand and squeezing it between both of his. "I'm ever so glad to see you again."

"Yes," said Mrs. Carrington, "Herbert always says nobody can tell him such beautiful stories as Elsie, and nobody but his mother and his old mammy was half so kind to run and wait on him when he was laid on his back for so many weeks. He missed you very much when we went home, and often wished he was at Roselands again."

"How is your hip now, Herbert?" asked Elsie looking pitying at the boy's pale face.

"Oh, a great deal better, thank you. I can take quite long walks sometimes now, though I still limp, and cannot run and leap like other boys."

They chatted a few moments longer, and then Elsie went to her room to have her hat taken off, and her hair made smooth before the tea bell should ring.

The two little girls were seated together at the table, Elsie's papa being on her other side.

"How nice these muffins are! Don't you like them, Elsie?" asked Lucy, as she helped herself to a third or fourth.

"Yes, very much," said Elsie, cheerfully.

"Then what are you eating that cold bread for? And you haven't got any butter either. Pompey, why don't you hand Miss Elsie the butter?"

"No, Lucy, I mustn't have it. Papa does not allow me to eat hot cakes nor butter," said Elsie, in the same cheerful tone in which she had spoken before.

Lucy opened her eyes very wide, and drew in her breath.

"Well!" she exclaimed, "I guess if my papa should try that on me, I'd make such a fuss he'd have to let me eat just whatever I wanted."

"Elsie knows better than to do that," said Mr. Dinsmore, who had overheard the conversation. "She would only get sent away from the table and punished for her naughtiness."

"I wouldn't do it anyhow, papa," said Elsie, raising her eyes beseechingly to his face.

"No, daughter, I don't believe you would," he replied in an unusually kind tone, and Elsie's face flushed with pleasure.

Several days passed away very pleasantly. Lucy shared Elsie's studies in the mornings, while Herbert remained with his mamma. Then in the afternoon all went walking or riding out together, unless the weather was too warm, when they spent the afternoon playing on the veranda, on the shady side of the house, and took their ride or walk after the sun went down.

Arthur and Walter paid but little attention to Herbert, as his lameness prevented him from sharing in the active sports which they preferred, for they had never been taught to yield their wishes to others, and they were consequently extremely selfish and overbearing. But Elsie was very kind, and did all in her power to interest and amuse him.

One afternoon they all walked out together, attended by Jim, but Arthur and Walter, unwilling to accommodate their pace to Herbert's slow movements, were soon far in advance, Jim following close at their heels.

"They're quite out of sight," said Herbert presently, "and I'm very tired. Let's sit down on this bank, girls. I want to try my new bow, and you may run and pick up my arrows for me."

"Thank you, sir," said Lucy, laughing. "Elsie may do it if she likes, but as for me, I mean to take a nap. This nice, soft grass will make an elegant couch." Throwing herself down, she soon was, or pretended to be, in a sound slumber, while Herbert, seating himself with his back against the tree, amused himself with shooting his arrows here and there. Elsie ran for them and brought them to him, until she was quite heated and out of breath.

"Now I must rest a little, Herbert," she said at length, sitting down beside him. "Shall I tell you a story?"

"Oh, yes, do! I like your stories, and I don't mind leaving off shooting till you're done," said he, laying down his bow.

Elsie's story lasted about ten minutes, and when she had finished, Herbert took up his bow again, saying, "I guess you're rested now, Elsie," and sent an arrow over into the meadow.

"There! Just see how far I sent that! Do run and bring it to me, Elsie," he cried, "and let me see if I can't hit that tree next time. I've but just missed it."

"I'm tired, Herbert, but I'll run and bring it to you once," replied Elsie, forgetting entirely her father's prohibition. "But then you must try to wait until Jim comes back before you shoot any more."

So saying, she darted away, and came back in a moment with the arrow in her hand. But a sudden recollection had come over her just as she left the meadow, and throwing down the arrow at the boy's feet, she exclaimed in an agitated tone, "Oh, Herbert! I must go home just as quickly as I can. I had forgotten—oh, how could I forget! Oh, what will papa say!"

"Why, what's the matter?" asked Herbert in alarm.

"Never mind," said Elsie, sobbing. "There are the boys coming. They will take care of you, and I must go home. Goodbye."

And she ran quickly up the road, Herbert following her retreating form with wondering eyes.

Elsie sped onward, crying bitterly as she went.

"Where is papa?" she inquired of a servant whom she met in the avenue.

"Dunno Miss Elsie, but I reckon Massa Horace am in de house, kase his horse am in de stable."

Elsie hardly waited for the answer, but hurrying into the house, went from room to room, looking and asking in vain for her father. He was not in the drawing room, nor the library, nor his own apartments. She had just come out of these, and meeting a chambermaid in the hall, she exclaimed, "Oh, Fanny! Where is papa? Can't you tell me? For I must see him."

"Here I am, Elsie. What do you want with me?" called out her father's voice from the veranda, where she had neglected to look.

"What do you want?" he repeated, as his little girl appeared before him with her flushed and tearful face.

Elsie moved slowly toward him, with a timid air and downcast eyes.

"I wanted to tell you something, papa," she said in a low tremulous tone.

"Well, I am listening," said he, taking hold of her hand and drawing her to his side. "What is it? Are you sick or hurt?"

"No, papa, not either. But—but, oh, papa! I have been a very naughty girl," she exclaimed, bursting into tears, and sobbing violently. "I disobeyed you, papa. I—I have been in the meadow.

"Is it possible?! Would you dare to do so when I so positively forbid it only the other day?" he said in his sternest tone, while a dark frown gathered on his brow. "Elsie, I shall have to punish you."

"I did not intend to disobey you, papa." she sobbed. "I quite forgot that you had forbidden me to go there."

"That is no excuse, no excuse at all," said he, severely. "You must remember my commands, and if your memory is so poor I shall find means to strengthen it."

He paused a moment, still looking at the little, trembling, sobbing girl at his side, then asked. "What were you doing in the meadow? Tell me the whole story, that I may understand just how severely I ought to punish you."

Elsie gave him all the particulars. When, upon questioning her closely, he perceived how entirely voluntary her confession had been, his tone and manner became less stern. He said quite mildly, "Well, Elsie, I shall not be very severe with you this time, as you seem to be very penitent, and have made so full and frank a confession, but beware how you disobey me again, for you will not escape so easily another time. And remember, I will not take forgetfulness as any excuse. Go now to Aunt

Chloe, and tell her from me that she is to put you immediately to bed."

"It is only the middle of the afternoon, papa," said Elsie, deprecatingly.

"If it were much earlier, Elsie, it would make no difference. You must go at once to your bed, and stay there until tomorrow morning."

"What will Lucy and Herbert think when they come in and can't find me, papa?" she said weeping afresh.

"You should have thought of that before you disobeyed me," he answered very gravely. "If you are hungry," he added, "you may ask Chloe to get you a slice of bread or a cracker for your supper, but you can have nothing else."

Elsie lingered, looking timidly up into his face as though wanting to say something, but afraid to venture.

"Speak, Elsie, if you have anything more to say," he said encouragingly.

"Dear papa, I am so sorry I have been so naughty," she murmured, leaning her head against the arm of his chair, while the tears rolled fast down her cheeks. "Won't you please forgive me, papa? It seems to me I can't go to sleep tonight if you are angry with me."

He seemed quite touched by her penitence. "Yes, Elsie," he said, "I do forgive you. I am not at all angry with you now, and you may go to sleep in peace. Good night, my little daughter," and he bent down and pressed his lips to her brow.

Elsie held up her face for another, and he kissed her lips.

"Good night, dear papa," she said. "I hope I shall never be such a naughty girl again." And she went to her room, made almost happy by that kiss of forgiveness.

Elsie was up quite early the next morning and had learned all her lessons before breakfast. As she came down the stairs she saw, through the open door, her papa standing with some of the men-servants, apparently gazing at some object lying on the ground. She ran out and stood on the steps of the portico, looking at them and wondering what they were doing.

Presently her father turned round, and seeing her, held out his hand, calling, "Come here, Elsie."

She sprang quickly down the steps, and running to him, put her hand in his, saying, "Good morning, papa."

"Good morning, daughter," said he. "I have something to show you."

And leading her forward a few paces, he pointed to a large rattlesnake lying there.

"Oh, papa," she cried, starting back and clinging to him.

"It will not hurt you now," he said. "It is dead. The men killed it this morning in the meadow. Do you see now why I forbid you to go there?"

"Oh, papa!" she murmured, in a low tone of deep feeling, laying her cheek affectionately against his hand. "I might have lost my life by my disobedience. How good God was to take care of me! Oh, I hope I shall never be so naughty again."

"I hope not," said he gravely, but not unkindly, "and I hope that you will always, after this, believe that your father has some good reason for his commands, although he may not choose to explain it to you."

"Yes, papa, I think I will," she answered, humbly.

The breakfast-bell had rung, and he now led her in and seated her at the table.

Lucy Carrington looked curiously at her, and soon took an opportunity to whisper, "Where were you last night, Elsie? I couldn't find you, and your papa wouldn't say what had become of you, though I am quite sure he knew."

"I'll tell you after breakfast," replied Elsie, blushing deeply.

Lucy waited rather impatiently until all had risen from the table, and then, putting her arm round Elsie's waist, she drew her out on to the veranda, saying, "Now, Elsie, tell me. You know you promised."

"I was in bed," replied Elsie, dropping her eyes, while the color mounted to her very hair.

"In bed! Before five o' clock!" exclaimed Lucy, in a tone of astonishment. "Why, what was that for?"

"Papa sent me," replied Elsie, with an effort. "I had been naughty, and disobeyed him."

"Why, how strange! Do tell me what you had done!" exclaimed Lucy, with a face full of curiosity.

"Papa had forbidden me to go into the meadow, and I forgot all about it, and ran in there to get Herbert's arrow for him," replied Elsie, looking very much ashamed.

"Was that all? Why, my papa wouldn't have punished me for that," said Lucy. "He might have scolded me a little if I had done it on purpose, but if I had told him I had forgotten, he would only have said, 'You must remember better next time.'"

"Papa says that forgetfulness is no excuse, that I am to remember his commands, and if I forget, he will have to punish me, to make me remember better next time," said Elsie.

"He must be very strict indeed. I'm glad he is not my papa," replied Lucy, in a tone of great satisfaction.

"Come, little girls, make haste and get ready. We are to start in half an hour," said Adelaide Dinsmore, calling to them from the hall door.

The whole family, old and young, including visitors, were on that day to go on a picnic up the river, taking their dinner along, and spending the day in the woods. They had been planning this excursion for several days, and the children especially had been looking forward to it with a great deal of pleasure.

"Am I to go, Aunt Adelaide? Did papa say so?" asked Elsie anxiously, as she and Lucy hastened to obey the summons.

"I presume you are to go of course, Elsie. We have been discussing the matter for the last three days, always taking it for granted that you were to make one of the party, and he has never said you were to make one of the party, and he has never said you should not," replied Adelaide, good-naturedly. "So make haste, or you will be too late. But here comes your papa now," she added, as the library door opened, and Mr. Dinsmore stepped out into the hall where they were standing.

"Horace, Elsie is to go of course?"

"I do not see the 'of course,' Adelaide," said he dryly. "No, Elsie is not to go. She must stay at home and attend to her lessons as usual."

A look of keen disappointment came over Elsie's face, but she turned away without a word and went upstairs, while Lucy, casting a look of wrathful indignation at Mr. Dinsmore, ran after her, and following her into her room, she put her arm round her neck, saying, "Never mind, Elsie. It's too bad, and I wouldn't bear it. I'd go in spite of him."

"No, no, Lucy, I must obey my father—God says so. And besides, I couldn't do that if I wanted to, for papa is stronger than I am, and would punish me severely if I were to attempt such a thing," replied Elsie hastily, brushing away a tear that would come into her eye.

"Then I'd coax him," said Lucy. "Come, I'll go with you, and we will both try."

"No," replied Elsie, with a hopeless shake of the head, "I have found out already that my papa never breaks his word, and nothing could induce him to let me go, now that he has once said I should not. But you will have to leave me, Lucy, or you will be too late."

"Goodbye, then," said Lucy, turning to go, "but I think it is a great shame, and I sha'n't half enjoy myself without you."

"Well, now, Horace, I think you might let the child go," was Adelaide's somewhat indignant rejoinder to her brother, as the two little girls disappeared. "I can't conceive what reason you can have for keeping her at home, and she looks so terribly disappointed. Indeed, Horace, I am sometimes half inclined to think you take pleasure in thwarting that child."

"You had better call me a tyrant at once, Adelaide," said he angrily, and turning very red, "but I must beg to be permitted to manage my own child in my own way. I cannot see that I am under any obligation to give my reasons either to you or to anyone else."

"Well, if you did not intend to let her go, I think you might have said so at first, and not left the poor child build her hopes upon it, only to be disappointed. I must say I think it was cruel."

"Until this morning, Adelaide," he replied, "I did intend to let her go, for I expected to go myself. But I find I shall not be able to do so, as I must meet a gentleman on business, and as I know that accidents frequently occur to such pleasure parties, I don't feel willing to let Elsie go, unless I could be there myself to take care of her. Whether you believe it or not, it is really regard for my child's safety, and not cruelty, that leads me to refuse her this gratification."

"You are full of notions about that child, Horace," said Adelaide, a little impatiently. "I'm sure some of the rest of us could take care of her."

"No, in case of accident you would all have enough to do to take care of yourselves, and I shall not think of trusting Elsie in the company, since I cannot be there myself," he answered decidedly. And Adelaide, seeing he was not to be moved from his determination, gave up the attempt, and left the room to prepare for her ride.

It was a great disappointment to Elsie, and for a few moments her heart rose up in rebellion against her father. She tried to put away the feeling, but it would come back, for she could not imagine any reason for his refusal to let her go, excepting the disobedience of the day before. It seemed hard and unjust to punish her twice for the same fault, especially as he would have known nothing about it but for her own frank and voluntary confession. It was a great pity she had not heard the reasons he gave her Aunt Adelaide, for then she would have been quite submissive and content. It is indeed true that she ought to have been as it was, but little Elsie, though sincerely desirous to do right, was not yet perfect, and had already strangely forgotten the lesson of the morning.

She watched from the veranda the departure of the pleasure-seekers, all apparently in the happiest spirits. She was surprised to see that her father was not with them, and it half reconciled her to staying at home, although she hardly expected to see much of him. But there was something pleasant in the thought that he wanted her at home because he was to be there himself; it looked as though he really had some affection for her, and even a selfish love was better than none. These were not Elsie's thoughts; no, she would have never dreamed of calling her father selfish, but the undefined feeling was there, as she watched him hand the ladies into the carriage, and then turn and re-enter the house as they drove off.

But Miss Day's bell rang, and Elsie gathered up her books and hastened to the schoolroom. Her patience and endurance were sorely tried that morning, for Miss Day was in an exceedingly bad humor, being greatly mortified and also highly indignant that she had not been invited to make one of the picnic party. Elsie had never found her more unreasonable and difficult to please, and her incessant fault finding and scolding were almost more than the little girl could bear in addition to her own disappointment. At last the morning, which had seldom seemed so long, was over, and Elsie was dismissed from the schoolroom for the day.

At dinner, instead of the usual large party, there were only her father and the gentleman with whom he was transacting business, Miss Day, and herself.

The gentleman was not one of those who care to notice little children, but continued to discuss business and politics with Mr. Dinsmore, without seeming to be in the least aware of the presence of the little girl. She sat in perfect silence, eating whatever her father saw fit to put upon her plate. Elsie was very glad indeed when at length Miss Day rose to leave the table and her papa told her she might go too.

He called her back though, before she had gone across the room, to say that he had intended to ride with her that afternoon, but found he should not be able to do so. She must take Jim for a protector, as he did not wish her either to miss her ride or to go entirely alone.

He spoke very kindly, and Elsie thought with remorse of the rebellious feelings of the morning, and, had she been alone with her father, would certainly have confessed them, expressing her sorrow and asking forgiveness. But she could not do so before a third person, more especially a stranger, and merely saying, "Yes, papa, I will," she turned away and left the room. Jim was bringing up her horse as she passed the open door, and she hastened upstairs to prepare for her ride.

"Oh, mammy!" she suddenly exclaimed, as Chloe was trying on her hat. "Is Pomp going to the city today?"

"Yes, darlin', he gwine start directly," said Chloe, arranging her nursling's curls to better advantage, and finishing her work with a fond caress.

"Oh, then, mammy! Take some money out of my purse, and tell him to buy me a pound of the very nicest candy he can find," said the little girl eagerly. "I haven't had any for a long time, and I feel hungry for it today. What they had bought for the picnic looked so good, but you know I didn't get any of it."

The picnic party returned just before teatime, and Lucy Carrington rushed into Elsie's room eager to tell her what a delightful day they had had. She gave a very glowing account of their sports and entertainment, interrupting herself every now and then to lament over Elsie's absence. She assured her again and again that it had been the only drawback upon her own pleasure, and that she thought that Elsie's papa was very unkind indeed to refuse her permission to go. And as Elsie listened the morning's feelings of vexation and disappointment returned in full force, and though she said nothing, she allowed her friend to accuse her father of cruelty and injustice without offering any remonstrance.

In the midst of their talk the tea bell rang, and they hurried down to take their places at the table. Lucy went on with her narrative, though in a rather subdued tone, Elsie now and then asking a question, until Mr. Dinsmore turned to his daughter, saying in his stern way; "Be quiet Elsie. You are talking entirely too much for a child of your age. Don't let me hear you speak again until you have left the table."

Elsie's face flushed, and her eyes fell, under the rebuke, and during the rest of the meal not a sound escaped her lips.

"Come, Elsie, let us go into the garden and finish our talk," said Lucy, putting her arm affectionately around her friend's waist as they left the table. "Your papa can't hear us there, and we'll have a good time."

"Papa only stopped us because we were talking too much at the table," said Elsie, apologetically. "I'm sure he is willing you should tell me all about what a nice time you all had. But, Lucy," she added, lowering her voice, "please don't say again that you think papa was unkind to keep me at home today. I'm sure he knows best, and I ought not to have listened to a word of that kind about him."

"Oh, well! Never mind, I won't talk so any more." said Lucy good-naturedly, as they skipped down the walk together. "But I think he's cross, and I wish you were my sister, that you might have my kind, good papa for yours too," she added, drawing her arm more closely about her fiend's waist.

"Thank you, Lucy," said Elsie, with a little sigh. "I would like to be your sister, but indeed I would not like to give up my own dear papa, for I love him, oh, so much!"

"Why, how funny, when he's so cross to you!" exclaimed Lucy laughing.

Elsie put her hand over her friend's mouth, and Lucy pushed it away, saying, "Excuse me, I forgot, but I'll try not to say it again."

While the little girls were enjoying their talk in the garden, a servant with a small bundle in her hand came out on the veranda, where Mr. Horace Dinsmore was sitting smoking a cigar, and, casting an inquiring glance around, asked if he knew where Miss Elsie was.

"What do you want with her?" he asked.

"Only to give her dis bundle, massa, dat Pomp jus brought from de city."

"Give it to me," he said, extending his hand to receive it.

A few moments afterward Elsie and her friend returned to the house, and meeting Pomp, she asked him if he had brought her candy.

He replied that he had got some that was very nice indeed, and he thought that Fanny had carried it to her, and seeing Fanny near, he called to her to know what she had done with it.

"Why, Pomp, Massa Horace he told me to give it to him," said the girl.

Elsie turned away with a very disappointed look.

"You'll go and ask him for it, won't you?" asked Lucy, who was anxious to enjoy a share of the candy as well as to see Elsie gratified.

"No," said Elsie, sighing. "I had rather do without it."

Lucy coaxed for a little while, but finding it impossible to persuade Elsie to approach her father on the subject, finally volunteered to do the errand herself.

Elsie readily consented, and Lucy, trembling a little in spite of her boast that she was not afraid of him, walked out on the veranda where Mr. Dinsmore was still sitting, and putting on the air of great confidence, said:

"Mr. Dinsmore, will you please give me Elsie's candy? She wants it."

"Did Elsie send you?" he asked in a cold, grave tone.

"Yes, sir," replied Lucy, somewhat frightened.

"Then, if you please, Miss Lucy, you may tell Elsie to come directly to me."

Lucy ran back to her friend, and Elsie received the message in some trepidation, but as no choice was now left her, she went immediately to her father.

"Did you want me, papa?" she asked timidly.

"Yes, Elsie. I wish to know why you send another person to me for what you want, instead of coming yourself. It displeases me very much, and you may rest assured that you will never get anything that you ask for in that way."

Elsie hung her head in silence.

"Are you going to answer me?" he asked, in his severe tone. "Why did you send Lucy instead of coming yourself?"

"I was afraid, papa," she whispered, almost under her breath.

"Afraid! Afraid of what?" he asked, with increasing displeasure.

"Of you, papa," she replied, in a tone so low that he could scarcely catch the words, although he bent down his ear to receive her reply.

"If I were a drunken brute, in the habit of knocking you about, beating and abusing you, there might some reason for your fear, Elsie," he said, coloring with anger, "but as it is, I see no excuse for it at all, and I am both hurt and displeased by it."

"I am very sorry, papa. I won't do so again," she said, trembling.

There was a moment's pause, and then she asked in a timid, hesitating way, "Papa, may I have my candy, if you please?"

"No, you may not," he said decidedly, "and understand and remember that I positively forbid you either to buy or eat anything of the kind again without my express permission."

Elsie's eyes filled, and she had a hard struggle to keep down a rising sob as she turned away and went slowly back to the place where she had left her friend.

"Have you got it?" asked Lucy eagerly.

Elsie shook her head.

"What a shame!" exclaimed Lucy, indignantly. "He's just as cross as he can be. He's a tyrant, so he is! Just a hateful old tyrant, and I wouldn't care a cent for him, if I were you, Elsie. I'm glad he is not my father, so I am."

"I'm afraid he doesn't love me much," sighed Elsie in low, tearful tones, "for he hardly ever lets me have anything, or go anywhere that I want to."

"Well, never mind, I'll send and buy a good lot tomorrow, and we'll have a regular feast," said Lucy, soothingly, as she passed her arm around her friend's waist and drew her down to a seat on the portico step.

"Thank you, Lucy, you can buy for yourself if you like, but not for me, for papa has forbidden me to eat anything of the sort."

"Oh, of course we'll not let him know anything about it," said Lucy.

But Elsie shook her head sadly, saying with a little sigh, "No, Lucy, you are very kind, but I cannot disobey papa, even if he would never know it, because that would be disobeying God, and He would know it."

"Dear me, how particular you are!" exclaimed Lucy a little peevishly.

"Elsie," said Mr. Dinsmore, speaking from the door, "what are you doing there? Did I not forbid you to be out in the evening air?"

"I did not know you meant the doorstep, papa. I thought I was only not to go down into the garden," replied the little girl, rising to go in.

"I see you intend to make as near an approach to disobedience as you dare," said her father.

"Go immediately to your room, and tell mammy to put you to bed."

Elsie silently obeyed, and Lucy, casting an indignant glance at Mr. Dinsmore, was about to follow her, when he said, "I wish her to go alone, if you please, Miss Lucy." With a frown and a pout the little girl walked into the drawing room and seated herself on the sofa beside her mamma.

Mr. Dinsmore walked out on to the portico, and stood there watching the moon which was just riding over the treetops.

"Horace," said Arthur, emerging from the shadow of a tree near by and approaching his brother, "Elsie thinks your a tyrant. She says you never let her have anything, nor go anywhere, and you're always punishing her. She and Lucy have had a fine time out there talking over your bad treatment of her, and planning to have some candy in spite of you."

"Arthur, I do not believe that Elsie would deliberately plan to disobey me. Whatever faults she may have, I am very sure she is above the meanness of telling tales," replied Mr. Dinsmore, in a tone of severity, as he turned and went into the house, while Arthur, looking sadly crestfallen, crept away out of sight.

When Elsie reached her room, she found that Chloe was not there, for, not expecting her services would be required at so early an hour, she had gone down to the kitchen to have a little chat with her fellow-servants. Elsie rang for her, and then walking to the window, stood looking down into the garden in an attitude of thoughtfulness and dejection. She was mentally taking a review of the manner in which she had spent the day, as was her custom before retiring. The retrospect had seldom been so painful to the little girl. She had a very tender conscience, and it told her that she had more than once during the day indulged in wrong feelings toward her father. She had also allowed another to speak disrespectfully of him, giving by her silence a tacit approval of the sentiments uttered, and, more than that, had spoken complaining of him herself.

"Oh!" she murmured half aloud as she covered her face with her hands, and the tears trickled through her fingers. "How soon I have forgotten the lesson papa taught me this morning and my promise to trust him without knowing his reasons. I don't deserve that he should love me or be kind and indulgent, when I am so rebellious."

"What de matter, darlin'?" asked Chloe's voice in pitiful tones, as she took her nursling in her arms and laid her little head against her bosom, passing her hand caressingly over her soft bright curls. "Your old mammy can't bear to see her love cryin' like dat."

"Oh, mammy, mammy! I've been such a wicked girl today! Oh, I'm afraid I shall never be good, never be like Jesus! I'm afraid He is angry with me, for I have disobeyed Him today," sobbed the child.

"Darlin'," said Chloe, earnestly, "didn't you read to your ole mammy dis very morning dese bressed words: 'If any man sin, we have an advocate with the Father, Jesus Christ the righteous,' an' de other: 'If we confess our sins, He is faithful and just to forgive us our sins.' Go to de dear, bressed Lord Jesus, darlin', an' ax Him to forgive you, an' I knows He will."

"Yes, He will," replied the little girl, raising her head and dashing away her tears, "He will forgive my sins, and take away my wicked heart, and give me right thoughts and feelings. How glad I am you remembered those sweet verses, you dear old mammy," she added, twining her arms lovingly around her nurse's neck. And then she delivered her papa's message, and Chloe began at once to prepare her for bed.

Elsie's tears had ceased to flow, but they were still trembling in her eyes, and the little face wore a very sad and troubled expression as she stood patiently passive in her nurse's hands. Chloe had soon finished her labors, and then the little girl opened her Bible, and, as usual, read a few verses aloud, though her voice trembled, and once or twice a tear fell on the page. Then, closing the book, she stole away to the side of the bed and knelt down.

She was a good while on her knees, and several times, as the sound of a low sob fell upon Chloe's ear, she sighed and murmured to herself, "Poor darlin'! Dear, bressed lamb, your ole mammy don't like to hear dat."

Then as the child rose from her kneeling posture, Chloe went to her, and taking her in her arms, folded her into a fond embrace. She called her by the most tender and endearing epithets, telling her that her old mammy loved her better than life—better than anything in the whole wide world.

Elsie flung her arms around the nurse's neck, and laid her head upon her bosom, saying, "Yes, my dear old mammy, I know you love me, and I love you too. But put me in bed now, or papa will be displeased."

"What makes you so restless, darlin'?" asked Chloe, half an hour afterward. "Can't you go to sleep no how?"

"Oh, mammy! If I could only see papa just for one moment to tell him something. Do you think he would come to me?" sighed the little girl. "Please, mammy, go down and see if he is busy. Don't say a word if he is, but if not, ask him to come to me for just one minute."

Chloe left the room immediately, but returned the next moment, saying, "I jes looked into de parlor, darlin', an Massa Horace he mighty busy playin' chess wid Miss Lucy's mamma, an' I didn't say nuffin' to him. Jes you go sleep, my love, an' tell Massa Horace all 'bout it in de mornin'."

Elsie sighed deeply, and turning over on her pillow, cried herself to sleep.

Chloe was just putting the finishing touches to the little girl's dress the next morning, when Lucy Carrington rapped at the door.

"Good morning, Elsie," she said. "I was in a hurry to come to you, because it is my last day, you know. Wasn't it too bad of your father to send you off to bed so early last night?"

"No, Lucy. Papa has a right to send me to bed whenever he pleases, and besides, I was naughty and deserved to be punished. And it was not much more than half an hour earlier than my usual bedtime."

"You naughty!" exclaimed Lucy, opening her eyes very wide. "Mamma often says she wishes I was half as good."

Elsie sighed, but made no answer. Her thoughts seemed far away. She was thinking of what she had been so anxious, the night before, to say to her father, and trying to gain courage to do it this morning. "If I could only get close to him when nobody was by, and he would look and speak kindly to me, I could do it then," she murmured to herself.

"Come, Aunt Chloe, aren't you done? I want to have a run in the garden before breakfast," said Lucy, somewhat impatiently, as Chloe tied and untied Elsie's sash several times.

"Well, Miss Lucy, I'se done now," she answered, passing her hand once more over the nursling's curls. "but Massa Horace he mighty pertickler 'bout Miss Elsie."

"Yes," said Elsie, "papa wants me always to look very nice and neat, and when I go down in the morning he just gives me one glance from head to toe. If anything is wrong he is sure to see it and send me back immediately to have it made right. Now, mammy, please give me my hat and let us go."

"You's got plenty of time, chillens. De bell won't go for to ring dis hour," remarked the old nurse, tying on Elsie's hat.

"My chile looks sweet an' fresh as a moss rosebud dis mornin'," she added, talking to herself, as she watched the two little girls tripping downstairs hand in hand.

They skipped up and down the avenue several times, and ran all around the garden before it was time to go in. Then Elsie went up to Chloe to have her hair made smooth again. She was just descending for the second time to the hall, where she had left Lucy, when they saw a carriage drive up to the front door.

"There's papa!" cried Lucy, joyfully, as it stopped and a gentleman sprang out and came up the steps into the portico. And in an instant she was in his arms, receiving such kisses and caresses as Elsie had vainly longed for all her life.

Lucy had several brothers, but was an only daughter, and a very great love, especially with her father.

Elsie watched them with a wistful look and a strange aching at her heart.

But presently Mr. Carrington set Lucy down, and turning to her, gave her a shake of the hand, and then a kiss, saying, "How do you do this morning, my dear? I'm afraid you are hardly glad to see me, as I come to take Lucy away, for I suppose you have been having fine times together."

"Yes, sir, indeed we have, and I hope you will let her come again."

"Oh, yes, certainly! But the visits must not be all on one side. I shall talk to your papa about it, and perhaps persuade him to let us take you along this afternoon to spend a week at Ashlands."

"Oh, how delightful!" cried Lucy, clapping her hands. "Elsie, do you think he will let you go?"

"I don't know, I'm afraid not," replied the little girl, doubtfully.

"You must coax him, as I do my papa," said Lucy.

But at this Elsie only shook her head, and just then the breakfast bell rang.

Mr. Dinsmore was already in the breakfast room, and Elsie, going up to him, said, "Good morning, papa."

"Good morning, Elsie," he replied, but his tone was so cold that even if no one else had been by, she could not have said another word.

He had not intended to be influenced by the information Arthur had so maliciously given him the night before, yet unconsciously he was, and his manner to his little daughter was many degrees colder that it had been for some time.

After breakfast Lucy reminded Elsie of a promise she had made to show her some beautiful shells which her father had collected in his travels, and Elsie led the way to the cabinet, a small room opening into the library, and filled with curiosities.

They had gone in alone, but were soon followed by Arthur, Walter, and Enna.

Almost everything in the room belonged to Mr. Horace Dinsmore, and Elsie, knowing that many of the articles were rare and costly, and that he was very careful of them, begged Enna and the boys to go out, lest they should accidentally do some mischief.

"I won't," replied Arthur. "I've just as good a right to be here as you."

As he spoke he gave her a push, which almost knocked her over, and in catching at a table to save herself from falling, she threw down a beautiful vase of rare old china, which Mr. Dinsmore prized very highly. It fell with a loud crash, and lay scattered in fragments at their feet.

"There, see what you've done!" exclaimed Arthur, as the little group stood aghast at the mischief.

It happened that Mr. Dinsmore was just then in the library, and the noise soon brought him upon the scene of action.

"Who did this?" he asked, in a wrathful tone, looking from one to the other.

"Elsie," said Arthur. "She threw it down and broke it."

"Troublesome, careless child! I would not have taken a hundred dollars for that vase," he exclaimed. "Go to your room! Go this instant, and stay there until I send for you. And remember, if you ever come in here again without permission I shall punish you."

He opened the door as he spoke, and Elsie flew across the hall, up the stairs, and into her own room, without once pausing or looking back.

"Now go out, every one of you, and don't come in here again. This is no place for children," said Mr. Dinsmore, turning the others into the hall, and shutting and locking the door upon them.

"You ought to be ashamed, Arthur Dinsmore," exclaimed Lucy indignantly. "It was all your own fault, and Elsie was not to blame at all, and you know it."

"I didn't touch the old vase, and I'm not going to take the blame for it either, I can tell you, miss," replied Arthur, moving off, followed by Walter and Enna. Lucy walked to the other end of the hall, and stood looking out of the window, debating in her own mind whether she had sufficient courage to face Mr. Dinsmore, and make him understand where the blame of the accident ought to lie.

At length she seemed to have solved the question, for turning about and moving noiselessly down the passage to the library door, she gave a timid little rap, which was immediately answered by Mr. Dinsmore's voice saying, "Come in."

Lucy opened the door and walked in, closing it after her.

Mr. Dinsmore sat at a table writing, and he looked up with an expression of mingled surprise and impatience.

"What do you want, Miss Lucy?" he asked. "Speak quickly, for I am very busy."

"I just wanted to tell you, sir," replied Lucy, speaking up quite boldly, "that Elsie was not at all to blame about the vase, for it was Arthur who pushed her and made her fall against the table, and that was the way the vase came to fall and break."

"What made him push her?" he asked.

"Just because Elsie asked him, and Walter, and Enna to go out, for fear they might do some mischief."

Mr. Dinsmore's pen was suspended over the paper for a moment while he sat thinking with a somewhat clouded brow. Presently turning to the little girl, he said quite pleasantly, "Very well, Miss Lucy, I am much obliged to you for your information, for I should be very sorry to punish Elsie unjustly. And now will you do me the favor to go to her and tell her that her papa says she need not stay in her room any longer?"

"Yes, sir, I will," replied Lucy, her face sparkling with delight as she hurried off with great alacrity to do his bidding.

She found Elsie in her room crying violently. Throwing her arms around her neck, she delivered Mr. Dinsmore's message, concluding with, "So now, Elsie, you see you needn't cry, nor feel sorry any more, but just dry your eyes and let us go down into the garden and have a good time."

Elsie was very thankful to Lucy, and very glad that her papa now knew that she was not to blame, but she was still sorry for his loss, and his words had wounded her too deeply to be immediately forgotten. Indeed, it was some time before the sore spot they had made in her heart was entirely healed. But she tried to forget it all and enter heartily into the sports proposed by Lucy.

The Carringtons were not to leave until the afternoon, and the little girls spent nearly the whole morning in the garden, coming into the drawing room a few moments before the dinner bell rang.

Mrs. Carrington sat on a sofa engaged with some fancy work, while Herbert, who had not felt well enough to join the other children, had stretched himself out beside her, putting his head in her lap.

Mr. Carrington and Mr. Horace Dinsmore were conversing near by.

Lucy ran up to her papa and seated herself upon his knee with her arm around his neck. Elsie stopped a moment to speak to Herbert, and then timidly approaching her father, with her eyes upon the floor, said in a low, half-frightened tone, that reached no ear but his, "I am very sorry about the vase, papa."

He took her hand, and drawing her close to him, pushed back the hair from her forehead with his other hand, and bending down to her, said almost in a whisper, "Never mind, daughter, we will forget all about it. I am sorry I spoke so harshly to you, since Lucy tells me you were not so much to blame."

Elsie's face flushed with pleasure, and she looked up gratefully, but before she had time to reply, Mrs. Carrington said, "Elsie, we want to take you home with us to spend a week. Will you go?"

"I should like to, very much, indeed, ma'am, if papa will let me," replied the little girl, looking wistfully up into his face.

"Well, Mr. Dinsmore, what do you say? I hope you can have no objection," said Mrs. Carrington, looking inquiringly at him.

Her husband added, "Oh, yes, Dinsmore! You must let her go by all means. You can certainly spare her for a week, and it need be no interruption to her lessons, as she can share with Lucy in the instructions of our governess, who is really a superior teacher."

Mr. Dinsmore was looking very grave, and Elsie knew from the expression of his countenance what his answer would be, before he spoke. He had noticed the indignant glance Lucy had once or twice bestowed upon him, and remembering Arthur's report of the conversation between the two little girls the night before, had decided in his own mind that the less Elsie saw of Lucy the better.

"I thank you both for your kind attention to my little girl," he replied courteously, "but while fully appreciating your kindness in extending the invitation, I must beg leave to decline it, as I am satisfied that home is the best place for her at present."

"Ah, no, I suppose we ought hardly to have expected you to spare her so soon after your return," said Mrs. Carrington, "but really, I am very sorry to be refused, for Elsie is such a good child that I am always delighted to have Lucy and Herbert with her."

"Perhaps you think better of her than she deserves, Mrs. Carrington. I find that Elsie is sometimes naughty and in need of correction, as well as other children, and therefore I think it best to keep her as much as possible under my own eye," replied Mr. Dinsmore, looking very gravely at his little daughter as he spoke.

Elsie's face flushed painfully, and she had hard work to keep from bursting into tears. It was a great relief to her that just at that moment the dinner bell rang, and there was a general movement in the direction of the dining room. Her look was touchingly humble as her father led her in and seated her at the table.

She was thinking, "Papa says that I am naughty sometimes, but, oh how very naughty he would think me if he knew all the wicked feelings I had yesterday."

As soon as they had risen from the table, Mrs. Carrington bade Lucy go up to her maid to have her bonnet put on, as the carriage was already at the door.

Elsie would have gone with her, but her father had taken her hand again, and he held it fast.

She looked up inquiringly into his face.

"Stay here," he said. "Lucy will be down again in a moment."

And Elsie stood quietly at his side until Lucy returned.

But even then her father did not relinquish his hold of her hand, and all the talking the little girls could do must be done close at his side.

Yet, as he was engaged in earnest conversation with Mr. Carrington, and did not seem to be listening to them, Lucy ventured to whisper to Elsie, "I think it's real mean of him. He might let you go."

"No," replied Elsie, in the same low tone, "I'm sure papa knows best, and besides, I have been naughty, and don't deserve to go, though I should like to, dearly."

"Well, goodbye," said Lucy, giving her a kiss.

It was not until Mr. Carrington's carriage was fairly on its way down the avenue, that Mr. Dinsmore dropped his little girl's hand, and then he said, "I want you in the library, Elsie. Come to me in half an hour."

"Yes, papa, I will," she replied, looking a little frightened.

"You need not be afraid," he said, in a tone of displeasure. "I am not going to hurt you."

Elsie blushed and hung her head, but made no reply, and he turned away and left her. She could not help wondering what he wanted with her, and though she tried not to feel afraid, it was impossible to keep from trembling a little as she knocked at the library door.

Her father's voice said, "Come in," and entering, she found him alone, seated at a table covered with papers and writing materials, while beside the account book in which he was writing lay a pile of money, in bank notes, and gold and silver.

"Here, Elsie," he said, laying down his pen, "I want to give you your month's allowance. Your grandfather has paid it to you heretofore, but of course, now that I am at home, I attend to everything that concerns you. You have been receiving eight dollars. I shall give you ten," and he counted out the money and laid it before her as he spoke, "but I shall require a strict account of all that you spend. I want you to learn to keep accounts, for if you live, you will someday have a great deal of money to take care of. Here is a blank book that I have prepared, so that you can do so very easily. Every time that you lay out or give away any money, you must set it down here as soon as you come home. Be particular about that, lest you should forget something. You must bring your book to me at the end of every month, and let me see how much you have spent, what is the balance in hand, and if you are not able to make it come out square. You must tell me what you have done with every penny. You will lose either the whole or a part of your allowance for the next month, according to the extent of your delinquency. Do you understand?"

"Yes, sir."

"Very well. Let me see how much you can remember of your last month's expenditure. Take the book and set down everything you can think of."

Elsie had a good memory, and was able to remember how she spent almost every cent during the time specified, and she set down one item after another, and then added up the column without any mistake.

"That was very well done," said her father approvingly. And then running over the items half aloud, "Candy, half a dollar. Remember, Elsie, there is to be no more money disposed of in that way, not as a matter of economy, by any means, but because I consider it very injurious. I am very anxious that you should grow up strong and healthy. I would not for anything have a miserable dyspeptic."

Then suddenly closing the book and handing it to her, he said inquiringly, "You were very anxious to go to Ashlands?"

"I would have liked to go, papa, if you had been willing," she replied meekly.

"I am afraid Lucy is not a suitable companion for you, Elsie. I think she puts bad notions into your head," he said very gravely.

Elsie flushed and trembled, and was just opening her lips to make her confession, when the door opened and her grandfather entered. She could not speak before him, and so remained silent.

"Does she not sometimes say naughty things to you?" asked her father, speaking so low that her grandfather could not have heard.

"Yes, sir," replied the little girl, almost under her breath.

"I thought so," said he, "and therefore I shall keep you apart as entirely as possible, and I hope there will be no murmuring on your part."

"No, papa, you know best," she answered, very humbly.

Then putting the money into her hands, he dismissed her. When she had gone out he sat for a moment in deep thought. Elsie's list of articles bought with her last month's allowance consisted almost entirely of gifts for others, generally the servants. There were some beads and sewing-silk for making a purse, and a few drawing materials, but with the exception of the candy, she had bought nothing else for herself. This was what her father was thinking of.

"She is a dear, unselfish, generous little thing," he said to himself. "However, I may be mistaken. I must not allow myself to judge from only one month. She seems submissive too,"—he had overheard what passed between her and Lucy at parting—"but perhaps that was for effect. She probably suspected I could hear her—and she thinks me a tyrant, and obeys from fear, not love."

And this thought drove away all the tender feeling that had been creeping into his heart. When he next met his little daughter, his manner was as cold and distant as ever, and Elsie found it impossible to approach him with sufficient freedom to tell him what was in her heart.

CHAPTER FIFTH

Man is unjust,
but God is just; and finally
justice Triumphs.

——*Longfellow's Evangeline*

How disappointment tracks
The steps of hope!

——*Miss Landon*

ONE AFTERNOON, THE NEXT WEEK after the Carringtons had left, the younger members of the family, Arthur, Elsie, Walter, and Enna, were setting out to take a walk, when Elsie, seeing a gold chain hanging from the pocket of Arthur's jacket, exclaimed, "Oh, Arthur! How could you take grandpa's watch? Do put it away, for you will be almost sure to injure it."

"Hold your tongue, Elsie. I'll do as I please," was the polite rejoinder.

"But, Arthur, you know that grandpa would never let you take it. I have often heard him say that it was very valuable, for it was seldom that so good a one could be had at any price, and I know that he paid a great deal for it."

"Well, if he prizes it so, he needn't have left it lying on his table, and so I'll just teach him a lesson. It's time he learned to be careful."

"Oh, Arthur! Do put it away," pleaded Elsie. "If anything should happen to it, what will grandpa say? I know he will be very angry, and ask us all who did it, and you know I cannot tell a lie, and if he asks me if it was you, I cannot say no."

"Yes, I'll trust you for telling tales," replied Arthur, sneeringly, "but if you do, I'll pay you for it."

He ran down the avenue as he spoke, Walter and Enna following, and Elsie slowly bringing up the rear, looking the picture of distress. For she knew not what to do, seeing that Arthur would not listen to her remonstrances, and, as often happened, all the older members of the family were out. Thus there was no authority that could be appealed to in time to prevent the mischief which she had every reason to fear would be done. Once she thought of turning back, that she might escape the necessity of being a witness in the case. But, remembering that her father told her she must walk with the others that afternoon, and also that, as she had already seen the watch in Arthur's possession, her testimony would be sufficient to convict him even if she saw no more, she gave up the idea. She hurried on with the faint hope that she might be able to induce Arthur to refrain from indulging in such sports as would be likely to endanger the watch, or else to give it into her charge. At any other time she would have trembled at the thought of touching it, but now she felt so sure it would be safer with her than with him, that she would gladly have taken the responsibility.

The walk was far from being a pleasure that afternoon. The boys ran so fast that it quite put her out of breath to keep up with them. Then every little while Arthur would cut some caper that made her tremble for the watch. He answered her entreaties that he would either give it into her care or walk along quietly, with sneers and taunts, and declarations of his determination to do just exactly as he pleased, and not be ruled by her.

But at length, while he was in the act of climbing a tree, the watch dropped from his pocket and fell to the ground, striking with considerable force.

Elsie uttered a slight scream, and Arthur, now thoroughly frightened himself, jumped down and picked it up.

The crystal was broken, the back dented, and how much the works were injured they could not tell, but it had ceased to run.

"Oh, Arthur! See what you've done!" exclaimed Walter.

"What will papa say?" said Enna, while Elsie stood pale and trembling, not speaking a word.

"You hush!" exclaimed Arthur fiercely. "I'll tell you what, if any of you dare to tell of me, I'll make you sorry for it to the last day of your life. Do you hear?"

The question was addressed to Elsie in a tone of defiance.

"Arthur," said she, "grandpa will know that somebody did it, and surely you would not wish an innocent person to be punished for your fault."

"I don't care who gets punished, so that papa does not find out that I did it," said he furiously, "and if you dare tell of me, I'll pay you for it."

"I shall say nothing, unless it becomes necessary to save the innocent, or I am forced to speak, but in that case I shall tell the truth," replied Elsie, firmly.

Arthur doubled up his fist, and made a plunge at her as if he meant to knock her down, but Elsie sprang behind the tree, and then ran so fleetly toward the house that he was not able to overtake her until his passion had had time to cool.

When they reached the house, Arthur replaced the watch on his father's table, whence he had taken it, and then they all awaited his return with what courage they might.

"I say, Wally," said Arthur, drawing his little brother aside and speaking in a low tone, having first sent a cautious glance around to assure himself that no one else was within hearing, "I say, what would you give me for that new riding whip of mine?"

"Oh, Arthur! Anything I've got," exclaimed the little boy eagerly. "But you wouldn't give it up, I know, and you're only trying to tease me."

"No, indeed, Wal, I mean to give it to you if you'll only be a good fellow and do as I tell you."

"What?" he asked, with intense interest.

"Tell papa that Jim broke the watch."

"But he didn't," replied the child, opening his eyes wide with astonishment.

"Well, what of that, you little goose?" exclaimed Arthur impatiently. "Papa doesn't know that."

"But Jim will get punished," said Walter, "and I don't want to tell such a big story either."

"Very well, sir, then you'll not get the whip, and, besides, if you don't do as I wish, I'm certain you'll see a ghost one of these nights, for there's one comes to see me sometimes, and I'll send him right off to you."

"Oh, don't, Arthur, don't! I'd die of fright," cried the little boy, who was very timid, glancing nervously around, as if he expected the ghost to appear immediately.

"I tell you I will, though, if you don't do as I say. He'll come this very night and carry you off, and never bring you back."

"O Arthur! Don't let him come, and I'll say anything you want me to," cried the little fellow in great terror.

"That's a good boy. I knew you would," said Arthur, smiling triumphantly. And turning away from Walter, he next sought out Enna, and tried his threats and persuasions upon her with even better success.

Elsie had gone directly to her own room, where she sat trembling every time a footstep approached her door, lest it should be a messenger from her grandfather. No one came, however, and at last the tea bell rang, and on going down she found to her relief that her grandfather and his wife had not yet returned.

"You look pale, Elsie," said her father, giving her a scrutinizing glance as she took her seat by his side. "Are you well?"

"Yes, papa, quite well," she replied.

He looked at her again a little anxiously, but said no more, and as soon as the meal was concluded, Elsie hastened away to her own room again.

It was still early in the evening when Mr. and Mrs. Dinsmore returned—for once, bringing no company with them—and he had not been many minutes in the house ere he took up his watch, and of course instantly discovered the injury it had sustained.

His suspicions at once fell upon Arthur, whose character for mischief was well established, and burning with rage, watch in hand, he repaired to the drawing room, which he entered, asking, in tones tremulous with passion, "Where is Arthur? Young rascal! This is some of his work," he added, holding up the injured article.

"My dear, how can you say so? Have you any proof?" asked his wife, deprecatingly adding in her softest tones, "My poor boy seems to get the blame for everything that goes wrong."

"He gets no more than he deserves," replied her husband angrily. "Arthur! Arthur I say, where are you?"

"He is in the garden, sir, I think. I saw him walking in the shrubbery a moment since," said Mr. Horace Dinsmore.

The father instantly dispatched a servant to bring him in, sending a second in search of the overseer, while a third was ordered to assemble all the house-servants. "I will sift this matter to the bottom, and child or servant, the guilty one shall suffer for it," exclaimed the old gentleman, pacing angrily up and down the room. "Arthur," said he sternly, as the boy made his appearance, looking somewhat pale and alarmed, "how dare you meddle with my watch?"

"I didn't, sir. I never touched it," he replied boldly, yet avoiding his father's eyes as he uttered the deliberate falsehood.

"There, my dear, I told you so," exclaimed his mother, triumphantly.

"I don't believe you," said the father, "and if you are guilty, as I strongly suspect, you had better confess it at once, before I find it out in some other way."

"I didn't do it, sir. It was Jim and I can prove it by Walter and Enna. We all saw it fall from his pocket when he was up in a tree. He cried like anything when he found it was broken, and said he didn't mean to do it any harm, he was only going to wear it a little while, and then put it back all safe, but now master would be dreadfully angry, and have him flogged."

"That I will, if it is true," exclaimed the old gentleman, passionately. "He shall be whipped and sent out to work on the plantation. I'll keep no such meddlers about my house."

He looked at Enna. "What do you know of this?" he asked.

"It is true, papa, I saw him do it," she replied with a slight blush, and sending an uneasy glance around the room.

"Did you see it, too, Walter?" asked his father.

"Yes, sir," replied the little fellow, in a low, reluctant tone, "but please, papa, don't punish him. I'm sure he didn't mean to break it."

"Hold your tongue! He shall be punished as he deserves," cried the old gentleman, furiously. "Here sir," turning to the overseer, and pointing to Jim, "take the fellow out, and give him such a flogging as he will remember."

Elsie was sitting in her room, trying to learn a lesson for the next day, but finding great difficulty in fixing her thoughts upon it, when she was startled by the sudden entrance of Aunt Chloe, who, with her apron to her eyes, was sobbing violently.

"O mammy, mammy! What's the matter? Has anything happened to you?" inquired the little girl, in a tone of great alarm, starting to her feet, and dropping her book in her haste and fright.

"Why," sobbed Chloe, "Jim he's been an' gone an' broke ole master's watch, an' he's gwine be whipped, an' ole Aunt Phoebe she's cryin' fit to break her ole heart 'bout her boy, kase—"

Elsie waited to hear no more, but darting out into the hall, and encountering her father on his way to his room, she rushed up to him. Pale and agitated, and seizing his hand, she looked up eagerly into his face, exclaiming with a burst of tears and sobs, "O papa, papa! Don't, oh, don't let them whip poor Jim."

Mr. Dinsmore's countenance was very grave, almost distressed.

"I am sorry it is necessary, daughter," he said, "but Jim has done very wrong, and deserves his punishment, and I cannot interfere."

"Oh, no, papa! He did not, indeed he did not break the watch. I know he didn't, for I was by and saw it all."

"Is it possible?" said he, in a tone of surprise. "Then tell me who did it. It could not have been you, Elsie?" and he looked searchingly into her face.

"Oh, no, papa! I would never have dared to touch it. But please don't make me tell tales. But I know it wasn't Jim. Oh, do stop them quickly, before they begin to whip him!"

"Aunt Chloe," said Mr. Dinsmore, "go down to my father and tell him it is my request that the punishment should be delayed a few moments until I come down."

Then taking Elsie's hand, he led her into her room again, and seating himself, drew her to his side, saying, with grave decision, "Now, my daughter, if you want to save Jim, it will be necessary for you to tell all you know about this affair."

"I don't like to tell tales, papa," pleaded the little girl. "I think it so very mean. Is it not enough for me to tell that I know Jim didn't do it?"

"No, Elsie. I have already said that it is quite necessary for you to tell all you know."

"Oh, papa! Don't make me. I don't like to do it," she urged with tears in her eyes.

"I should be very much ashamed of you, and quite unwilling to own you as my child, if under any other circumstances you were willing to tell tales," he replied, in a tone of kindness that quite surprised Elsie. She always trembled at the very thought of opposing the slightest resistance to his will. "But," he added, firmly, "it is the only way to save Jim. If you do not now make a full disclosure of all you know, he will be severely whipped and sent away to work on the plantation, which will distress his poor old mother exceedingly. Elsie, I think you would be doing very wickedly to allow an innocent person to suffer when you can prevent it. Besides, I will add the weight of my authority, and say you must do it at once; and you well know, my daughter, that there can be no question as to the duty of obedience to your father."

He paused, gazing earnestly down into the little tearful, downcast, blushing face at his side.

"Have I not said enough to convince you of your duty?" he asked.

"Yes, papa; I will tell you all about it," she answered in a tremulous tone.

Her story was told with evident reluctance, but in a simple, straightforward manner, that attested its truthfulness.

Mr. Dinsmore listened in silence, but with an expression of indignation on his handsome features, and the moment she had finished he rose, and again taking her hand, led her from her room, saying, as he did so:

"You must repeat this story to your grandfather."

"Oh, papa! Must I? Won't you tell him? Please don't make me do it," she pleaded tremblingly, and hanging back.

"My daughter, you must," he replied, so sternly that she dared not make any further resistance, but quietly submitted to be led into her grandfather's presence.

He was still in the drawing room, walking about in a disturbed and angry manner, and now and then casting a suspicious glance upon Arthur, who sat pale and trembling in a corner. He looked the picture of guilt and misery, for he had heard Chloe deliver his brother's message, and feared that exposure awaited him.

Walter had stolen away to cry over Jim's punishment. He wished that he had had the courage to tell the truth at first, but saying to himself that it was too late now, his father wouldn't believe him, and he would make it up to Jim somehow, even if it took his pocket-money for a month.

None of the other members of the family had left the room, and all wore an anxious, expectant look, as Mr. Dinsmore entered, leading Elsie by the hand.

"I have brought you another witness, sir," he said, "for it seems Elsie was present when the mischief was done."

"Ah!" exclaimed the old gentleman. "Then I may hope to get at the truth. Elsie, who broke my watch?"

"It was not Jim, grandpa, indeed, indeed it was not. But oh, please don't make me say who it was," replied the little girl, beseechingly.

"Elsie!" exclaimed her father, in a tone of stern reproof.

"Oh, papa! How can I?" she sobbed, trembling and clinging to his hand as she caught a threatening look from Arthur.

"Come, come, child, you must tell us all you know about it," said her grandfather, "or else I can't let Jim off."

Mr. Dinsmore was looking down at his little girl, and, following the direction of her glance, perceived the cause of the terror. "Don't be afraid to speak out and tell all you know, daughter, for I will protect you," he said, pressing the little trembling hand in his, and at the same time giving Arthur a meaning look.

"Yes, yes, speak out, child. Speak out at once. No one shall hurt you for telling the truth," exclaimed her grandfather, impatiently.

"I will, grandpa," she said, trembling and weeping, "but please don't be angry with Arthur. If you will forgive him this time, I think he will never meddle any more, and I am quite sure he did not mean to break it."

"So it was you, after all, you young rascal! I knew it from the first!" cried the old gentleman, striding across the room, seizing the boy by the shoulder and shaking him roughly.

"But go on, Elsie, let us have the whole story," he added, turning to her again, but still keeping his hold upon Arthur. "You young dog!" he added, when she had finished. "Yes, I'll forgive you when you've had a good, sound flogging and a week's solitary confinement on bread and water, but not before."

So, saying, he was about to lead him from the room, when Elsie suddenly sprang forward, and with clasped hands, and flushed eager face, she pleaded earnestly, beseechingly, "Oh, grandpa! Don't whip him, don't punish him! He will never be so naughty again. Will you, Arthur? Let me pay for the watch, grandpa, and don't punish him. I would so like to do it."

"It isn't the moneyed value of the watch I care for, child," replied the old gentleman, contemptuously. "And besides, where would you get so much money?"

"I am rich, grandpa, am I not? Didn't my mamma leave me a great deal of money?" asked the little girl, casting down her eyes and blushing painfully.

"No, Elsie," said her father very gravely, as he took her hand and led her back to the side of his chair again, "you have nothing but what I choose to give you, until you come of age, which will not be for a great many years yet."

"But you will give me the money to pay for the watch, papa, won't you?" she asked, pleadingly.

"No, I certainly shall not, for I think Arthur should be left to suffer the penalty of his own misdeeds," he replied in a very decided tone. "And, besides," he added, "your grandfather has already told you that it is not the pecuniary loss he cares for."

"No, but I will teach this young rascal to let my property alone," said the elder gentleman with almost fierce determination, as he tightened his grasp upon the boy's arm and dragged him from the room.

Arthur cast a look of hatred and defiance at Elsie as he went out, that made her grow pale with fear and tremble so that she could scarcely stand.

Her father saw both the look and the effect, and drawing the little trembler closer to him, he put his arm around her, and stroking her hair, said in a low, soothing voice: "Don't be frightened, daughter. I will protect you."

She answered him with a grateful look and a long sigh of relief, and he was just about to take her on his knee when visitors were announced, and, changing his mind, he dismissed her to her room, and she saw no more of him that evening.

"Oh, if they only hadn't come just now," thought the sorely disappointed child, as she went out with slow, reluctant steps. "I'm sure they wouldn't, if they had only known. I'm sure, quite sure papa was going to take me on his knee, and they prevented him. Oh, will he ever think of doing it again? Dear, dear papa, if you could only know how I long to sit there!" But Mrs. Dinsmore, who had hastily retired on the exit of Arthur and his father from the drawing room, was now sailing majestically down the hall, on her return thither. Elsie, catching sight of her, and being naturally anxious to avoid a meeting just then, at once quickened her pace very considerably, almost running up the stairs to her own room, where she found old Aunt Phoebe, Jim's mother, waiting to speak with her.

The poor old creature was overflowing with gratitude, and her fervent outpouring of thanks and blessings almost made Elsie forget her disappointment for the time.

Then Jim came to the door, asking to see Miss Elsie and poured out his thanks amid many sobs and tears. The poor fellow had been terribly frightened—indeed, so astounded by the unexpected charge, that he had not had a word to say in his own defense, beyond an earnest and reiterated assertion of his entire innocence, to which, however, his angry master had paid no attention.

But at length Phoebe remembered that she had some baking to do, and calling on Jim to come right along and split up some dry wood to heat her oven, she went down to the kitchen followed by her son, and Elsie was left alone with her nurse.

Chloe sat silently knitting, and the little girl, with her head leaning upon her hand and her eyes fixed thoughtfully upon the floor, was rehearsing again and again in her own mind all that had just passed between her papa and herself. She dwelt with lingering delight upon everything approaching to a caress, every kind word, every soothing tone of his voice, and then picturing to herself all that he might have done and said if those unwelcome visitors had not come in and put an end to the interview. And half hoping that he would send for her when they had gone, she watched the clock and listened intently for every sound.

But her bedtime came and she dared not stay up any longer, for his orders had been peremptory that she should always retire precisely at that hour, unless she had his express permission to remain up longer.

She lay awake for some time, thinking of his unwonted kindness, and indulging fond hopes for the future, and then fell asleep to dream that she was on her father's knee, and felt his arms folded lovingly about her, and his kisses warm upon her cheek.

Her heart beat quickly as she entered the breakfast room the next morning.

The family were just taking their places at the table, and her half-eager, half-timid "Good morning, papa," was answered by a grave, absent "Good morning, Elsie." Turning to his father and entering into a conversation with him on some business matter he took no further notice of his little daughter, excepting to see that her plate was well supplied with such articles of food as he allowed her to eat.

Elsie was sadly disappointed, and lingered about the room in the vain hope of obtaining a smile or caress, but presently her father went out, saying to the elder Mr. Dinsmore that he was going to ride over to Ion, and would probably not return before night. Then, with a sigh, the little girl went back to her room to prepare her morning lessons.

Elsie was now happily free from Arthur's persecutions for a time, for even after his release, he was too much afraid of his brother, openly to offer her any serious annoyance, though he plotted revenge in secret. Yet the little girl's situation was far from comfortable, and her patience often severely tried. Mrs. Dinsmore was excessively angry with her on Arthur's account, and whenever her father was not present, treated her in the most unkind manner. From the same cause the rest of the family, with the exception of her grandpa and Aunt Adelaide, were unusually cold and distant. Her father, although careful to see that all her wants were attended to, seldom took any further notice of her, unless to reprove her for some childish fault which, however trifling, never escaped his eye.

"You seem," said Adelaide to him one day, as he sent Elsie from the room for some very slight fault, "to expect that child to be a great deal more perfect than any grown person I ever saw, and to understand all about the rules of etiquette."

"If you please, Adelaide," said he haughtily, "I should like to be allowed to manage my own child as I see proper, without any interference from others."

"Excuse me," replied his sister, "I had no intention of interfering. But really, Horace, I do think you have no idea how eagle-eyed you are for faults in her, nor how very stern is the tone in which you always reprove her. I have known Elsie a great deal longer than you have, and I feel very certain that a gentle reproof would do her quite as much good, and not wound her half as much."

"Enough, Adelaide!" exclaimed her brother, impatiently. "If I were ten years younger than yourself, instead of that much older, there might be some propriety in your advising and directing me thus. As it is, I must say I consider it simply impertinent." And he left the room with an angry stride, while Adelaide looked after him with the thought, "I am glad you have no authority over me."

All that Adelaide had said was true. Yet Elsie never complained, never blamed her father, even in her heart, but, in her deep humility, thought it was all because she was "so very naughty or careless." She was continually making resolutions to be "oh, so careful always to do just right, and please dear papa," so that someday he might learn to love her.

But, alas! That hope was daily growing fainter and fainter. His cold and distant manner to her and his often repeated reproofs had so increased her natural timidity and sensitiveness that she was now very constrained in her approaches to him, and seldom ventured to move or speak in his presence. He would not see that this timidity and embarrassment were the natural results of his treatment, but attributed it all to want of affection. He saw that she feared him, and to that feeling alone he gave credit for her uniform obedience to his commands. He had no conception of the intense, but now almost despairing love for him that burned in that little heart, and made the young life one longing, earnest desire and effort to gain his affection.

CHAPTER SIXTH

Yea, though I walk through the valley of the shadow
of death, I will fear no evil; for thou art with me;
thy rod and thy staff, they comfort me.

—*Psalm 23:4*

'Tis but the cruel artifice of fate,
Thus to refine and vary on our woes,
To raise us from despair and give us hopes,
Only to plunge us in the gulf again.
And make us doubly wretched.

—*Trap's Abramuh*

IT WAS SABBATH MORNING, and Elsie, ready dressed for church, stood in the portico waiting for her father to come down and lift her into the carriage, in which Adelaide, Louisa, and Enna were already seated.

The coachman was in his seat, and the horses, a pair of young and fiery steeds purchased by Mr. Dinsmore only a few days before, were impatiently stamping and tossing their heads, requiring quite an exertion of strength to hold them in.

"I don't exactly like the actions of those horses, Ajax," remarked Mr. Dinsmore, as he came out putting on his gloves. "I did not intend to have them out in harness today. Why did you not give us the old bays?"

"Kase, marster Horace, ole Kate she's got a lame foot, an ole marster he say dese youngsters is got to be used some time or nuther, an' I reckoned I mout jis as well use 'em today."

"Do you feel quite sure of being able to hold them in?" asked his master, glancing uneasily first at the horses and then at Elsie.

"Ki! Marster, dis here chile ben able to hold in almost anything," exclaimed the Negro, exhibiting a double row of dazzlingly white teeth. "An' besides, I'se drove dese here hosses twice 'fore now, an' dey went splendid. Hold 'em in? Yes, sah, easy as nuffin."

"Elsie," said her father, still looking a little uneasy, in spite of Ajax's boasting, "I think it will be just as well for you to stay at home."

Elsie made no reply in words, but her answering look spoke such intense disappointment, such earnest entreaty, that, saying, "Ah, well! I suppose there is no real danger, and since you seem so anxious to go, I will not compel you to stay at home," he lifted her into the carriage, and seating himself beside her, ordered the coachman to drive on as carefully as he could.

"Elsie, change seats with me," said Enna. "I want to sit beside Brother Horace."

"No," replied Mr. Dinsmore, laying his hand on his little daughter's shoulder. "Elsie's place is by me, and she shall sit nowhere else."

"Do you think we are in any danger of being run away with?" asked Adelaide a little anxiously, as she observed him glancing once or twice out of the window, and was at the same time sensible that their motion was unusually rapid.

"The horses are young and fiery, but Ajax is an excellent driver," he replied, evasively, adding "You may be sure that if I had thought the danger very great I would have left Elsie at home."

They reached the church without accident, but on their return the horses took fright while going down a hill, and rushed along at a furious rate, which threatened every instant to upset the carriage.

Elsie thought they were going very fast, but did not know that there was real danger until her father suddenly lifted her from her seat, and placing her between his knees, held her tightly, as though he feared she would be snatched from his grasp.

Elsie looked up into his face. It was deadly pale, and his eyes were fixed upon her with an expression of anguish.

"Dear papa," she whispered, "God will take care of us."

"I would give all I am worth to have you safe at home," he answered hoarsely, pressing her closer and closer to him.

Oh! Even in that moment of fearful peril, when death seemed just at hand, those words, and the affectionate clasp of her father's arm, sent a thrill of intense joy to the love-famished heart of the little girl.

But destruction seemed inevitable. Lora was leaning back, half fainting with terror, Adelaide scarcely less alarmed, while Enna clung to her, sobbing most bitterly.

Elsie alone preserved a cheerful serenity. She had built her house upon the rock, and knew that it would stand. Her destiny was in her Heavenly Father's hands, and she was content to leave it there. Even death had no terrors to the simple, unquestioning faith of the little child who had put her trust in Jesus.

But they were not to perish thus, for at that moment a powerful Negro, who was walking along the road, hearing an unusual sound, turned about, caught sight of the vehicle coming toward him at such a rapid rate. Instantly comprehending the peril of the travelers, planted himself in the middle of the road, and, at the risk of life and limb, caught the horses by the bridle — the sudden and unexpected check throwing them upon their haunches, and bringing the carriage to an instant stand-still.

"Thank God, we are saved! That fellow shall be well rewarded for his brave deed," exclaimed Mr. Dinsmore, throwing open the carriage door.

They were almost at the entrance of the avenue, and all preferred to walk the short distance to the house rather than again trust themselves to the horses.

Mr. Dinsmore lingered a moment to speak to the man who had done them such good service, and to give some directions to the coachman. Then taking the hand of his little girl, who had been waiting for him, he walked slowly on, neither of them speaking a word until they reached the house, when he stooped and kissed her cheek, asking very kindly if she had recovered from the fright.

"Yes, papa," she answered in a quiet tone. "I knew that God would take care of us. Oh, wasn't He good to keep us all from being killed?"

"Yes," he said, very gravely. "Go now and let mammy get you ready for dinner."

As Elsie was sitting alone in her room that afternoon she was surprised by a visit from Lora, it being very seldom that the elder girls cared to enter her apartment.

Lora looked pale, and more grave and thoughtful than Elsie had ever seen her. For a while she sat in silence, then suddenly burst out, "Oh, Elsie, I can't help thinking all the time, what if we had been killed! Where would we all be now? Where would I have been? I believe you would have gone straight to Heaven, Elsie, but I—oh! I should have been with the rich man the minister read about this morning, lifting up my eyes in torment." And Lora buried her face in her hands and shuddered.

Presently she went on again. "I was terribly frightened, and so were the rest—all but you, Elsie. Tell me, do—what kept you from being afraid?"

"I was thinking," said Elsie gently, turning over the leaves of her little Bible as she spoke, "of this sweet verse: 'Yea, though I walk through the valley of the shadow of death, I will fear no evil; for Thou art with me;' and oh, Lora! It made me so happy to think that Jesus was there for me, and that if I were killed, I should only fall asleep, to wake up again in His arms. Then how could I be afraid?"

"Ah! I would give anything to feel as you do," said Lora, sighing. "But tell me, Elsie, did you not feel afraid for the rest of us? I'm sure you must know that we are not Christians. We don't even pretend to be."

Elsie blushed and looked down.

"It all passed so quickly, you know, Lora, almost in a moment," she said, "so that I only had time to think of papa and myself, and I have prayed so much for him that I felt quite sure God would spare him until he should be prepared to die. It was very selfish, I know," she added with deep humility, "but it was only for a moment, and I can't tell you how thankful I was for all our spared lives."

"Don't look so as if you had done something very wicked, Elsie," replied Lora, sighing again. "I'm sure we have given you little enough reason to care whatever becomes of us. But oh, Elsie, if you can only tell me how to become a Christian, I mean now to try very hard. Indeed, I am determined never to rest until I am one."

"Oh, Lora, how glad I am!" cried Elsie, joyfully. "For I know that if you are really in earnest, you will succeed, for no one ever yet failed who tried aright. Jesus said, 'Every one that asketh, receiveth; and he that seeketh, findeth; and to him that knocketh, it shall be opened.' Is not that encouraging? And listen to what God says here in this verse: 'Ye shall seek Me, and find Me, when ye shall search for Me with all your heart.' So you see, dear Lora, if you will only seek the Lord with your whole heart, you may be sure, quite sure of finding Him."

"Yes," said Lora, "but you have not answered my question: How am I to seek? That is, what means am I to use to get rid of my sins, and get a new heart? How do I make myself pleasing in the sight of God? What must I do to be saved?"

"That is the very question the jailer put to Paul, and he answered, 'Believe on the Lord Jesus Christ, and thou shalt be saved,'" replied Elsie, quickly turning to the chapter and pointing out the verse with her finger, that Lora might see that she had quoted it correctly. "And in answer to your other question, 'How shall I get rid of my sins?' see here: 'In that day there shall be a fountain opened to the house of David and to the inhabitants of Jerusalem for sin and for uncleanness.' That is in Zechariah. Then John tells us what that fountain is when he says, 'The blood of Jesus Christ His Son cleanseth us from all sin,' and again, 'Unto Him that loved us, and washed us from our sins in His own blood.'"

"Yes, Elsie, but what must I do?" asked Lora eagerly.

"Do, Lora? Only believe," replied Elsie, in the same earnest tone. "Jesus has done and suffered all that is necessary; and now we have nothing at all to do but to go to Him and be washed in that fountain. Believe Him when He says, 'I give unto them eternal life.' Just accept the gift, and trust and love Him. That is the whole of it, and it is so simple that even such a little girl as I can understand it."

"But surely, Elsie, I can, I must do something."

"Yes, God tells us to repent. Then He says, 'Give me thine heart.' You can do that; you can love Jesus. At least He will enable you to, if you ask Him, and He will teach you to be sorry for your sins. The Bible says, 'He is exalted to give repentance and remission of sins;' and if you ask Him He will give them to you. It is true we cannot do anything good of ourselves. Without the help of the Holy Spirit we can do nothing right, because we are so very wicked, but then we can always get help if we ask for it. Jesus said, 'Your Heavenly Father is more willing to give His Holy Spirit to them that ask Him, than parents are to give good gifts unto their children.' Oh, Lora! Don't be afraid to ask for it. Don't be afraid to come to Jesus, for He says, 'Him that cometh unto me, I will in no wise cast out,' and

He is such a precious Saviour, so kind and loving. But remember that you must come humbly, feeling that you are a great sinner, and not worthy to be heard, and only hoping to be forgiven because Jesus died. The Bible says, 'God resisteth the proud, but giveth grace unto the humble.'"

Lora lingered the greater part of the afternoon in Elsie's room, asking her questions, or listening to her while she read the Scriptures, or repeated some beautiful hymn, or spoke, in her sweet, childish way, of her own peace and joy in believing in Jesus.

But at last Lora went to her own room, and Elsie had another quiet half hour to herself before the tea bell again called the family together.

Elsie answered the summons with a light heart — a heart that thrilled with a new and strange sense of happiness as she remembered her father's evident anxiety for her safety during their perilous ride, recalling each word and look, and feeling again, in imagination, the clasp of his arm about her waist.

"Ah! Surely papa does love me," she murmured to herself over and over again. When he met her at the table with a kind smile, and laying his hands caressingly on her head, asked in an affectionate tone, "How does my little daughter do this evening?" her cheeks flushed. Her eyes grew bright with happiness, and she longed to tell him how very, very much she loved him.

But that was quite impossible, at the table, and before all the family, so she merely raised her glad eyes to his face and answered, "I am very well, thank you, papa."

But after all, this occurrence produced but little change in Elsie's condition. Her father treated her a little more affectionately for a day or two, and then gradually returned to his ordinary stern, cold manner; indeed, before the week was out, she was again in sad disgrace.

She was walking alone in the garden one afternoon, when her attention was attracted by a slight fluttering noise which seemed to proceed from an arbor near by, and on hastily turning in to ascertain the cause, she found a tiny and beautiful humming-bird confined under a glass vase. In its struggles to escape it was fluttering and beating against the walls of its prison, thus producing the sound the little girl had heard in passing.

Elsie was very tenderhearted, and could never see any living creature in distress without feeling a strong desire to relieve its sufferings. She knew that Arthur was in the habit of torturing every little insect and bird that came in his way. She had often drawn his persecutions upon herself by interfering in behalf of the poor victims, and now the thought instantly flashed upon her that this was some of his work, and that he would return ere long to carry out his cruel purposes. Then at once arose the desire to release the little prisoner and save it further suffering, and without waiting to reflect a moment she raised the glass, and the bird was gone.

Then she began to think with a little tremor, how angry Arthur would be, but it was too late to think of that now. After all, she did not stand in very great dread of the consequences, especially as she felt nearly sure of her father's approval of what she had done, having several times heard him reprove Arthur for his cruel practices.

Not caring to meet Arthur then, however, she hastily retreated to the house, where she seated herself in the veranda with a book. It was a very warm afternoon, and that, being on the east side of the house and well protected by trees, shrubbery, and vines, was as cool a spot as could be found on the place.

Arthur, Walter, and Enna sat on the floor playing jack stones—a favorite game with them—and Louise was stretched full length on a settee, buried in the latest novel.

"Hush!" she said, as Walter gave a sudden shout at a successful toss Enna had just made. "Can't you be quiet? Mamma is taking her afternoon nap, and you will disturb her. And besides, I cannot read in such a noise."

Elsie wondered why Arthur did not go to see after his bird, but soon forgot all about it in the interest with which she was poring over the story of the Swiss Family Robinson.

The jack stone players were just finished their game when they were all startled by the sudden appearance of Mr. Horace Dinsmore upon the scene. He was asking in a tone of great wrath who had been down in the garden and liberated the humming bird he had been at such pains to catch, because it was one of a rare species, and he was anxious to add it to his collection of curiosities.

Elsie was terribly frightened, and would have been glad at that moment to sink through the floor. She dropped her book in her lap, and clasping her hands over her beating heart, grew pale and red by turns, while she seemed choking with the vain effort to speak and acknowledge herself the culprit, as conscience told her she ought.

But her father was not looking at her; his eye was fixed on Arthur.

"I presume it was you, sir," he said very angrily, "and if so, you may prepare yourself for either a flogging or a return to your prison, for one or the other I am determined you shall have."

"I didn't do any such thing," replied the boy, fiercely.

"Of course you will deny it," said his brother, "but we all know that your word is good for nothing."

"Papa," said a trembling little voice, "Arthur did not do it. It was I."

"You!" exclaimed her father, in a tone of mingled anger and astonishment, as he turned his flashing eye upon her. "You, Elsie! Can it be possible that this is your doing?"

Elsie's book fell on the floor, and, covering her face with both hands, she burst into sobs and tears.

"Come here to me this instant," he said, seating himself on the settee, from which Louise had risen on his entrance. "Come here and tell me what you mean by meddling with my affairs in this way."

"Please, papa, please don't be so very angry with me," sobbed the little girl, as she rose and came forward in obedience to his commands. "I didn't know it was your bird, and I didn't mean to be naughty."

"No, you never mean to be naughty, according to your own account," he said. "Your badness is all accident, but nevertheless, I find you a very troublesome, mischievous child. It was only the other day you broke a valuable vase"—he forgot in his anger how little she had really been to blame for that. "And now you have caused me the loss of a rare specimen which I had spent a great deal of time and effort in procuring. Really, Elsie, I am sorely tempted to administer a very severe punishment."

Elsie caught at the arm of the settee for support.

"Tell me what you did it for. Was it pure love of mischief?" asked her father, sternly, taking hold of her arm and holding her up by it.

"No, papa," she answered almost under her breath. "I was sorry for the little bird. I thought Arthur had put it there to torture it, and so I let it go. I did not mean to do wrong, papa, indeed I did not," and the tears fell faster and faster.

"Indeed," said he, "you had no business to meddle with it, let who would have put it there. Which hand did it?"

"This one, papa," sobbed the child, indicating her right hand.

He took it in his and held it a moment, while the little girl stood trembling awaiting what was to come next. He looked at the downcast, tearful face, the bosom heaving with sobs, and then at the little trembling hand he held, so soft, and white, and tender, and the sternness of his countenance relaxed somewhat. It seemed next to impossible to inflict pain upon anything so tender and helpless, and for a moment he was half inclined to kiss and forgive her. But no, he had been very much irritated at his loss, and the remembrance of it again aroused his anger, and well nigh extinguished the little spark of love and compassion that had burned for a moment in his heart. She should be punished, though he would not inflict physical pain.

"See, Elsie," laughed Louise, maliciously, "he is feeling in his pocket for his knife. I suspect he intends to cut your hand off."

Elsie started, and the tearful eyes were raised to her father's face with a look of half terrified entreaty, half of confidence that such could not be in his intention.

"Hush, Louise!" exclaimed her brother, sternly. "You know you are not speaking truly, and that I would as soon think of cutting off my own hand as my child's. You should never speak anything but truth, especially to children."

"I think it is well enough to frighten them a little sometimes and I thought that was what you were going to do," replied Louise, looking somewhat mortified at the rebuke.

"No," said her brother, "that is a very bad plan, and one which I shall never adopt. Elsie will learn in time, if she does not know it now, that I never utter a threat which I do not intend to carry out, and never break my word."

He had drawn a handkerchief from his pocket while speaking.

"I shall tie this hand up, Elsie," he said, proceeding to do so. "Those who do not use their hands aright must be deprived of the use of them. There! Let me see if that will keep it out of mischief. I shall tie you up hand and foot before long, if you continue such mischievous pranks. Now go to your room, and stay there until teatime."

Elsie felt bitterly disgraced and humiliated as she turned to obey, and it needed not Arthur's triumphant chuckle nor the smirk of satisfaction on Enna's face to add to the keen suffering of her wounded spirit. This slight punishment was more to her than a severe chastisement would have been to many another child, for the very knowledge of her father's displeasure was enough at any time to cause great pain to her sensitive spirit and gentle, loving heart.

Walter, who was far more tenderhearted than either his brother or sister, felt touched by the sight of her distress, and ran after her to say, "Never mind, Elsie. I am ever so sorry for you, and I don't think you were the least bit naughty."

She thanked him with a grateful look, and a faint attempt to smile through her tears. Then she hurried on to her room, where she seated herself in a chair by the window, and laying her arms upon the sill, rested her head upon them, and while the bitter tears fell fast from her eyes she murmured half loud, "Oh, why am I always so naughty? Always doing something to displease my dear papa? How I wish I could be good, and make him love me! I am afraid he never will if I vex him so often."

Then an earnest, importunate prayer for help to do right, and wisdom to understand how to gain her father's love, went up from the almost despairing little heart to Him whose ear is ever open unto the cry of his suffering children. And thus between weeping, mourning, and praying, an hour passed slowly away, and the tea bell rang.

Elsie started up, but sat down again, feeling that she would much rather do without her supper than show her tear-swollen eyes and tied-up hand at the table.

But she was not to be left to her choice in the matter, for presently there came a messenger bringing a peremptory command from her father to "come down immediately" to her supper.

"Did you not hear the bell?" he asked, in his sternest tone, as she tremblingly took her seat at his side.

"Yes, sir," she answered, in a low tremulous tone.

"Very well, then. Remember that you are always to come down the moment the bell rings, unless you are directed otherwise, or are sick, and the next time you are so late, I shall send you away without your meal."

"I don't want any supper, papa," she said, humbly.

"Hush," he replied, severely. "I will have no pouting or sulking. You must just eat your supper and behave yourself. Stop this crying at once," he added, in an undertone, as he spread some preserves on a piece of bread and laid it on her plate, "or I shall take you away from the table, and if I do, you will be very sorry."

He watched her a moment while she made a violent effort to choke back her tears.

"What is your hand tied up for, Elsie?" asked her grandfather. "Have you been hurt?"

Elsie's face flushed painfully, but she made no reply.

"You must speak when you are spoken to," said her father. "Answer your grandfather's question at once."

"Papa tied it up, because I was naughty," replied the little girl, vainly striving to suppress a sob.

Her father made a movement as if about to lead her from the table.

"Oh, papa, don't!" she cried, in terror. "I will be good.

"Let me have no more crying, then," said he, "this is shameful behavior for a girl eight years old. It would be bad enough in a child of Enna's age."

He took out his handkerchief and wiped her eyes, "Now," said he, "begin to eat your supper at once, and don't let me have to reprove you again.

Elsie tried to obey, but it seemed very difficult, indeed almost impossible, while she knew that her father was watching her closely, and felt that everybody else was looking at her and thinking, "What a naughty little girl you are!"

"Oh!" thought the poor child. "If papa would only quit looking at me, and the rest would forget all about me and eat their suppers, maybe I could keep from crying." Then she sent up a silent prayer for help, struggled hard to keep back the tears and sobs that were almost suffocating her, and taking up her slice of bread, tried to eat.

She was very thankful to her Aunt Adelaide for addressing a question to her papa just at that moment, thus taking his attention from her, and then adroitly setting them all to talking until the little girl had had time to recover her composure, at least in a measure.

"May I go to my room now, papa?" asked the timid little voice as they rose from the table.

"No," he said, taking her hand and leading her out to the veranda, where he settled himself in an easy chair, and lighted a cigar.

"Bring me that book that lies yonder on the settee," he commanded.

She brought it.

"Now," said he, "bring that stool and set yourself down here close at my knee, and let me see if I can keep you out of mischief for an hour or two."

"May I get a book to read, papa?" she asked timidly.

"No," said he shortly. "You may just do what I bid you, and nothing more nor less."

She sat down as he directed, with her face turned toward him, and tried to amuse herself with her own thoughts. She watched the expression of his countenance as he read on and on, turning leaf after leaf, too much interested in his book to take any further notice of her.

"How handsome my papa is!" thought the little girl, gazing with affectionate admiration into his face. And then she sighed and tears trembled in her eyes again. She admired her father, and loved him, "oh so dearly," as she often whispered to herself, but would she ever meet with anything like a return of her fond affection? There was an aching void in her heart which nothing else could fill: must it always be thus? Was her craving for affection never to be satisfied? "Oh, papa! My own papa, will you never love me?" mourned the sad little heart. "Ah! If I could only be good always, perhaps he would, but I am so often naughty. Whenever he begins to be kind I am sure to do something to vex him, and then it is all over. Oh, I wish I could be good! I will try very, very hard. Ah! If I might climb on his knee now, and lay my head on his chest, and put my arms around his neck, and tell him how sorry I am that I have been naughty, and made him lose his bird, and how much—oh, how much I love him! But I know I could never tell him that—I don't know how to express it—no words could, I am sure. If he would forgive me, and kiss me, and call me his dear little daughter—oh, will he ever call me that? Or if I might only stand beside him and lay my head on his shoulder, and he would put his arm around me, it would make me so happy."

An exclamation from Enna caused Elsie to turn her head, and suddenly springing to her feet, she exclaimed in an eager, excited way, "Papa, there is a carriage coming up the avenue—it must be visitors. Please, please, papa, let me go to my room."

"Why?" he asked coolly, looking up from his book. "Why do you wish to go?"

"Because I don't want to see them, papa," she said, hanging her head and blushing deeply. "I don't want them to see me."

"You are not usually afraid of visitors," he replied in the same cool tone.

"But they will see that my hand is tied up, and they will ask what is the matter. Oh, papa! Do, please do let me go quickly, before they get here," she pleaded in an agony of shame and haste.

"No," said he, "I shall not let you go, if it were only to punish you for getting off the seat where I bid you stay, without permission. You will have to learn that I am to be obeyed at all times, and under all circumstances. Sit down, and don't dare to move again until I give you leave."

Elsie sat down without another word, but two bitter, scalding tears rolled quickly down her burning cheeks.

"You needn't cry, Elsie," said her father. "It is only an old gentleman who comes to see your grandfather on business, and who, as he never notices children, will not be at all likely to ask any questions. I hope you will learn someday, Elsie, to save your tears until there is really some occasion for them."

The old gentleman had alighted while Mr. Dinsmore was speaking. Elsie saw that he was alone, and the relief was so great that for once she scarcely needed her father's rebuke.

Another half-hour passed, and Mr. Dinsmore still sat reading, taking no notice of Elsie, who, afraid to speak or move, was growing very weary and sleepy. She longed to lay her head on her father's knee, but dared not venture to take such a liberty, but at length she was so completely overpowered by sleep as to do so unconsciously.

The sound of his voice pronouncing her name aroused her.

"You are tired and sleepy," said he. "If you would like to go to bed you may do so."

"Thank you, papa," she replied, rising to her feet.

"Well," he said, seeing her hesitate, "speak, if you have anything to say."

"I am very sorry I was naughty, papa. Will you please forgive me?" The words were spoken very low, and almost with a sob.

"Will you try not to meddle in the future, and not to cry at the table, not pout and sulk when you are punished?" he asked in a cold, grave tone.

"Yes, sir, I will try to be a good girl always," said the humble little voice.

"Then I will forgive you," he replied, taking the handkerchief off her hand.

Still Elsie lingered. She felt as if she could not go without some little token of forgiveness and love, some slight caress.

He looked at her with an impatient "Well?" Then, in answer to her mute request, "No," he said, "I will not kiss you tonight. You have been entirely too naughty. Go to your room at once."

Aunt Chloe was absolutely frightened by the violence of her child's grief, as she rushed into the room and flung herself into her arms weeping and sobbing most vehemently.

"What's de matter, darlin'?" she asked in great alarm.

"Oh, mammy, mammy!" sobbed the child. "Papa wouldn't kiss me! He said I was too naughty. Oh, mammy! Will he ever love me now?"

❦❧❦❧❦❧❦❧

CHAPTER SEVENTH

The smallest worm will turn, being trodden on.

—Shakespeare's Richard iii

A blossom full of promise is life's joy,
That never comes to fruit. Hope, for a time,
Suns the young flow'ret in its gladsome light,
And it looks flourishing—a little while—
'Tis pass'd, we know not whither, but 'tis gone.

—Miss Landon

IT WAS MISS DAY'S CUSTOM to present to the parents of her pupils a monthly report of their conduct and recitations. The regular time for this had occurred once since Mr. Horace Dinsmore's return, when she, of course, handed Elsie's to him.

It was very satisfactory, for Elsie was a most diligent scholar, carrying her religious principles into that as well as everything else, and disposed as Miss Day was to find fault with her, she could seldom see any excuse for so doing, in either her conduct or recitations.

Mr. Dinsmore glanced over the report and handed it back, saying, "It is all very good—very satisfactory indeed. I am glad to see that she is industrious and well behaved, for I wish her to grow up an intelligent and amiable woman."

Elsie, who was standing near, heard the words, and they sent a glow of pleasure to her cheek. She looked up eagerly, but her father turned and walked away without taking any notice of her, and the glow of happiness faded, and the soft eyes filled with tears of wounded feeling.

It was now time for a second report; but, alas, the past month had been a most unfortunate one for the little girl. The weather was very warm, and she had felt languid and weak. So much were her thoughts occupied with the longing desire to gain her father's love, so depressed were her spirits by her constant failure to do so, that she often found it impossible to give her mind to her lessons.

Arthur, too, during much of the time before and since the week of his imprisonment, had been more than usually annoying. He had been shaking her chair and jogging her elbow so frequently when she was writing, that her copybook presented by no means as good an appearance as usual, and never had Miss Day made out so poor a report for her. She carried it with much secret satisfaction to the little girl's father, and entered a long complaint of the child's idleness and inattention.

"Send her to me," he said, angrily. "She will find me in my own room."

Miss Day had left Elsie in the schoolroom putting her desk in order after the day's work, and she found her still there on her return.

"Elsie," said she, with a malicious smile, "your father wishes to see you immediately. He is in his room."

The child turned red and pale by turns, trembling so violently that for a moment she was quite unable to move, for she guessed from Miss Day's countenance what was probably in store for her.

"I advise you to go at once," said that lady, "for no doubt the longer you wait the worse it will be for you."

At the same moment Mr. Dinsmore's voice was heard calling in a stern, angry tone, "Elsie!"

Making a violent effort to control her feelings, she started up and hastened to obey.

The door of his room stood open, and she walked in, asking in a trembling voice, "Did you call me, papa?"

"Yes," said he, "I did. Come here to me."

He was sitting with the copybook and report in his hand, and there was much severity in both tone and look as he addressed her.

She obeyed instantly, but trembling violently, and with a face pale as death, and eyes filled with tears. She lifted them pleadingly to his face, and, touched by her evident terror and distress, he said in a tone somewhat less stern, "Can you tell me, Elsie, how it happens that your teacher brings me so bad a report of your conduct and lessons during the past month? She says you have been very idle, and the report tells the same story, and this copybook presents a shameful appearance."

The child answered only by tears and sobs.

They seemed to irritate him.

"Elsie," he said, sternly, "when I ask a question, I require an answer and that instantly."

"Oh, papa!" she answered, pleadingly. "I couldn't study. I'm very sorry—I'll try to do better—only don't be very angry with me, dear papa."

"I am angry with you, very angry, indeed," said he in the same severe tone, "and very strongly inclined to punish you. You couldn't study, eh? What reason can you assign, pray? Were you not well?"

"I don't know, sir," sobbed the little girl.

"You don't know? Very well, then, I think you could not be very ill without knowing it, and so you seem to have no excuse at all to offer. However, I will not inflict any punishment upon you this time, as you seem to be really sorry, and have promised to do better. But beware how you let me see such a report, unless you wish to be severely punished; and I warn you that unless your next copybook presents a better appearance than this, I certainly shall punish you.

"There are a number of pages here that look quite well," he continued, turning over the leaves. "That shows what you can do, if you choose. Now there is an old saying, 'A bird that can sing, and won't sing, must be made to sing.' Hush!" as Elsie seemed about to speak. "Not a word. You may go now." And throwing himself back in his easy chair, he took up a newspaper and began to read.

Yet Elsie lingered. Her heart so yearned for one word or look of sympathy and love. She so longed to throw herself into his arms and tell him how dearly, how very dearly she loved him. She did so hunger and thirst for one fond caress. Ah, how could she go away without it now, when for the very first time she found herself alone with him in his own room, where she had never ventured before, but where she had often been in her brightest dreams.

And so she lingered, trembling, hoping, fearing; but presently he looked up with a cold "Why do you stand there? I gave you permission to go. Go at once." And with a sinking heart she turned away and sought the solitude of her own room, there to weep, and mourn, and pray that she might one day possess the love she so pined for, and bitterly to reproach herself for having by the failures of the past month put it farther from her.

And soon a thought came to her which added greatly to her distress. If Arthur continued his persecutions, how could she make the next copybook more presentable? And in case it were not, her father had said positively that he would punish her, and oh, how could she bear punishment from him, when a word or look of displeasure almost broke her heart?

Miss Day seldom remained in the schoolroom during the whole of the writing hour, and sometimes the older girls were also absent. That meant Arthur had ample opportunity to indulge his mischievous propensities, for Elsie was above the meanness of telling tales, and had she not been, Arthur was so great a favorite with his mother that she would have brought a great deal of trouble upon herself by so doing.

She therefore saw no escape from the dreaded punishment, unless she could persuade the perverse boy to cease his annoyances; and of that there was little hope.

But she carried her trouble to her Heavenly Father, and asked Him to help her. She was still on her knees, pouring out her sobs and prayers, when someone knocked at the door.

She rose and opened it to find her Aunt Adelaide standing there.

"Elsie," she said, "I am writing to Miss Rose. Have you any word to send? You may write a little note, if you choose, and I will enclose it in my letter. But what is the matter, child?" she suddenly exclaimed, kindly taking the little girl's hand in hers.

With many tears and sobs Elsie told her the whole story, not omitting her papa's threat, and her fear that she could not, on account of Arthur's persecutions, avoid incurring the punishment.

Adelaide's sympathies were enlisted and she drew the sobbing child to her side, saying, as she pressed a kiss on her cheek, "Never mind, Elsie, I will take my book or needlework to the schoolroom every day, and sit there during the writing hour. But why don't you tell your papa about it?"

"Because I don't like to tell tales, Aunt Adelaide, and it would make your mamma so angry with me, and besides, I can't tell papa anything."

"Ah, I understand! And it's no wonder. He is strangely stern to the poor child. I mean to give him a good talking to," murmured Adelaide, more as if thinking aloud than talking to Elsie.

Then kissing the little girl again, she rose hastily and left the room, with the intention of seeking her brother. But he had gone out, and when he returned he brought several gentlemen with him, and she had no opportunity until the desire to interfere in the matter had passed from her mind.

"And it shall come to pass, that before they call, I will answer, and while they are yet speaking, I will hear." The promise had been fulfilled to Elsie, and help had been sent to her in her trouble.

When her Aunt Adelaide left her, Elsie—first carefully locking the door to guard against a surprise visit from Enna—went to her bureau, and unlocking a drawer, took out her purse she was knitting for her father, to replace the one she had given to Miss Allison.

She had commenced it before his return, and having spent upon it nearly every spare moment since, when she could feel secure from intrusion, she now had it nearly completed. Ah! Many a silent tear had fallen as she worked, and many a sigh over disappointed hopes had been woven into its bright meshes of gold and blue.

But now she had been much comforted and encouraged by her aunt's sympathy and kind promise of assistance, and, though there were still traces of tears upon it, the little face looked quite bright and cheerful again as she settled herself in her little sewing chair, and began her work.

The small white fingers moved right briskly, the bright shining needles glancing in and out, while the thoughts, quite as busy, ran on something in this fashion: "Ah! I am so sorry I have done so badly the past month. No wonder papa was vexed with me. I don't believe I ever had such a bad report before. What has come over me? It seems as if I can't study, and must have a holiday. I wonder if it is all laziness? I'm afraid it is, and that I ought to be punished. I wish I could shake it off, and feel industrious as I used to. I will try very hard to do better this month, and perhaps I can. It is only one month, and then June will be over, and Miss Day is going North to spend July and August, and maybe

September, and so we shall have a long holiday. Surely I can stand it one month more. It will soon be over, though it does seem a long time, and besides, this month we are not to study so many hours, because it is so warm, and there's to be no school on Saturdays—none tomorrow, so that I can finish this. Ah! I wonder if papa will be pleased?" And she sighed deeply. "I'm afraid it will be a long, long time before he will be pleased with me again. I have displeased him twice this week—first about the bird, and now this bad report, and that shameful copybook. But oh, I will try so hard next month, and dear Aunt Adelaide will keep Arthur from troubling me, and I'm determined my copybook shall look neat, and not a single blot in it.

"I wonder how I shall spend the vacation? Last summer I had such a delightful visit at Ashlands, and then they were here all the rest of the time. It was then poor Herbert had such a dreadful time with his hip. Ah, how thankful I ought to be that I am not lame, and have always been so healthy. But I'm afraid papa won't let me go there this summer, nor ask them to visit me, because he said he thought Lucy was not a suitable companion for me. I was very naughty when she was here, and I've been naughty a great many times since. Oh, dear! Shall I never, never learn to be good? It seems to me I am naughty now much oftener than I used to be before papa came home. I'm afraid he will soon begin to punish me severely, as he threatened today. I wonder what he means?"

A crimson tide suddenly swept over the fair face and neck, and dropping her work, she covered her face with her hands. "Oh, he couldn't, couldn't mean that! How could I ever bear it! And yet if it would make me really good, I think I wouldn't mind the pain—but the shame and disgrace! Oh, it would break my heart! I could never hold up my head again! Oh, can he mean that? But I must try to be so very good that I will never deserve punishment, and then it will make no difference to me what he means." And with this consolatory reflection she took up her work again.

"Mammy, is papa in his room?" asked Elsie, the next afternoon, as she put the finishing touches to her work.

"No, darlin', Marster Horace he rode out wid de strange gentlemen more than an hour ago."

Elsie laid her needles away in her work-basket, and opening her writing-desk, selected a bit of notepaper, in which she wrote in her very best hand, "A present for my dear papa, from his little daughter Elsie!" This she carefully pinned to the purse, and then carried it to her papa's room, intending to leave it on his dressing table.

Fearing that he might possibly have returned, she knocked gently at the door, but receiving no answer, opened it, and went in. But she had not gone more than halfway across the room when she heard his voice behind her, asking, in a tone of mingled surprise and displeasure, "What are you doing here in my room, in my absence, Elsie?"

She started, and turned round, pale and trembling, and lifting her eyes pleadingly to his face, silently placed the purse in his hands.

He looked first at it, and then at her.

"I made it for you, dear papa," she said, in a low tremulous tone. "Do please take it."

"It is really very pretty," he said, examining it. "Is it possible it is your work? I had no idea you had so much taste and skill. Thank you, daughter. I shall take it, and use it with a great deal of pleasure."

He took her hand as he spoke, and sitting down, lifted her to his knee, saying, "Elsie, my child, why do you always seem so afraid of me? I don't like it."

With sudden impulse she threw her arms around his neck, and pressed her lips to his cheek, then dropping her head on his chest, she sobbed, "Oh, papa! Dear papa, I do love you so very dearly! Will you not love me? Oh, papa! Love me a little. I know I've been naughty very often, but I will try to be good."

Then for the first time he folded her in his arms and kissed her tenderly, saying, in a moved tone, "I do love you, my darling, my own little daughter."

Oh! The words were sweeter to Elsie's ear than the most delicious music! Her joy was too great for words, for anything but tears.

"Why do you cry so, my darling?" he asked, soothingly, stroking her hair, and kissing her again and again.

"Oh, papa! Because I am so happy, so very happy," she sobbed.

"Do you indeed care so very much for my love?" he asked. "Then, my daughter, you must not tremble and turn pale whenever I speak to you as though I were a cruel tyrant."

"Oh, papa! I cannot help it, when you look and speak so sternly. I love you so dearly I cannot bear to have you angry with me. But I am not afraid of you now."

"That is right," he said, caressing her again. "But there is the tea bell," he said, setting her down. "Go into the dressing room there, and bathe your eyes, and then come to me."

She hastened to do his bidding, and then taking her hand he led her down and seated her in her usual place by his side.

There were visitors, and all the conversation was addressed to them and the older members of the family, but he now and then bestowed a kind look upon his little girl, and attended carefully to all her wants, and Elsie was very happy.

Everything now went on very pleasantly Elsie for some days. She did not see a great deal of her father, as he was frequently away from home for a day or two, and, when he returned, generally brought a number of visitors with him. But whenever he did notice her it was very kindly, and she was gradually overcoming her fear of him, and constantly hoping that the time would soon come when he would have more leisure to bestow upon her. She was happy now, and with a mind at ease, was able to learn her lessons well. And her Aunt Adelaide faithfully kept her promise, and thus freed her from Arthur's annoyances. She was enabled to do justice to her writing. She took great pains, and her copybook showed a marked improvement in her penmanship, and its pages had not yet been defaced by a single blot, so that she was looking forward with pleasing anticipations to the time when her report should again be presented to her father.

But, alas! One unfortunate morning it happened that Miss Day was in a very bad humor indeed — peevish, fretful, irritable, and unreasonable to the last degree, and as usual, Elsie was the principal sufferer from her ill-humor. She found fault with everything the little girl did. She scolded her, shook her, refused to explain the manner of working out a very difficult example, or to permit her to apply to anyone else for assistance, and then punished her because it was done wrong. And when the child could no longer keep back her tears, called her a baby for crying, and a dunce for not understanding her arithmetic better.

All this Elsie bore meekly and patiently, not answering a word. But her meekness seemed only to provoke the governess the more, and finally, when Elsie came to recite her last lesson, she took pains to put her questions in the most perplexing form. She scarcely allowed the child an instant to begin her reply, answered them herself, and then, throwing down the book, scolded her vehemently for her bad lesson, and marked it in her report as a complete failure.

Poor Elsie could bear no more, but bursting into tears and sobs, said, "Miss Day, I did know my lesson, every word of it, if you had asked the question as usual, or had given me time to answer."

"I say you did not know it, that it was a complete failure," replied Miss Day, angrily, "and shall just sit down and learn it, every word over."

"I do know it, if you would hear me right," said Elsie, indignantly, "and it is very unjust of you to mark it a failure."

"Impudence!" exclaimed Miss Day, furiously. "How dare you contradict me? I shall take you to your father."

And seizing her by the arm, she dragged her across the room, and opening the door, pushed her into the passage.

"Oh, don't, Miss Day!" pleaded the little girl, turning toward her, pale and tearful. "Don't tell papa."

"I will! So just walk along with you," was the angry rejoinder, as she pushed her before her to Mr. Dinsmore's door. It stood open, and he sat at his desk, writing.

"What is the matter?" he asked, looking up as they appeared before the door.

"Elsie has been very impertinent, sir," said Miss Day. "She not only accused me of injustice, but contradicted me flatly."

"Is it possible?" said he, frowning angrily. "Come here to me, Elsie, and tell me, is it true that you contradicted your teacher?"

"Yes, papa," sobbed the child.

"Very well, then, I shall certainly punish you, for I will never allow anything of the kind."

As he spoke he picked up a small ruler that lay before him, at the same time taking Elsie's hand as though he meant to use it on her.

"Oh, papa!" she cried, in a tone of entreaty.

But he laid it down again, saying, "No, I shall punish you by depriving you of your play this afternoon, and giving you only bread and water for your dinner. Sit down there," he added, pointing to a stool. Then with a wave of his hand to the governess, "I think she will not be guilty of the like again, Miss Day."

The governess left the room, and Elsie sat down on her stool, crying and sobbing violently, while her father went on with his writing.

"Elsie," he said, presently, "cease that noise. I have had quite enough of it."

She struggled to suppress her sobs, but it was almost impossible, and she felt it a great relief when a moment later the dinner bell rang, and her father left the room.

In a few moments a servant came in, carrying on a small waiter a tumbler of water, and a plate with a slice of bread on it.

"Dis am dreffful poor fare, Miss Elsie," he said, setting it down beside her, "but Massa Horace he say it all you can hab. But if you say so, dis chile tell ole Phoebe to send up somethin' better fore Massa Horace gits through his dinner."

"Oh, no, thank you, Pompey! You're very kind, but I would not disobey, nor deceive papa," replied the little girl, earnestly, "and I am not at all hungry."

He lingered a moment, seeming loath to leave her to dine upon such fare.

"You had better go now, Pompey," she said gently. "I am afraid you will be wanted."

He turned and left the room muttering something about "disagreeable, good-for-nothing Miss Day!"

Elsie felt no disposition to eat, and when her father returned, half an hour afterward, the bread and the water were still untouched.

"What is the meaning of this?" he asked in a stern, angry tone. "Why have you not eaten what I sent you?"

"I am not hungry, papa," she said humbly.

"Don't tell me that," he replied. "It is nothing but stubbornness, and I shall not allow you to show such a temper. Take up that bread this moment, and eat it. You shall eat every crumb of the bread, and drink every drop of the water."

She obeyed him instantly, breaking off a bit of bread and putting it in her mouth, while he stood watching her with an air of stern, cold determination, but when she attempted to swallow, it seemed utterly impossible.

"I cannot, papa," she said. "It chokes me."

"You must," he replied. "I am going to be obeyed. Take a drink of water, and that will wash it down."

It was a hard task, but seeing that there was no escape she struggled to obey, and at length every crumb of bread and drop of water had disappeared.

"Now, Elsie," said her father, in a tone of great severity, "never dare to show me such a temper as this again. You will not escape so easily next time. Remember I am to be obeyed always; and when I send you anything to eat, you are to eat it."

It had not been temper at all, and his unjust severity almost broke her heart, but she could not say one word in her own defense.

He looked at her a moment as she sat there trembling and weeping, then saying, "I forbid you to leave this room without permission. Don't venture to disobey me, Elsie. Sit where you are until I return." He turned to go.

"Papa," she asked, pleadingly, "may I have my books, to learn my lessons for tomorrow?"

"Certainly," he said. "I will send a servant with them."

"And my Bible too, please, papa."

"Yes, yes," he answered impatiently, as he went out and shut the door.

Jim was just bringing up Elsie's horse, as Mr. Dinsmore passed through the hall, and he stepped out to order it back to the stable, saying that Miss Elsie was not going to ride.

"What is the trouble with Elsie?" asked his sister Adelaide, as he returned to the drawing room and seated himself beside her.

"She has been impertinent to her governess, and I have confined her to my room for the rest of the day," he replied rather shortly.

"Are you sure, Horace, that Elsie was so much to blame?" asked his sister, speaking in a tone too low to reach any ear but his. "I am certain, from what Lora tells me, that Miss Day is often cruelly unjust to her, more so than to any other of her pupils."

He looked at her with a good deal of surprise.

"Are you not mistaken?" he asked.

"No! It is a positive fact that she does at times really abuse her."

"Indeed! I shall certainly not allow that," he said, coloring with anger.

"But in this instance, Adelaide," he added, thoughtfully, "I think you must be mistaken, for Elsie acknowledged that she had been impertinent. I did not condemn her unheard, stern and severe as you think me."

"If she was, Horace, believe me it must have been only after great provocation, and her acknowledgment of it is no proof at all, to my mind, for Elsie is so humble, she would think she must have been guilty of impertinence if Miss Day accused her of it."

"Surely not, Adelaide. She is by no means wanting in sense," he replied, in a tone of incredulity, not unmixed with annoyance.

Then he sat thinking a moment, half inclined to go to his child and inquire more particularly into the circumstances. But soon relinquished the idea, saying to himself, "No, if she does not choose to be frank with me, and say what she can in her own defense, she deserves to suffer. And besides, she showed such stubbornness about eating that bread."

He was very proud, and did not like to acknowledge even to himself that he had punished his child unjustly—much less to her, and it was not until near teatime that he returned to his room, entering so softly that Elsie did not hear him.

She was sitting just where he had left her, bending over her Bible, an expression of sadness and deep humility on the sweet little face, so young and fair and innocent. She did not seem aware of his presence until he was close beside her, when, looking up with a start, she said in a voice full of tears, "Dear papa, I am very sorry for all my naughtiness. Will you please forgive me?"

"Yes," he said, "certainly I will, if you are really sorry." And stooping, he kissed her coldly, saying, "Now go to your room, and let Chloe dress you for tea."

She rose at once, gathered up her books, and went out.

The little heart was very sad, for her father's manner was so cold she feared he would never love her again. And she was particularly distressed by the bad mark given her for recitation that day, because she knew the time was now drawing very near when her report must be handed in to her papa. The delight with which she had hitherto looked forward to receiving his well-merited approbation, was now changed to fear, and dread of his displeasure. Yet she knew she had not deserved the bad mark, and again and again she determined that she would tell her father all about it, but his manner had now become so cold and stern that she could not summon up courage to do so. But she put it off from day to day, until it was too late.

❦❦❦❦❦❦❦

CHAPTER EIGHTH

He that pursues an act that is attended
With doubtful issues, for the means, had need
Of policy and force to make it speed.

—*T. Nabb's Unfortunate Mother*

Joy never feasts so high,
As when the first course is of misery.

—*Suckling's Aglaura*

IT WAS FRIDAY, AND THE NEXT MORNING was the time when the reports were to be presented. School had closed, and all but Elsie had already left the room, but she was carefully arranging the books, writing and drawing materials in her desk for she was very neat and orderly in her habits.

When she had quite finished her work she took up her report book, and glanced over it. As her eye rested for an instance upon the one bad mark, she sighed a little, and murmured to herself, "I am so sorry. I wish papa knew how little I really deserved it. I don't know why I never can get the courage to tell him."

Then laying it aside, she opened her copybook and turned over the leaves with unalloyed pleasure, for not one of its pages was defaced by a single blot, and from beginning to end it gave evidence of painstaking carefulness and decided improvement.

"Ah, surely this will please dear papa!" she exclaimed, half loud. "How good Aunt Adelaide was to sit here with me!"

Then putting it carefully in its place, she closed and locked the desk, and carrying the key to her room, laid it on the mantel, where she was in the habit of keeping it.

Now it so happened that afternoon that Arthur, who had made himself sick of over-indulgence in sweetmeats, and had in consequence been lounging about the house doing nothing for the last day or two, remained at home while all the rest of the family were out, walking, riding, or visiting.

He was not usually very fond of reading, but while lying on the lounge in the nursery, very much in want of some amusement, it suddenly occurred to him that he would like to look at a book he had seen Elsie reading that morning.

To be sure the book belonged to her, and she was not there to be consulted as to her willingness to lend it, but that made no difference to Arthur, who had very little respect for the rights of property, excepting where his own were concerned.

Elsie, he knew, was out, and Chloe in the kitchen, so feeling certain there would be no one to interfere with him, he went directly to the little girl's room to look for the book. He soon found it lying on the mantel, but the desk key lay right beside it. As he caught sight of that he gave a half scream of delight, for he guessed at once to what lock it belonged, and felt that he could accomplish the revenge he had plotted ever since the affair of the watch.

He put his hand to take it, but drew it back again, and stood for a moment balancing in his mind the chances of detection.

He could deface Elsie's copybook, but Adelaide could testify to the little girl's carefulness, and the neatness of her work up to that very day, for she had been in the schoolroom that morning during the writing hour. But then Adelaide had just left home to pay a visit to a friend living at some distance, and would not return for several weeks, so there was little danger from that quarter. Miss Day, to be sure, knew the appearance of Elsie's book quite as well, but there was still less danger of her interference, and he was pretty certain no one else knew.

So he decided to run the risk, and laying down the book, he took the key, went to the door, looked carefully up and down the hall to make sure of not being seen by any of the servants, and having satisfied himself on that point, hurried to the schoolroom. He unlocked Elsie's desk, took out her copybook, and dipping a pen in the ink, proceeded deliberately to blot nearly every page in it. On some he made a large blot, on others a small one, and on some two or three, and also scribbled between the lines and on the margin, so as completely to deface poor Elsie's work.

But to do Arthur justice, though he knew his brother would be pretty sure to be very angry with Elsie, he did not know of the threatened punishment. He stopped once or twice as he thought he heard a footstep, and shut down the lid until it had passed, when he raised it again and went on with his wicked work. It did not take long, however, and he soon replaced the copybook in the precise spot in which he had found it, wiped the pen, and put it carefully back in its place. He relocked the desk, hurried back to Elsie's room, put the key just where he had found it, and taking the book, returned to the nursery without having met anyone.

He threw himself down on a couch and tried to read, but in vain. He could not fix his attention upon the page — could think of nothing but the mischief he had done, and its probable consequences, and now, when it was too late, he more than half repented. Yet as to confessing and thus saving Elsie from unmerited blame, he did not for a single moment entertain the thought. But at length it suddenly occurred to him that if it became known that he had been into Elsie's room to get the book he might be suspected, and he started up with the intention of replacing it. But he found that it was too late. She had already returned, for he heard her voice in the hall, so he lay down again, and kept the book until she came in search of it.

He looked very guilty as the little girl came in, but not seeming to notice it, she merely said, "I am looking for my book. I thought perhaps someone might have brought it in here. Oh, you have it, Arthur! Well, keep it, if you wish. I can read it just as well another time."

"Here, take it," said he roughly, pushing it toward her. "I don't want it. 'Tisn't a bit pretty."

"I think it is very interesting, and you are quite welcome to read it if you wish," she answered mildly. "But if you don't care to, I will take it."

"Young ladies and gentlemen," said the governess, as they were about closing their exercises the next morning, "this is the regular day for the reports, and they are all made out. Miss Elsie, here is yours. Bring your copybook, and carry both to your papa."

Elsie obeyed, not without some trembling, yet hoping, as there was but one bad mark in the report and the copybook showed such evident marks of care and painstaking, her papa would not be very seriously displeased.

It being the last day of the term, the exercises of the morning had varied somewhat from the usual routine, and the writing hour had been entirely omitted. Thus it happened that Elsie had not opened her copybook, and was in consequence still in ignorance of its sadly altered appearance.

She found her father in his room. He took the report first from her hand, and glancing over it, said with a slight frown, "I see you have one very bad mark for recitation, but as there is only one, and the others are remarkably good, I will excuse it."

Then taking the copybook and opening it, much to Elsie's surprise and alarm he gave her a glance of great displeasure, turned rapidly over the leaves, then laying it down, said in his sternest tones, "I see I shall have to keep my promise, Elsie."

"What, papa?" she asked, turning pale with terror.

"What!" said he. "Do you ask me what? Did I not tell you positively that I would punish you if your copybook this month did not present a better appearance than it did last?"

"Oh, papa! Does it not? I tried so very hard; and there are no blots in it."

"No blots?" said he. "What do you call these?" and he turned over the leaves again, holding the book so that she could see them, and showing that almost every one was blotted in several places.

Elsie gazed at them in unfeigned astonishment. Then looking up into his face, she said earnestly but fearfully, "Papa, I did not do it."

"Who did, then?" he asked.

"Indeed, papa, I do not know," she replied.

"I must inquire into this business," he said, rising, "and if it is not your fault you shall not be punished, but if I find you have been telling me a falsehood, Elsie, I shall punish you much more severely than if you had not denied your fault."

And taking her by the hand as she spoke, he led her back to the schoolroom.

"Miss Day," said he, showing the book, "Elsie says these blots are not her work. Can you tell me whose they are?"

"Miss Elsie generally tells the truth, sir," replied Miss Day, sarcastically, "but I must say that in this instance I think she has failed, as her desk has a good lock, and she herself keeps the key."

"Elsie," he asked, turning to her, "is this so?"

"Yes, papa."

"And have you ever left your desk unlocked, or the key lying about?"

"No, papa. I am quite certain I have not," she answered unhesitatingly, though her voice trembled, and she grew very pale.

"Very well then, I am quite certain you have told me a falsehood, since it is evident this must have been your work. Elsie, I can forgive anything but falsehood, but that I never will forgive. Come with me. I shall teach you to speak the truth to me, at least, if to no one else," and taking her hand again, he led, or rather dragged, her from the room, for he was terribly angry, his face fairly pale with passion.

Lora came in while he was speaking, and, certain that Elsie would never be caught in a falsehood, her eye quickly sought Arthur's desk.

He was sitting there with a very guilty countenance.

She hastily crossed the room, and speaking in a low tone, said, "Arthur, you have had a hand in this business I very well know. Now confess it quickly, or Horace will half kill Elsie."

"You don't know anything about it," said he doggedly.

"Yes I do," she answered, "and if you do not speak out at once, I shall save Elsie, and find means to prove your guilt afterward, so you had much better confess."

"Go away," he exclaimed angrily. "I have nothing to confess."

Seeing it was useless to try to move him, Lora turned away and hurried to Horace's room, which, in her haste, she entered without knocking, he having fortunately neglected to fasten the door. She was just in time: he had a small riding whip in his hand, and Elsie stood beside him pale as death, too much frightened even to cry, and trembling so that she could scarcely stand.

He turned an angry glance on his sister as she entered, but taking no notice of it, she exclaimed eagerly, "Horace, don't punish Elsie, for I am certain she is innocent."

He laid down the whip, asking, "How do you know it? What proof have you? I shall be very glad to be convinced," he added, his countenance relaxing somewhat in its stern and angry expression.

"In the first place," replied his sister, "there is Elsie's established character for truthfulness. In all the time she has been with us, we have ever found her perfectly truthful in word and deed. And then, Horace, what motive could she have had for spoiling her book, knowing as she did that certain punishment would follow? Besides, I am sure Arthur is at the bottom of this, for though he will not acknowledge, he does not deny it. Ah, yes! And now I recollect, I saw and examined Elsie's book only yesterday, and it was then quite free from blots."

A great change had come over her brother's countenance while she was speaking.

"Thank you, Lora," he said cordially, as soon as she had done, "you have quite convinced me, and saved me from punishing Elsie as unjustly as severely. The last assurance I consider quite sufficient of itself to establish her innocence."

Lora turned and went out feeling very happy, and as she closed the door, Elsie's papa took her in his arms, saying in loving, tender tones, "My poor little daughter! My own darling child! I have been cruelly unjust to you, have I not?"

"Dear papa, you thought I deserved it," she said, with a burst of tears and sobs, throwing her arms around his neck, and laying her head on his chest.

"Do you love me, Elsie, dearest?" he asked, folding her closer to his heart.

"Ah, so very, very much! Better than all the world beside. Oh, papa, if you would only love me!" The last word was almost a sob.

"I do, my darling, my own precious child," he said, caressing her again and again. "I do love my little girl, although I may at times seem cold and stern, and I am more thankful than words can express that I have been saved from punishing her unjustly. I could never forgive myself if I had done it. I would rather have lost half I am worth. Ah! I fear it would have turned all her love for me into hatred, and justly, too."

"No, papa, oh, no, no! Nothing could ever do that!" and the little arms were clasped closer and closer about his neck, and the tears again fell like rain, as she timidly pressed her quivering lips to his cheek.

"There, there daughter! Don't cry any more. We will try to forget all about it, and talk of something else," he said soothingly. "Elsie, dear, your Aunt Adelaide thinks perhaps you were not so very much to blame the other day, and now I want you to tell me all the circumstances. Though I should be very sorry to encourage you to find fault with your teacher, I am by no means willing to have you abused."

"Please, papa, don't ask me," she begged. "Aunt Lora was there, and she will tell you all about it."

"No, Elsie," he said, very decidedly, "I want the story from you; and remember, I want every word that passed between you and Miss Day, as far as you can possibly recall it."

Seeing that he was determined, Elsie obeyed him, though with evident reluctance, and striving to put Miss Day's conduct in as favorable a light as consistent with truth, while she by no means extended her own. Yet her father listened with feelings of strong indignation.

"Elsie," he said when she had done, "if I had known all this at the time, I should not have punished you at all. Why did you not tell me, my daughter, how you have been ill treated and provoked?"

"Oh, papa! I could not. You know you did not ask me."

"I did ask you if it was true that you contradicted her, did I not?"

"Yes, papa, and it was true."

"You ought to have told me the whole story though. But I see how it was—I frightened you by my sternness. Well, daughter," he added, kissing her tenderly, "I shall endeavor to be less stern in the future, and you must try to be less timid and more at your ease with me."

"I will, papa," she replied meekly, "but indeed I cannot help feeling frightened when you are angry with me."

Mr. Dinsmore sat there a long time with his little daughter on his knee, caressing her more tenderly than ever before. Elsie was very happy, and talked more freely to him than she ever had done, telling him her joys and her sorrows. She told how dearly she loved Miss Allison—what happy hours they spent together in studying the Bible and in prayer—how grieved she was when her friend went away—and how intensely she enjoyed the little letter now and then received from her. And he listened to it all, apparently both pleased and interested, encouraging her to go on by an occasional question or a word of assent or approval.

"What is this, Elsie?" he asked, taking hold of the chain she always wore around her neck, and drawing the miniature from her bosom.

But as he touched the spring and the case flew open, revealing the sweet, girlish face, it needed not

Elsie's low murmured "Mamma" to tell him who that lovely lady was.

He gazed upon it with emotion, carried back in memory to the time when for a few short months she had been his own most cherished treasure. Then, looking from it to his child, he murmured, "Yes, she is very like—the same features, the same expression, complexion, hair, and all—will be the very counterpart of her if she lives."

"Dear papa, am I like mamma?" asked Elsie, who had caught a part of his words.

"Yes, darling, very much indeed, and I hope you will grow more so."

"You loved mamma?" she said inquiringly.

"Dearly, very dearly."

"Oh, papa! Tell me about her! Do, dear papa," she pleaded eagerly.

"I have not much to tell," he said, sighing. "I knew her only for a few short months ere we were torn asunder, never to meet again on earth."

"But we may hope to meet her in heaven, dear papa," said Elsie softly, "for she loved Jesus, and if we love Him we shall go there too when we die. Do you love Jesus, papa?" she timidly inquired, for she had seen him do a number of things which she knew to be wrong—such as riding out for pleasure on the Sabbath, reading secular newspapers, and engaging in worldly conversation—and she greatly feared he did not.

But instead of answering her question, he asked, "Do you, Elsie?"

"Oh, yes, sir! Very, very much, even better than I love you, my own dear papa."

"How do you know?" he asked, looking keenly into her face.

"Just as I know that I love you, papa, or anyone else," she replied, lifting her eyes to his face in evident surprise at the strangeness of the question. "Ah, papa," she added in her own sweet, simple way, "I do so love to talk to Jesus, to tell Him all my troubles, and ask Him to forgive my sins and make me holy. And then it is so sweet to know that He loves me, and will always love me, even if no one else does."

He kissed her very gravely, and set her down, saying, "Go now, my daughter, and prepare for dinner. It is almost time for the bell."

"You are not displeased, papa?" she inquired, looking up anxiously into his face.

"No, darling, not at all," he replied, stroking her hair. "Shall I ride with my little girl this afternoon?"

"Oh, papa! Do you really mean it? I shall be so glad!" she exclaimed joyfully.

"Very well, then," he said, "it is settled. But go now, there is the bell. No, stay," he added quickly, as she turned to obey. "Think a moment and tell me where you put the key of your desk yesterday, for it must have been then the mischief was done. Had you it with you when you rode out?"

Suddenly Elsie's face flushed, and she exclaimed eagerly, "Ah! I remember now! I left it on the mantelpiece, papa, and —"

But here she paused, as if sorry she had said so much.

"And what?" he asked.

"I think I had better not say it, papa! I'm afraid I ought not, for I don't really know anything, and it seems so wrong to suspect people."

"You need not express any suspicions." said her father. "I do not wish you to do so, but I must insist upon having all the facts you can furnish me with. Was Aunt Chloe in your room all the time you were away?"

"No, sir, she told me she went down to the kitchen directly after I left, and did not come up again until after I returned."

"Very well. Do you know whether anyone else entered the room during your absence?"

"I do not know, papa, but I think Arthur must have been in, because when I came home I found him reading a book which I left lying on the mantelpiece," she answered in a low, reluctant tone.

"Ah, ha! That is just it! I see it all now," he exclaimed, with a satisfied nod. "There, that will do, Elsie. Go now and make haste down to your dinner."

But Elsie lingered, and, in answer to a look of kind inquiry from her father, said coaxingly, "Please, papa, don't be very angry with him. I think he did not know how much I cared about my book."

"You are very forgiving, Elsie. But go, child, I shall not abuse him," Mr. Dinsmore answered, with an imperative gesture, and the little girl hurried from the room.

It happened that just at this time the elder Mr. Dinsmore and his wife were paying a visit to some friends in the city, and thus Elsie's papa had been left head of the house for the time. Arthur, knowing this to be the state of affairs, and that though his father was expected to return that evening, his mother would be absent for some days, was beginning to be a good deal fearful of the consequences of his misconduct. This was not without reason, for his brother's wrath was now fully aroused, and he was determined that the boy should not on this occasion escape the penalty of his misdeeds.

Arthur was already in the dining room when Mr. Dinsmore came down.

"Arthur," he said, "I wish you to step into the library a moment. I have something to say to you."

"I don't want to hear it," muttered the boy, with a dogged look, and standing perfectly still.

"I dare say not, sir, but that makes no difference," replied his brother. "Walk into the library at once." Arthur returned a scowl of defiance, muttering almost under his breath, "I'll do as I please about that," but cowed by his brother's determined look and manner, he slowly and reluctantly obeyed.

"Now, sir," said Mr. Dinsmore, when he had him fairly in the room, and had closed the door behind them, "I wish to know how you came to meddle with Elsie's copybook?"

"I didn't," was the angry rejoinder.

"Take care, sir. I know all about it," said Mr. Dinsmore, in a warning tone. "It is useless for you to deny it. Yesterday, while Elsie was out and Aunt Chloe in the kitchen, you went to her room, took the key of her desk from the mantelpiece where she had left it, went to the schoolroom and did the mischief, hoping to get her into trouble thereby. And then, relocking the desk and returning the key to its proper place, thought you had escaped detection, and I was very near giving my poor innocent little girl the whipping you so richly deserve."

Arthur looked up in astonishment. "Who told you?" he asked. "Nobody saw me," then catching himself, said hastily, "I tell you I didn't do it. I don't know anything about it."

"Will you dare to tell me such a falsehood as that again?" exclaimed Mr. Dinsmore, angrily, taking him by the collar and shaking him roughly.

"Let me alone now," whined the culprit. "I want my dinner, I say."

"You'll get no dinner today, I can tell you," replied his brother. "I am going to lock you into your bedroom, and keep you there until your father comes home, and then if he doesn't give you the flogging you deserve, I will, for I intend you shall have your deserts for once in your life. I know that all this is in revenge for Elsie's forced testimony in the affair of the watch, and I gave you fair warning then that I would see to it that any attempt to abuse my child should receive its just reward."

He took the boy by the arm as he spoke, to lead him from the room.

At first Arthur seemed disposed to resist, but soon seeing how useless it was to contend against such odds, he resigned himself to his fate, saying sullenly, "You wouldn't treat me this way if mamma was at home."

"She is not, however, as it happens, though I can tell you that even she could not save you now," replied his brother, as he opened the bedroom door, and pushing him in, locked it upon him, and put the key in his pocket.

Mr. Horace Dinsmore had almost unbounded influence over his father, who was very proud of him. The old gentleman also utterly despised everything mean and underhanded, and upon being made acquainted by Horace with Arthur's misdemeanors he inflicted upon him as severe a punishment as anyone could have desired.

CHAPTER NINTH

*Keep the Sabbath day to sanctify it, as the
Lord thy God hath commanded thee.*

—Deut. 5:12

*She is mine own;
And I as rich in having such a jewel
As twenty seas, if all their sand were pearl,
The water nectar, and the rocks pure gold.*

—Shakespeare's Two Gentlemen of Verona

AND NOW HAPPY DAYS HAD COME to the
little Elsie. Her father treated her with the
tenderest affection, and kept her with him almost
constantly, seeming scarcely willing to have her out
of his sight for an hour. He took her with him
wherever he went on his rides and walks and visits
to the neighboring planters.

She was much admired for her beauty and
sweetness of disposition, much caressed and
flattered, but, through it all, lost none of her native
modesty, but was ever the same meek, gentle little
girl. She felt grateful for all the kindness she
received, and liked to visit with her papa. But her
happiest days were spent at home on those rare
occasions when they were free from visitors, and
she could sit for hours on his knee, or by his side,

talking or reading to him, or working at her embroidery, or knitting and listening while he read. He helped her with all her studies, taught her something of botany and geology in their walks, helped her to see and correct the faults of her drawings, sang with her when she played, bought her quantities of new music, and engaged the best masters to instruct her. In short, he took a lively interest in all her pursuits and pleasures, gave her every indulgence, and lavished upon her the tenderest caresses. He was very proud of her beauty, her sweetness, her intelligence, and talent, and nothing pleased him better than to hear them spoken of by others in terms of praise.

And Elsie was very happy. The soft eyes grew bright with happiness, and the little face lost its pensive expression, and became as round and rosy and merry as Enna's.

Miss Day went north, expecting to be absent several months, and Elsie's papa took her traveling, spending some time at different watering places. It was her first journey since she had been old enough to care for such things, and she enjoyed it exceedingly. They left home in July, and did not return until September, so that the little girl had time to rest and recoup, both mentally and physically, and was ready to begin her studies again with zeal and energy. Yet it was so pleasant to be her papa's constant companion, and she had enjoyed her freedom from the restraints of the schoolroom, that she was not at all sorry to learn, on her arrival at Roselands, that the governess would still be absent for some weeks.

"How bright and happy the child looks!" was Adelaide's remark on the day of their return, as from the opposite side of the room, she watched the speaking countenance of the little girl, who was giving Enna and the boys an animated description of her journey.

"Yes," said Lora, "and how entirely she seems to have overcome her fear of her father!" For at that instant Elsie suddenly left the little group, and running to him, leaned confidingly on his knee, while apparently urging some request, which he answered with a smile and a nod of acquiescence, when she left the room, and presently returned carrying a richly bound book of engravings.

Yes, Elsie had lost her fear of her father, and could now talk to him, and tell him her feelings and wishes, as freely as Enna ever did. And no wonder, for in all these weeks he had never given her one harsh word or look, but indeed he had had no occasion to do so, for she was always docile and obedient.

It was Sabbath afternoon—the first Sabbath after their return—and Elsie was in her own room alone with the books she loved best—her Bible, hymn-book, and *Pilgrim's Progress*.

She had spent a very happy hour in self-examination, reading, and prayer, and was singing to herself in a low tone her favorite hymn, "I Lay My Sins on Jesus." She was turning over the leaves of her Bible to find the story of Elijah, which she had promised to read to Chloe that afternoon, when a child's footsteps were heard coming down the hall. The handle of the door was turned hastily, and then, as it refused to yield, Enna's voice called out in a fretful, imperious tone, "Open this door, Elsie Dinsmore. I want in, I say."

Elsie sighed, as she thought, "There is an end to my nice afternoon," but she arose at once, and quickly crossing the room, opened the door, asking pleasantly, "What do you want, Enna?"

"I told you I wanted to come in," replied Enna, saucily, "and now you've got to tell me a story to amuse me. Mamma says so, because you know I've got a cold, and she won't let me go out."

"Well, Enna," said Elsie, patiently, "I am going to read a very beautiful story to mammy, and you are quite welcome to sit here and listen."

"I sha'n't have it read! I said you were to tell it. I don't like to hear reading," replied Enna in her imperious way. At the same time she took quiet possession of Elsie's little rosewood rocking-chair—a recent present from her papa, and highly prized by the little girl on that account—and beginning to scratch with her thumb nail upon the arm.

"Oh, don't scratch my pretty new chair, Enna!" Elsie entreated. "It is papa's present, and I wouldn't have it spoiled for a great deal."

"I will. Who cares for your old chair?" was the reply in a scornful tone, as she gave another and harder dig with her nail. "You're a little old maid—so particular with all your things—that's what mamma says you are. Now tell me that story."

"I will you tell you a story if you stop scratching my chair, Enna," said Elsie, almost with tears in her eyes. "I will tell you about Elijah on Mount Carmel, or Belshazzar's feast, or the children in the fiery furnace, or—"

"I sha'n't hear any of those! I don't want any of your Bible stories," interrupted Enna, insolently. "You must tell me that pretty fairy tale Herbert Carrington is so fond of."

"No, Enna, I cannot tell you that today," replied Elsie, speaking gently, but very firmly.

"I say you shall!" screamed Enna, springing to her feet. "I'll just go and tell mamma, and she'll make you do it."

"Stay, Enna," said Elsie, catching her hand to detain her, "I will tell you any story I know that is suitable for the Sabbath, but I cannot tell the fairy tale today, because you know it would be wrong. I will tell you tomorrow, though, if you will wait."

"You're a bad girl, and I'll just tell mamma of you," exclaimed Enna, passionately, jerking her hand away and darting from the room.

"Oh, if papa was only at home," sighed Elsie, sinking into her rocking chair, pale and trembling. But she knew that he had gone riding, and would probably not return for some time. He had invited her to accompany him, but she had begged to be allowed to stay at home, and he had let her have her wish.

As she feared, she was immediately summoned to Mrs. Dinsmore's presence.

"Elsie," said that lady, severely, "are you not ashamed of yourself, to refuse Enna such a small favor? Especially when the poor child is not well. I must say you are the most selfish, disobliging child I ever saw."

"I offered to tell her a Bible story, or anything suitable for the Sabbath day," replied Elsie, meekly, "but I cannot tell the fairy tale, because it would be wrong."

"Nonsense! There's no harm at all in telling fairy tales today, any more than any other day. That is just an excuse, Elsie," said Mrs. Dinsmore angrily.

"I don't want her old Bible stories. I won't have them. I want that pretty fairy tale," sobbed Enna passionately. "Make her tell it, mamma."

"Come, come, what is all this fuss about?" asked the elder Mr. Dinsmore, coming in from an adjoining room.

"Nothing," said his wife, "except that Enna is not well enough to go out, and wants a fairy story to pass away the time, which Elsie alone is acquainted with, but is too lazy or too self-willed to relate."

He turned angrily to his granddaughter.

"Ah, indeed! Is that it? Well, there is an old saying, 'A bird that can sing, and won't sing, must be made to sing.'"

Elsie was opening her lips to speak, but Mrs. Dinsmore bade her be silent, and then went on. "She pretends it is all on account of conscientious scruples. 'It isn't fit for the Sabbath,' she says. Now I say it is a great piece of impertinence for a child of her years to set up her opinion against yours and mine, and I know very well it is nothing but an excuse, because she doesn't choose to be obliging."

"Of course it is—nothing in the world but an excuse," responded Mr. Dinsmore, hotly.

Elsie's face flushed, and she answered a little indignantly, "No, grandpa, indeed it is not merely an excuse, but—"

"Do you dare to contradict me, you impertinent little hussy!" cried the old gentleman, interrupting her in the middle of her sentence. And catching her by the arm, he shook her violently. Then picking her up and setting her down hard upon a chair, he said, "Now, miss, sit you there until your father comes home, then we will see what he thinks of such impertinence, and if he doesn't give you the complete whipping you deserve, I miss my guess."

"Please, grandpa, I—"

"Hold your tongue! Don't dare to speak another word until your father comes home," said he, threateningly. "If you don't choose to say what you're wanted to, you shall not talk at all."

Then going to the door, he called a servant and bade him to tell "Mr. Horace," as soon as he returned, that he wished to see him.

For the next half-hour—and a very long one it seemed for her—Elsie sat there wishing for, and yet dreading, her father's coming. Would he inflict upon her the punishment which her grandfather evidently wished for her to receive, without pausing to inquire into the merits of the case? Or would he listen patiently to her story? And even if he did, might he not still think her deserving of punishment? She could not answer these questions to her own satisfaction. A few months ago she would have been certain of a very severe chastisement, and even now she trembled with fear, for though she knew beyond a doubt that he loved her dearly, she knew also that he was a strict and severe disciplinarian, and never excused her faults.

At last her ear caught the sound of his step in the hall, and her heart beat fast and faster as it drew nearer, until he entered, and addressing his father, asked, "Did you wish to see me, sir?"

"Yes, Horace, I want you to attend to this girl," replied the old gentleman, with a motion of the head toward Elsie. "She has been very impertinent to me."

"What! Elsie impertinent! Is it possible? I certainly expected better things of her."

His tone expressed great surprise, and turning to his little daughter, he regarded her with a grave, sad look that brought the tears to her eyes. Dearly as she loved him, it seemed almost harder to bear than the old expression of stern severity.

"It is hard to believe," he said, "that my little Elsie would be guilty of such conduct, but if she has been, of course she must be punished, for I cannot allow anything of the kind. Go, Elsie, to my dressing room and remain there until I come to you."

"Papa—" she began, bursting into tears.

"Hush!" he said, with something of the old sternness. "Not a word, but obey me instantly."

Then as Elsie went sobbing from the room, he seated himself, and turning to his father, said, "Now, sir, if you please, I should like to hear the whole story—precisely what Elsie has done and said, and what was the provocation, for that must also be taken into the account, in order that I may be able to do her justice."

"If you do her justice, you will whip her well," remarked the elder Mr. Dinsmore in a tone of asperity.

Horace colored violently, for nothing aroused his ire sooner than any interference between him and his child, but controlling himself, he replied quite calmly, "If I find her deserving a punishment, I will not spare her, but I should be sorry indeed to punish her unjustly. Will you be so good as to tell me what she has done?"

Mr. Dinsmore referred him to his wife for the commencement of the trouble, and she made out as bad a case against Elsie as possible, but even then there seemed to her father to be very little to condemn. And when Mrs. Dinsmore was obliged to acknowledge that it was Elsie's refusal to amuse Enna in her desire for a particular story which Elsie thought it not best to relate on the Sabbath, he bit his lip with vexation. He told her in a haughty tone, that though he did not approve of Elsie's strict notions regarding such matters, yet he wished her to understand that his daughter was not to be made a slave to Enna's whims. If she chose to tell her a story, or do anything else for her amusement, he had no objection, but she was never to be forced to do it against her inclinations, and Enna must understand that it was done as a favor, and not at all as her right.

"You are right enough there, Horace," remarked his father, "but that does not excuse Elsie for her impertinence to me. In the first place, I must say I agree with my wife in thinking it quite a piece of impertinence for a child of her years to set up her opinion against mine, and besides, she contradicted me flatly."

He then went on to repeat what he had said, and Elsie's denial of the charge, using her exact words, but quite a different tone, and suppressing the fact that he had interrupted her before she had finished her sentence.

Elsie's tone, though slightly indignant, had still been respectful, but from her grandfather's rehearsal of the scene her father received the impression that she had been exceedingly saucy, and he left the room with the intention of giving her almost as severe as punishment as her grandfather would have prescribed.

On the way up to his room, however, his anger had a little time to cool, and it occurred to him that it would be no more than just to hear her side of the story ere he condemned her.

Elsie was seated on a couch at the far side of the room, and as he entered she turned on him a tearful, pleading look, that went straight to his heart.

His face was grave and sad, but there was very little sternness in it, as he sat down and took her in his arms.

For a moment he held her without speaking, while she lifted her eyes timidly to his face. Then he said, as he gently stroked the hair back from her forehead, "I am very sorry, very sorry indeed, to hear so bad an account of my little daughter. I am afraid I shall have to punish her, and I don't like to do it."

She answered not a word, but burst into tears, and hiding her face on his chest, sobbed aloud.

"I will not condemn you unheard, Elsie," he said after as moment's pause. "Tell me how you came to be so impertinent to your grandfather."

"I did not mean to be saucy, papa, indeed I did not," she sobbed.

"Stop crying then, daughter," he said kindly, "and tell me all about it. I know there was some trouble between you and Enna, and I want you to tell me all that occurred, and every word spoken by either of you, as well as all that passed between Mrs. Dinsmore, your grandfather, and yourself. I am very glad I can trust my little girl to speak the truth. I am quite sure she would not tell a falsehood even to save herself from punishment," he added tenderly.

"Thank you, dear papa, for saying that," said Elsie, raising her head and almost smiling through her tears. "I will try to tell it just as it happened."

She then told her story simply and truthfully, repeating as he bade her, every word that had passed between Enna and herself, and between her and her grandparents. Her words to her grandfather sounded very different, repeated in her quiet, respectful tones. And when she had added that if he would have allowed her, she was going on to explain that it was not any unwillingness to oblige Enna, but the fear of doing wrong, that led her to refuse her request, her father thought that after all she deserved very little blame.

"Do you think I was very saucy, papa?" she asked anxiously, when she had finished her story.

"So much depends upon the tone, Elsie," he said, "that I can hardly tell. If you used the same tone in speaking to your grandpa that you did in repeating your words to me just now, I don't think it was very impertinent, though the words themselves were not as respectful as they ought to have been. You must always treat my father quite as respectfully as you do me. And I think with him, too, that there is something quite impertinent in a little girl like you setting up her opinion against that of her elders. You must never try it with me, my daughter."

Elsie laid down her head in silence for a moment, then said in a tremulous tone, "Are you going to punish me, papa?"

"Yes," he said, "but first I am going to take you downstairs and make you beg your grandfather's pardon. I see you don't want to do it," he added, looking keenly into her face, "but you must, and I hope I shall not be obliged to enforce obedience to my commands."

"I will do whatever you bid me, papa," she sobbed, "but I do not mean to be saucy. Please, papa, tell me what to say."

"You must say, 'Grandpa, I do not mean to be impertinent to you, and I am very sorry for whatever may have seemed saucy in my words or tones. Will you please forgive me, and I will try always to be perfectly respectful in the future.' You can say all that with truth, I think?"

"Yes, papa, I am sorry, and I do intend to be respectful to grandpa always," she answered, brushing away her tears, and putting her hand in his.

He then led her into her grandfather's presence, saying, "Elsie has come to beg your pardon, sir."

"That is as it should be," replied the old gentleman, glancing triumphantly at his wife. "I told her you would not uphold her in any such impertinence."

"No," said his son, with some displeasure in his tone, "I will neither uphold her in wrong doing, nor suffer her to be imposed upon. Speak, my daughter, and say what I bade you."

Elsie sobbed out the required words.

"Yes, I must forgive you, of course," replied her grandfather, coldly, "but I hope your father is not going to let you off without proper punishment."

"I will attend to that. I certainly intend to punish her as she deserves," said his son, laying a marked emphasis upon the concluding words of his sentence.

Elsie wholly misunderstood him, and so trembled with fear as he led her from the room, that she could scarcely walk, seeing which, he took her in his arms and carried her upstairs, she sobbing on his shoulder.

He did not speak until he had locked the door, carried her across the room, and seated himself upon the couch again, with her upon his knee.

Then he said, in a soothing tone, as he wiped away her tears and kissed her kindly, "You need not tremble so, my daughter. I am not going to be severe with you."

She looked up in glad surprise.

"I said I would punish you as you deserve," he said, with a smile, "and I intend to keep you shut up here with me until bedtime. I shall not allow you to go downstairs to tea, and besides, I am going to give you a long lesson to learn, which I shall require you to recite to me quite perfectly before you can go to bed."

Elsie grew frightened again at the mention of the lesson, for she feared it might be something which she could not conscientiously study on the Sabbath. But all her fear and trouble vanished as she saw her father take up a Bible that lay on the table, and turn over the leaves as though selecting a passage.

Presently he put it into her hands, and pointing to the thirteenth and fourteenth chapters of John's Gospel, bade her carry the book to a low seat by the window, and sit there until she had learned them perfectly.

"Oh, papa, what a nice lesson!" she exclaimed, looking up delightedly into his face. "But it won't be any punishment, because I love these chapters dearly, and have read them so often that I almost know every word already."

"Hush, hush!" he said, pretending to be very stern. "Don't tell me that my punishments are no punishment. I don't allow you to talk so. Just take the Book and learn what I bid you, and if you know those two already, you may learn the next."

Elsie laughed, kissed his hand, and tripped away to her window. Meanwhile he threw himself down on the couch and took up a newspaper, more as a screen to his face, however, than for the purpose of reading. He lay there closely watching his little daughter, as she sat in the rich glow of the sunset, with her sweet, grave little face bending over the Holy Book.

"The darling!" he murmured to himself. "She is lovely as an angel, and she is mine, mine only, mine own precious one, and loves me with her whole soul. Ah, how can I ever find it in my heart to be stern to her? Ah! If I were but half as good and pure as she is, I should be a better man than I am." And he heaved a deep sigh.

Half an hour had passed, and still Elsie bent over her book. The tea bell rang, and Mr. Dinsmore started up, and crossing the room, bent down and stroked her hair.

"Do you know it, darling?" he asked.

"Almost, papa," and she looked up into his face with a bright, sweet smile, full of affection.

With a sudden impulse he caught her in his arms, and kissing her again and again, said with emotion, "Elsie, my darling, I love you too well. I could never bear to lose you."

"You must love Jesus better, my own precious papa," she replied, clasping her little arms around his neck, and returning his caresses.

He held her a moment, and then putting her down, said, "I shall send you up some supper, and I want you to eat it. Don't behave as you did about the bread and water once, a good while ago."

"Will it be bread and water this time, papa?" she asked, with a smile.

"You will see," he said laughingly, and left the room.

Elsie turned to her book again, but in a few moments was interrupted by the entrance of a servant carrying on a silver waiter a plate of hot, buttered muffins, a cup of jelly, another of hot coffee, and a piece of broiled chicken. Elsie was all astonishment.

"Why, Pomp," she asked, "did papa send it?"

"Yes, Miss Elsie, 'deed he did," replied the servant, with a grin of satisfaction, as he set down his burden. "I reckon you been berry nice gal dis day, or else Marster Horace tink you little bit sick."

"Papa is very good, and I am much obliged to you too, Pomp," said the little girl, laying aside her book, and seating herself before the waiter.

"Jes ring de bell, Miss Elsie, ef you want more, and dis chile fotch 'em up. Marster Horace say so hisself." And the grinning Negro bowed himself out, chuckling with delight, for Elsie had always been a great favorite with him.

"Dear papa," Elsie said, when he came in again and smilingly asked if she had eaten her prison fare, "what a good supper you sent me! But I thought you didn't allow me such things!"

"Don't you know," said he playfully, laying his hand upon her head, "that I am absolute monarch of this small kingdom, and you are not to question my doings or decrees?"

Then in a more serious tone, "No daughter, I do not allow it as a regular thing, because I do not think it for your good. But for once, I thought it would not hurt you. I know you are not one to presume upon favors, and I wanted to indulge you a little, because I fear my little girl has been made to suffer perhaps more than she quite deserved this afternoon."

His voice had a very tender tone as he uttered the concluding words, and stooping, he pressed his lips to her forehead.

"Don't think, though," he added the next moment, "that I am excusing you for impertinence. Not at all. But it was what you have had to suffer from Enna's insolence. I shall put a stop to that, for I will not have it."

"I don't mind it much, papa," said Elsie gently. "I am quite used to it, for Enna has always treated me so."

"And why did I never hear of it before?" he asked, half angrily. "It is abominable! Not to be endured!" he exclaimed. "And I shall see that Miss Enna is made to understand that my daughter is fully equal in every respect, and always to be treated as such."

He paused, but Elsie, half frightened at his vehemence, made no reply, and he went on: "I have no doubt your grandfather and his wife would have been better pleased had I forced you to yield to Enna's whim, but I had no idea of such a thing. You shall use your own pleasure whenever she is concerned. But if I had bidden you tell her that story it would have been a very difficult matter. You need never set up your will, or your opinion of right and wrong, against mine, Elsie, for I shall not allow it. I don't altogether like some of those strict notions you have got into your head, and I give you fair warning, that should they ever come into collision with my wishes and commands, they will have to be given up. But don't look so alarmed, daughter. I hope it may never happen, and we will say no more about it tonight," he added, kindly, for she had grown very pale and trembled visibly.

"Oh, papa, dear papa! Don't ever bid me do anything wrong. It would break my heart," she said, laying her head on his shoulder as he sat down and drew her to his side.

"I never intend to bid you do wrong, but, on the contrary, wish you always to do right. But then, daughter, I must be the judge of what is wrong or right for you. You must remember that you are only a very little girl, and not yet capable of judging for yourself, and all you have to do is to obey your father without murmuring or hesitation, and then there will be no trouble."

His tone, though mild, and not unkind, was very firm and decided, and Elsie's heart sank. She seemed to feel herself in the shadow of some great trouble laid up in store for her in the future. But she strove, and ere long with success, to banish the foreboding of evil which oppressed her, and give herself up to the enjoyment of present blessings.

Her father loved her dearly—she knew that—and he was not now requiring her to do ought against her conscience, and perhaps he never might. He had said so himself, and God could incline his heart to respect her scruples, or if, in His infinite wisdom, He saw that the dreaded trial was needed, He would give her strength to bear it, for had He not promised, "As thy day, so shall thy strength be?"

Her father's arm was around her, and she had been standing silent, with her face hidden on his shoulder, while these thoughts were passing through her mind, and the little heart going up in prayer to God for him and for herself.

"What is my little girl thinking of?" he asked presently.

"A good many things, papa," she said, raising her face, now quite peaceful and happy again. "I was thinking of what you had just been saying to me, and that I am so glad I know that you love me dearly. And I was asking God to help us both to do His will, and that I might always be able to do what you bid me, without disobeying Him," she added simply. Then she asked, "May I say my lesson now, papa? I think I know it quite perfectly."

"Yes," he said in an absent way. "Bring me the Book."

Elsie brought it, and putting it into his hands, drew up a stool and sat down at his feet, resting her arm on his knee, and looking up into his face. Then in her sweet, low voice, she repeated slowly and feelingly, with true and beautiful emphasis, the chapters he had given her to learn — that most touching description of the Last Supper, and our Savior's farewell address to His sorrowing disciples.

"Ah, papa! Is it not beautiful?" she exclaimed, laying her head upon his knee, while the tears trembled in her eyes. "Is not that a sweet verse, 'having loved His own which were in the world, He loved them unto the end?' It seems so strange that He could be so thoughtful for them, so kind and loving, when all the time He knew what a dreadful death He was just going to die. And He knew besides that they were all going to run away and leave Him alone with His cruel enemies. Oh, it is so sweet to know that Jesus is so loving, and that He loves me, and will always love me, even to the end, forever."

"How did you know that, Elsie?" he asked.

"I know that He loves me, papa, because I love Him, and He has said, 'I love them that love me.' And I know that He will love me always, because He has said, 'I have loved thee with an everlasting love,' and in another place, 'I will never leave thee, nor forsake thee.'"

"But do you think that you are good enough, daughter, for Jesus to love you?"

"Ah, papa! I know I am not at all good. I have a very wicked heart, and often my thoughts and feelings are all wrong, and Jesus knows all about it, but it does not keep Him from loving me, for you know it was sinners He died to save. Ah, papa, how good and kind He was! Who could help loving Him? I used to feel so lonely and sad sometimes, papa, that I think my heart would have broken quite, and I should have died, if I had not had Jesus to love me."

"When were you so sad and lonely, darling?" he asked in a moved tone, as he laid his hand gently on her head, and stroked her hair caressingly.

"Sometimes when you were away, papa, and I had never seen you. But then I used to think of you, heart would long and ache so to see you, you call me daughter, and to lay my head against your chest and feel your arms folding me close to your heart, as you do so often now."

She paused a moment, and struggled hard to keep down the rising sobs, as she added, "But when you came, papa, and I saw you did not love me, oh, papa, that was the worst! I thought I could never, never, bear it. I thought my heart would break, and I wanted to die and go to Jesus, and to mamma."

The little frame shook with sobs.

"My poor darling! My poor little love," he said taking her in his arms again, and caressing her with the greatest tenderness. "It was very hard, very cruel. I don't know how I could steel my heart so against my own little child, but I had been very much prejudiced, and led to suppose that you looked upon me with fear and dislike, as a hated tyrant."

Elsie lifted her eyes to his face with a look of extreme surprise.

"Oh, papa!" she exclaimed. "How could you think that? I have always loved you, ever since I can remember."

When Elsie went to her room that evening she thought very seriously of all that had occurred during the afternoon, and all that her papa had said to her. And to her usual petitions was added a very fervent one that he might never bid her break any command of God, or if he did, that she might have strength given her according to her day.

A shadow had fallen on her pathway, faint, but perceptible; a light, fleecy cloud obscured the brightness of her sun. Yet it was not for some weeks that even the most distant mutterings of the coming storm could be heard.

CHAPTER TENTH

If thou turn away thy foot from the Sabbath, from doing thy pleasure on my holy day, and call the Sabbath a Delight, the Holy of the Lord, Honorable, and shalt honor him, not doing thine own ways, not finding thine own pleasure, nor speaking thine own words.

—Isaiah 58:13

Whether it be right in the sight of God to hearken unto you, more than unto God, judge ye.

—Acts 4:19

QUITE A NUMBER OF GUESTS had dined at Roselands. They were nearly all gentlemen, and were now collected in the drawing room, laughing, jesting, talking politics, and conversing with each other and the ladies upon various worldly topics. They were apparently quite forgetful that it was the Lord's day, which He has commanded to be kept holy in thought and word, as well as deed.

"May I ask what you are in search of, Mr. Eversham?" inquired Adelaide, as she noticed one of the guests glance around the room with a rather disappointed air.

"Yes, Miss Adelaide, I was looking for little Miss Elsie. Travilla has given me so very glowing an account of her precocious musical talent, that I have conceived a great desire to hear her play and sing."

"Do you hear that, Horace?" asked Adelaide, turning to her brother.

"Yes, and I shall be most happy to gratify you, Eversham," replied the young father, with a proud smile.

He crossed the room to summon a servant, but as he placed his hand upon the bell rope, Mrs. Dinsmore arrested his movement.

"Stay, Horace," she said. "You had better not send for her."

"May I be permitted to ask why, madam?" he inquired in a tone of mingled surprise and annoyance.

"Because she will not sing," answered the lady, coolly.

"Pardon me, madam, but I think she will, if I bid her to do it," he said with flashing eyes.

"No, she will not," persisted Mrs. Dinsmore, in the same cold, quiet tone. "She will tell you she is wiser than her father, and that it would be a sin to obey him in this. Believe me, she will most assuredly defy your authority, so you had better take my advice and let her alone—thus sparing yourself the mortification of exhibiting before your guests your inability to govern your child."

Mr. Dinsmore bit his lip with vexation.

"Thank you," he said, haughtily, "but I prefer convincing you that that inability lies wholly in your imagination, and I am quite at a loss to understand upon what you found your opinion, as

Elsie has never yet made the very slightest resistance to my authority."

He had given the bell rope a vigorous pull while speaking, and a servant now appeared in answer to the summons. He sent him with a message to Elsie, requiring her presence in the drawing room.

Then turning away from his stepmother, who looked after him with a gleam of triumph in her eye, he joined the group of gentlemen already gathered about the piano, where Adelaide had just taken her seat and begun a brilliant overture.

Yes, outwardly calm and self-satisfied as his demeanor may have been, Horace Dinsmore was even now regretting the step he had just taken. For remembering Elsie's conscientious scruples regarding the observance of the Sabbath—which he had for the moment forgotten—he foresaw that there would be a struggle, probably a severe one. And though, having always found her docile and yielding, he left no doubt of the final result, he would willingly have avoided the contest, could he have done so without a sacrifice of pride. But, as he said to himself, with a slight sigh, he had now gone too far to retreat, and then he had all along felt that this struggle must come some time, and perhaps it was as well now as at any other.

Elsie was alone in her own room, spending the Sabbath afternoon in her usual manner, when the servant came to say that her papa wished to see her in the drawing room. The little girl was a good deal alarmed at the summons, for the thought instantly flashed upon her, "He is going to bid me play and sing, or do something else which it is not right to do on the Sabbath day."

But remembering that he never had done so, she hoped he might not now, yet ere she obeyed the call she knelt down for a moment, and prayed earnestly for strength to do right, however difficult it might be.

"Come here, daughter," her father said as she entered the room. He spoke in his usual pleasant affectionate tone, yet Elsie started, trembled, and turned pale, for catching sight of the group at the piano, and her Aunt Adelaide just vacating the music stool, she at once perceived what was in store for her.

"Here, Elsie," said her father, selecting a song which she had learned during their absence, and sang remarkably well, "I wish you to sing this for my friends. They are anxious to hear it."

"Will not tomorrow do, papa?" she asked, in a low, tremulous tone.

Mrs. Dinsmore, who had drawn near to listen, now looked at Horace with a meaning smile, which he affected not to see.

"Certainly not, Elsie," he said. "We want it now. You know it quite well enough without any more practice."

"I did not want to wait for that reason, papa," she replied in the same low, trembling tones, "but you know this is the holy Sabbath day."

"Well, my daughter, and what of that? I consider this song perfectly proper to be sung today, and that ought to satisfy you that you will not be doing wrong to sing it. Remember what I said to you some weeks ago. And now sit down and sing it at once, without any more ado."

"Oh, papa! I cannot sing it today. Please let me wait until tomorrow."

"Elsie," he said in his sternest tones, "sit down to the piano instantly, and do as I bid you, and let me have no more of this nonsense."

She sat down, but raising her pleading eyes, brimful of tears, to his face, she repeated her refusal. "Dear papa, I cannot sing it today. I cannot break the Sabbath."

"Elsie, you must sing it," said he, placing the music before her. "I have told you that it will not be breaking the Sabbath, and that is sufficient. You must let me judge for you in these matters."

"Let her wait until tomorrow, Dinsmore. Tomorrow will suite us quite as well," urged several of the gentlemen, while Adelaide good-naturedly said,

"Let me play it, Horace. I have no such scruples, and presume I can do it nearly as well as Elsie."

"No," he replied, "when I give my child a command, it is to be obeyed. I have said she should play it, and play it she must. She is not to suppose that she may set up her opinion of right and wrong against mine."

Elsie sat with her little hands folded in her lap, the tears streaming from her downcast eyes over her pale cheeks. She was trembling, but though there was no stubbornness in her countenance, the expression meek and humble, she made no movement toward obeying her father's order.

This was a moment of silent waiting. Then he said in his severest tone, "Elsie, you shall sit there till you obey me, though it should be until tomorrow morning."

"Yes, papa," she replied in a scarcely audible voice, and they all turned away and left her.

"You see now that you had better have taken my advice, Horace," remarked Mrs. Dinsmore, in a triumphant aside. "I knew very well how it would end."

"Excuse me," said he, "but it has not ended, and ere it does, I think she will learn that she has a stronger will than her own to deal with."

Elsie's position was a most uncomfortable one, her seat high and uneasy, and seeming to grow more and more so as the weary moments passed slowly away. No one came near her or seemed to notice her, yet she could hear them conversing in other parts of the room, and knew that they were sometimes looking at her, and, timid and bashful as she was, it seemed hard to bear. Then, too, her little heart was very sad as she thought of her father's displeasure, and feared that he would withdraw from her the affection which had been for the last few months the very sunshine of her life. Besides all this, the excitement of her feelings, and the close and sultry air—for it was a very warm day— had brought on a nervous headache. She leaned forward and rested her head against the instrument, feeling in momentary danger of falling from her seat.

Thus two long hours had passed when Mr. Travilla came to her side, and said in a compassionate tone, "I am really very sorry for you, my little friend, but I advise you to submit to your papa. I see you are getting very weary sitting there, and I warn you not to hope to conquer him. I have known him for years, and a more determined person I never saw. Had you not better sing the song? It will not take five minutes, and then your trouble will be all over."

Elsie raised her head and answered gently, "Thank you for your sympathy, Mr. Travilla. You are very kind. But I could not do it, because Jesus says, 'He that loveth father or mother more than Me, is not worthy of Me,' and I cannot disobey Him, even to please my own dear papa."

"But, Miss Elsie, why do you think it would be disobeying Him? Is there any verse in the Bible which says you must not sing songs on Sunday?"

"Mr. Travilla, it says the Sabbath is to be kept holy unto the Lord, that we are not to think our own thoughts, nor speak our own words, nor do our own actions, but all the day must be spent in studying God's word, or worshipping and praising Him. And there is no praise in that song—not one word about God or heaven."

"That is very true, Elsie, but still it is such a very little thing, that I cannot think there would be much harm in it, or God would be very angry with you for doing it."

"Oh, Mr. Travilla!" she said, looking up at him in great surprise. "Surely you know that there is no such thing as a little sin, and don't you remember about the man who picked up sticks on the Sabbath day?"

"No. What was it?"

"God commanded that he should be stoned to death, and it was done. Would you not have thought that a very little thing, Mr. Travilla?"

"Yes, I believe that I should," said he, turning away with a very grave face.

"Dinsmore," he said, going up you his friend, "I am sure that child is conscientious. Had you not better give up to her in this instance?"

"Never, Travilla," he answered, with stern decision. "This is the first time she has rebelled against my authority, and if I let her conquer now, she will think she is always to have her own way. No, cost what it may, I must subdue her. She will have to learn that my will is law."

"Right, Horace," said the elder Mr. Dinsmore, approvingly. "Let her understand from the first that you are to be master. It is always the best plan."

"Excuse me, Dinsmore," said Travilla, "but I must say that I think a parent has no right to coerce a child into doing violence to its conscience."

"Nonsense!" replied his friend, a little angrily. "Elsie is entirely too young to set up her opinion against mine. She must allow me to judge for her in these matters for some years to come."

Eversham, who had been casting uneasy glances at Elsie all the afternoon, now drew his chair to Adelaide. He said to her in an undertone, "Miss Adelaide, I am deeply sorry for the mischief I have unwittingly caused, and if you can tell me how to repair it you will lay me under lasting obligations."

Adelaide shook her head. "There is no moving Horace when he has once set his foot down," she said, "and as to Elsie, I doubt whether any power on earth can make her do what she considers wrong."

"Poor little thing!" said Eversham, sighing. "Where in the world did she get such odd notions?"

"Partly from a pious Scotch woman, who had a good deal to do with her in her infancy, and partly from studying the Bible, I believe. She is always at it."

"Indeed!" and he relapsed into thoughtful silence.

Another hour passed slowly away, and then the tea bell rang.

"Elsie," asked her father, coming to her side, "are you ready to obey me now? If so, we will wait a moment to hear the song, and then you can go to your tea with us."

"Dear papa, I cannot break the Sabbath," she replied, in a low, gentle tone, without lifting her head.

"Very well then, I cannot break my word. You must sit there until you will submit, and until then you must fast. You are not only making yourself miserable by your disobedience and obstinacy, Elsie, but are mortifying and grieving me very much," he added in a subdued tone. This sent a sharp pang to the loving little heart, and caused some very bitter tears to fall, as he turned away and left her.

The evening passed wearily away to the little girl. The drawing room was but dimly lighted, for the company had all deserted it to wander about the grounds, or sit in the portico enjoying the moonlight and the pleasant evening breeze, and the air indoors seemed insupportably close and sultry. At times Elsie could scarcely breathe, and she longed intensely to get out into the open air. Every moment her seat grew more uncomfortable and the pain in her head more severe. Her thoughts began to wander, she forgot where she was, everything became confused, and at length she lost all consciousness.

Several gentlemen, among who were Mr. Horace Dinsmore and Mr. Travilla, were conversing together on the portico, where they were suddenly startled by a sound as of something falling.

Travilla, who was nearest the door, rushed into the drawing room, followed by the others.

"A light! Quick, quick, a light!" he cried, raising Elsie's insensible form in his arms. "The child has fainted."

One of the others, instantly snatching a lamp from a distant table, brought it near. The increased light showed Elsie's little face, ghastly as that of a corpse, while a stream of blood was flowing from a wound in the temple, made by striking against some sharp corner of the furniture as she fell.

She was a pitiable sight indeed, with her fair face, her curls, and her white dress all dabbed in blood.

"Dinsmore, you're a brute!" exclaimed Travilla indignantly, as he placed her gently on a sofa.

Horace made no reply, but, with a face almost as pale as her own, bent over his little daughter in speechless alarm, while one of the guests, who happened to be a physician, hastily dressed the wound, and then applied restoratives.

It was some time ere consciousness returned, and the father trembled with the agonizing fear that the gentle spirit had taken its flight.

But at length the soft eyes unclosed, and gazing with a troubled look into his face, bent so anxiously over her, she asked, "Dear papa, are you angry with me?"

"No, darling," he replied in tones made tremulous with emotion, "not at all."

"What was it?" she asked in a bewildered way. "What did I do? What has happened?"

"Never mind, daughter," he said, "you have been ill, but you are better now, so don't think any more about it."

"She had better be put to bed at once," said the physician.

"There is blood on my dress," cried Elsie in a startled tone. "Where did it come from?"

"You fell and hurt your head," replied her father, raising her gently in his arms. "But don't talk any more now."

"Oh! I remember," she moaned, an expression of keen distress coming over her face. "Papa—"

"Hush! Hush! Not a word more. We will let the past go," he said, kissing her lips. "I shall carry you to your room now, and see you put to bed."

He held her on his knee, her head resting on his shoulder, while Chloe prepared her for rest.

"Are you hungry, daughter?" he asked

"No, papa, I only want to go to sleep."

"There, Aunt Chloe, that will do," he said, as the old nurse tied on the child's night-cap, and raising her again in his arms, he carried her to the bed and was about to place her on it.

"Oh, papa! My prayers first, you know," she cried eagerly.

"Never mind them tonight," said he. "You are not able."

"Please let me, dear papa," she pleaded. "I cannot go to sleep without."

Yielding to her entreaties, he placed her on her knees, and stood beside her, listening to her murmuring petitions, in which he more than once heard his own name coupled with a request that he might be made to love Jesus.

When she had finished, he again raised her in his arms, kissed her tenderly several times, and then laid her carefully on the bed, saying, as he did so, "Why did you ask, Elsie, that I might love Jesus?"

"Because, papa, I do so want you to love Him; it would make me so happy. And besides, you cannot go to Heaven without. The Bible says so."

"Does it? And what makes you think I don't love Him?"

"Dear papa, please don't be angry," she pleaded tearfully, "but you know Jesus says, 'He that keepeth my commandments, he it is that loveth me.'"

He stooped over her. "Good night, daughter," he said.

"Dear, dear papa," she cried, throwing her arms round his neck, and drawing down his face close to hers, "I do love you so very, very much!"

"Better then anybody else?" he asked.

"No, papa, I love Jesus best. You next."

He kissed her again, and with a half sigh turned away and left the room. He was not entirely pleased, not quite willing that she should love even her Saviour better than himself.

Elsie was very weary, and was soon asleep. She awoke the next morning feeling nearly as well as usual. And after she had had her bath and been dressed by Chloe's careful hands, the curls being arranged to conceal the plaster that covered the wound on her temple, there was nothing in her appearance, except a slight paleness, to remind her friends of the last night's accident.

She was sitting reading her morning chapter when her father came in, and taking a seat by her side, lifted her to his knee, saying as he caressed her tenderly, "My little daughter is looking pretty well this morning. How does she feel?"

"Quite well, thank you, papa," she replied, looking up into his face with a sweet, loving smile.

He raised the curls to look at the wounded temple. Then, as he dropped them again, he said, with a shudder, "Elsie, do you know that you were very near being killed last night?"

"No, papa, was I?" she asked with an awestruck countenance.

"Yes, the doctor says if that wound had been made half an inch nearer your eye—I should have been childless."

His voice trembled almost too much for utterance as he finished his sentence, and he strained her to his heart with a deep sigh of thankfulness for her escape.

Elsie was very quiet for some moments, and the little face was almost sad in its deep thoughtfulness.

"What are you thinking of, darling?" he asked.

She raised her eyes to his face, and he saw that they were brimful of tears.

"Oh, papa!" she said, dropping her head on his chest while the bright drops fell like rain down her cheeks. "Would you have been so very sorry?"

"Sorry, darling! Do you not know that you are more precious to me than all my wealth, all my friends and relatives put together? Yes, I would rather part with everything else than lose this one little girl," he said, kissing her again and again.

"Dear, dear papa! How glad I am that you love me so much," she replied, and then relapsed into silence.

He watched her changing countenance for some time, then asked, "What is it, darling?"

"I was just thinking," she said, "whether I was ready to go to Heaven, and I believe I was, for I know that I love Jesus. And then I was thinking how glad mamma would have been to see me. Don't you think she would, papa?"

"I can't spare you to her yet," he replied with emotion, "and I think she loves me too well to wish it."

As Miss Day had not yet returned, Elsie's time was still pretty much at her own disposal, excepting when her papa gave her something to do. So, after breakfast, finding that he was engaged with someone in the library, she took her Bible, and seeking out a shady retreat in the garden, sat down to read.

The Bible was ever the Book of Books to her, and this morning the solemn, tender feelings naturally caused by the discovery of the recent narrow escape from sudden death made it even more than usually touching and beautiful in her eyes. She had been alone in the arbor for some time, when, hearing a step at her side, she looked up, showing a face all wet with tears.

It was Mr. Travilla who stood beside her.

"In tears, little Elsie! Pray, what may the book be that affects you so?" he asked, sitting down by her side and taking it from her hand. "The Bible, I declare!" he exclaimed in surprise. "What can there be in it that you can find so affecting?"

"Oh, Mr. Travilla!" said the little girl. "Does it not make your heart ache to read how the Jews abused our dear, dear Saviour? And then to think that it was all because of our sins," she sobbed.

He looked half distressed, half puzzled. It seemed a new idea to him.

"Really, my little Elsie," he said, "you are quite original in your ideas. I suppose I ought to feel unhappy about these things, but indeed the truth is, I have never thought much about them."

"Then you don't love Jesus," she answered, mournfully. "Ah, Mr. Travilla, how sorry I am!"

"Why Elsie, what difference can it make to you whether I love him or not?"

"Because, Mr. Travilla, the Bible says, 'If any man love not the Lord Jesus Christ, let him be anathema, maranatha,' accursed from God. Oh, sir! Think how dreadful! You cannot be saved unless you love Jesus, and believe on Him. 'Believe on the Lord Jesus Christ, and thou shalt be saved.' That is what God says in His Word."

She spoke with deep solemnity, and the tears trembling in her eyes. He was touched, but for a while sat perfectly silent.

Then he said, with an effort to speak lightly, "Ah, well, my little friend, I certainly intend to repent and believe before I die, but there is time enough yet."

"Mr. Travilla," she said, laying her hand on his arm and looking earnestly into his face, "how do you know that there is time enough yet? Don't put it off, I beg of you."

She paused a moment, then asked, "Do you know Mr. Travilla, how near I came to being killed last night?"

He nodded.

"Well, suppose I had been killed, and had not loved Jesus. Where would I be now?"

He put his arm around her, and giving her a kiss, said, "I don't think you would have been in any bad place, Elsie. A sweet, amiable little girl, who has never harmed anyone, would surely not fare very badly in another world."

She shook her head very gravely.

"Ah, Mr. Travilla, you forgot the anathema, maranatha. If I had not loved Jesus, and had my sins washed away in His blood, I could not have been saved."

Just at this moment a servant came to tell Elsie that her papa wanted her in the drawing room, and Mr. Travilla, taking her hand, led her into the house.

They found the company again grouped about the piano, listening to Adelaide's music.

Elsie went directly to her father and stood by his side, putting her hand in his with a gesture of confiding affection.

He smiled down at her, and kept fast hold of it until his sister had risen from the instrument, when putting Elsie in her place, he said, "Now, my daughter, let us have that song."

"Yes, papa," she replied, beginning the prelude at once, "I will do my very best."

And so she did. The song was both well played and well sung, and her father looked proud and happy as the gentlemen expressed their pleasure and asked for another and another.

Thus the clouds which had so suddenly obscured little Elsie's sky, seemed to have vanished as speedily as they had arisen.

Her father again treated her with all his wonted affection, and there even seemed to be a depth of tenderness in his love which it had not known before, for he could not forget how nearly he had lost her.

CHAPTER ELEVENTH

In that hour Jesus rejoiced in spirit, and said,
"I thank thee, O Father, Lord of heaven and earth,
that thou hast hid these things from the wise
and prudent, and hast revealed them unto babes;
even so, Father; for so it seemed
good in thy sight."

—*Luke* 10:21

SAYS THE APOSTLE PAUL, "I say the truth in Christ, I lie not, my conscience also bearing me witness in the Holy Ghost, that I have great heaviness and continual sorrow in my heart, for I could wish that myself were accursed from Christ, for my brethren, my kinsmen according to the flesh . . . Brethren, my heart's desire and prayer to God for Israel is, that they might be saved."

And such is, in greater or less degree, the feeling of every renewed heart: loving Jesus, it would fain have others love Him too. It desires the salvation of all, but for that of its own dear ones it longs and labors and prays; it is like Jacob wrestling with the angel, when he said, "I will not let thee go except thou bless me."

And thus it was with Elsie. She knew now that her father was not a Christian, that he had no real love for Jesus, none of the true fear of God before his eyes. She saw that if he permitted her to read to him from God's word, as he sometimes did, it was not that he felt any pleasure in listening, but only to please her. She had no reason to suppose he ever prayed, and though he went regularly to church, it was because he considered it proper and respectable to do so, and not that he cared to worship God, or to learn His will.

This conviction, which had gradually dawned upon Elsie, until now it amounted to certainty, caused her great grief. She shed many tears over it in secret, and very many and very earnest were the prayers she offered up for her dear father's conversion.

She was sitting on his knee one evening in the drawing room, while he and several other gentlemen were conversing on the subject of religion. They were discussing the question whether or not a change of heart were necessary to salvation.

The general opinion seemed to be that it was not, and Elsie listened with pain while her father expressed his decided conviction that all who led an honest, upright, moral life, and attended to the outward observances of religion, were quite safe.

He could see "no necessity for a change of heart," he "did not believe in the doctrine of total depravity," not he, no indeed. He thought the world "much better than many people would have us believe."

Elsie fixed her eyes on his face with a very mournful gaze while he was speaking, but he was busy with his argument and did not notice her.

But one of the guests was just expressing his approval of Mr. Dinsmore's sentiments, when catching sight of Elsie's face, he stopped, remarking, "Your little girl looks as if she had something to say on the subject. What is it, my dear?"

Elsie blushed, hesitated, and looked at her father.

"Yes, speak, my daughter, if you have anything to say," he said encouragingly.

Elsie lifted her eyes timidly to the gentlemen's face as she replied, "I was just thinking, sir, of what our Saviour said to Nicodemus: 'Verily, verily I say unto thee, except a man be born again, he cannot see the kingdom of God.' 'Marvel not that I said unto thee, Ye must be born again.'"

She repeated these words of inspiration with a deep, earnest solemnity that seemed to impress every hearer.

For a moment there was a deep hush in the room.

Then the gentleman asked, "Well, my little lady, and what is meant by being born again?"

"Oh, sir!" she replied. "Surely you know that it means to have the image of God, lost in Adam's fall, restored to us. It means what David asked for when he prayed, 'Create in me a clean heart, O God, and renew a right spirit within me.'"

"Where did you learn all this?" he asked, looking at her with mingled surprise and admiration.

"In the Bible, sir," she modestly replied.

"You seem to have read it to some purpose," said he, "and now since you consider that change so necessary, can you tell me how it is to be brought about?"

"God's Holy Spirit, alone, can change a sinner's heart, sir."

"And how am I to secure His aid?" he asked.

Elsie answered with a text: "God is more willing to give His Holy Spirit to them that ask Him, than parents are to give good gifts unto their children."

He paused a moment, then asked, "Have you obtained this new heart, Miss Elsie?"

"I hope I have, sir," she replied, the sweet little face all suffused with blushes, and the soft, downcast eyes filling with tears.

"Why do you think so?" he asked again. "I think there is a text that says you must be able always to give a reason for the hope that is in you, or something to that effect, is there not?"

"Yes, sir: 'Be ready always to give an answer to every man that asketh you a reason for the hope that is in you, with meekness and fear.'" Then raising her eyes to his face with a touching mixture of deep humility and holy boldness, she continued, "And this, sir, is my answer: Jesus says, 'Him that cometh unto me, I will in no wise cast out,' and I believe Him. I did go to Him, and He did not cast me out, but forgave my sins, and taught me to love Him and desire to serve Him all my life."

This conversation between the gentleman and the little girl had drawn attention of all present, and now Mrs. Dinsmore, who had more than once shown signs of impatience, said, "Well, Elsie, I think you have now talked quite enough for a child of your age." Then, pulling out her watch, "It is high time for little folks to be in bed."

Elsie, blushing deeply, would have retired immediately, but her father held her fast, saying, as he gave his stepmother an angry glance, "You need not go, Elsie, unless you choose. I am quite capable of judging when it is time to send you to bed."

"I would rather go, if you please, papa," whispered Elsie, who had a great dread of Mrs. Dinsmore's anger.

"Very well, then, you may do as you like," he replied, giving her a goodnight kiss. And with a graceful goodnight to the company, the little girl left the room.

Her questioner followed her with an admiring glance, then turning to her father, exclaimed warmly, "She is a remarkably intelligent child, Dinsmore! One that any father might be proud of. I was astonished at her answers."

"Yes," remarked Travilla, "a text has been running in my head ever since you commenced your conversation—something about these things being hid from the wise and prudent, and revealed unto babes. And," he added, "I am sure if ever I saw one who possessed that new nature of which she spoke, it is she herself. Has she any faults, Dinsmore?"

"Very few, I think, though she would tell you a different story," replied her father with a gratified smile.

The next morning Elsie was sitting reading her Bible, when she suddenly felt a hand laid on her head, and her father's voice said, "Good morning, little daughter."

"Ah, papa! Is that you?" she asked, raising her head to give him a smile of joyful welcome. "I did not know you were there."

"Ah? I have been watching you for several minutes," he said. "Always poring over the same Book, Elsie. Do you never tire of it?"

"No, indeed, papa. It is always new, and I do love it so, it is so very sweet. May I read a little to you?" she added, coaxingly.

"Yes, I love to listen to anything read by my darling," he said, sitting down and taking her on his knee.

She opened at the third chapter of John's Gospel, and read it through. At the sixteenth verse, "For God so loved the world, that He gave His only begotten Son, that whosoever believeth in Him should not perish, but have everlasting life," she paused, and asked, "Was not that a wonderful gift, papa? And wonderful love that prompted it?"

"Yes," he said, absently, stroking her hair.

She finished the chapter, and closing the book, laid her head on his chest, asking, "Dear papa, don't you believe the Bible?"

"Certainly, daughter. I am not an infidel," he replied in a careless tone.

"Well, then, papa," she continued, half hesitatingly, "does not this chapter teach very plainly that we must love Jesus, and have new hearts, if we want to go to heaven?"

"Yes," he said, "I dare say it does."

Then taking the book from her, he laid it aside, and giving her a kiss, said, "I was much pleased with your intelligent answers to Mr. Lee, last evening."

Elsie sighed, and her eyes filled with tears. It was not what she wanted.

"What an odd child you are!" he said, laughing. "You really look as though I had been scolding, instead of praising you."

She dropped her head on his chest, and burst into tears and sobs.

"Why, Elsie, my own darling, what ails you?"

"Oh, papa!" she sobbed, "I want you to love Jesus."

"Oh! Is that all?" he said.

And setting her on her feet, he took her by the hand and led her out into the garden. There they met Mr. Travilla and another gentleman, who immediately entered into conversation with Mr. Dinsmore, while Elsie wandered about amongst the flowers and shrubs, gathering a nosegay for her Aunt Adelaide.

CHAPTER TWELFTH

She had waited for their coming,
She had kiss'd them o'er and o'er—
And they were so fondly treasured
For the words of love they bore,
Words that whispered in the silence,
She had listened till his tone
Seemed to linger in the echo
"Darling, thou art all mine own!"

—*Mrs. J. C. Neal.*

"PRAY, WHAT WEIGHTY MATTER is troubling your young brain, birdie?" asked Adelaide, laughingly laying her hand on Elsie's shoulder. "Judging from the exceeding gravity of your countenance, one might imagine that the affairs of the nation had been committed to your care."

"Oh, auntie! Can't you help me? Won't you?" answered the little girl, looking up coaxingly into the bright, cheerful face bent over her.

"Help you in what? Reading with your book upside down, eh?" asked Adelaide, pointing with a quizzical look at the volume of fairy tales in her little niece's lap.

"Oh!" cried Elsie, coloring and laughing in her turn. "I was not reading, and did not know that my book was wrong side up. But, Aunt Adelaide, you know Christmas is coming soon, and I want to give papa something, and I am quite puzzled about it. I thought of slippers, but he has a very handsome pair, and besides there would hardly be time to work them, as I have so many lessons. A purse won't do either, because I have given him one already, and I would like it to be something worth more than either slippers or purse. But you are so much wiser than I, can't you help me think?"

"So this is what has kept you so quiet and demure all day that I have scarcely once heard you laugh or sing—quite an unusual state of things of late," and Adelaide playfully pinched the round, rosy cheek. "Ahem! Let me put on my thinking cap," assuming an air of comic gravity. "Ah, yes, I have it! Your miniature, little one, of course. What could please him better?"

"Oh, yes!" cried Elsie, clapping her hands. "That will do nicely. Why didn't I think of it? Thank you, auntie. But then," she added, her countenance falling, "how can I get it taken without his knowledge? You know the surprise is half the fun."

"Never mind, my dear, I'll find a way to manage that," replied Adelaide, confidently. "So just run away with you now, and see how much money you can scrape together to spend on it."

"It won't take long to count it," Elsie said with a merry laugh. "But here is papa just coming in at the door. I hope he won't suspect what we have been talking about," and she bounded away to meet him and claim the kiss he never refused her now.

Once Adelaide would not have been surprised at Elsie's quietness. Patient and sweet tempered the little girl had always been, but more especially after her father's return from Europe—very quiet and timid, seeming to shrink from observation, with a constant dread of incurring reproof or punishment. But the last few happy months, during which her father had continued to lavish upon her every proof of the tenderest affection, had wrought a great change in her. Her manner had lost its timidity. She moved about the house with a light and joyous step, and it was no unusual thing to hear her merry, silvery laugh ring out, or her sweet voice caroling like some wild bird of the wood — the natural outgrowth of her joy and thankfulness. For the little heart that had so long been famishing for love, that had often grown so weary and sick in its hungering and thirsting for it, was now fully satisfied, and reveled in its newfound happiness.

"I have got it all arranged nicely, Elsie," Adelaide said, coming into the room with a very pleased face as the little girl was preparing for bed that evening. "Your papa is going away in a day or two to attend to some business matters connected with your property, and will be absent at least two weeks, so, unless he should take it into his head to carry you along, we can easily manage about the picture."

Elsie looked up with a countenance of blank dismay.

"Why," said Adelaide, laughing, "I thought you'd be delighted with my news, and instead of that, you look as if I had read you your death warrant."

"Oh, Aunt Adelaide! Two whole weeks without seeing papa! Just think how long."

"Pooh! Nonsense, child! It will be gone before you know it. But tell me, how much money have you?"

"I have saved my allowance for two months. That makes twenty dollars, you know, auntie, and I have a little change besides. Do you think it will be enough?"

"Hardly, I'm afraid, but I can lend you some if necessary."

"Thank you, auntie," Elsie answered gratefully, "you are very kind, but I couldn't take it, because papa has told me expressly that I must never borrow money, nor run into debt in any way."

"Dear me!" exclaimed Adelaide, a little impatiently. "Horace certainly is the most absurdly strict person I ever met with. But never mind, I think we can manage it somehow," she added, in a livelier tone, as she stooped to kiss her little niece goodnight.

Elsie's gentle rap was heard very early at her papa's door the next morning.

He opened it immediately, and springing into his arms, she asked, almost tearfully, "Are you going away, papa?"

"Yes, darling," he said, caressing her fondly. "I must leave home for a few weeks, and though I at first thought of taking you with me, upon further consideration I have decided that it will be better to leave you here. Yet, if you desire it very much, my love, I will take you along. Shall I?"

"You know I would rather be with you than anywhere else, papa," she answered, laying her head on his shoulder, "but you know best, and I am quite willing to do whatever you say."

"That is right, daughter. My little Elsie is a good, obedient child," he said, pressing her closer to him.

"When are you going, papa?" she asked, her voice trembling a little.

"Tomorrow, directly after dinner, daughter."

"So soon," she sighed.

"The sooner I leave you the sooner I shall return, you know, darling," he said, patting her cheek, and smiling kindly on her.

"Yes, papa, but two weeks seems such a long, long time."

He smiled. "At your age I suppose it does, but when you are as old as I am, you will think it very short. But to make it pass more quickly, you may write me a little letter every day, and I will send you one just as often."

"Oh, thank you, papa! That will be so pleasant," she answered, with a brightening countenance. "I do so love to get letters, and I would rather have one from you than from anybody else."

"Ah, then I think you ought to be willing to spare me for two weeks. I have been thinking my little girl might perhaps be glad of a little extra pocket money for buying Christmas gifts," he said, taking out his purse. "Would you?"

"Yes, papa, oh, very much, indeed!"

He laughed at her eager tone, and putting a fifty-dollar note into her hand, asked, "Will that be enough?"

Elsie's eyes opened wide with astonishment.

"I never before had half so much as this," she exclaimed. "May I spend it all, papa?"

"Provided you don't throw it away," he answered gravely. "But don't forget that I require a strict account of all your expenditure."

"Must I tell you every thing that I buy?" she asked, her countenance falling considerably.

"Yes, my child, you must. Not until after Christmas, however, if you would rather not."

"I will not mind it so much then," she answered, looking quite relieved, "but indeed, papa, it is a great deal of trouble."

"Ah! My little girl must not be lazy," he said, shaking his head gravely.

This was Elsie's first parting from her father since they had learned to know and love each other, and when the time came to say goodbye, she clung to him, and seemed so loath to let him go, that he quite repented of his determination to leave her at home.

"O papa, papa! I cannot bear to have you go, and leave me behind," she sobbed. "I feel as if you were never coming back."

"Why, my own darling," he said, kissing her again and again, "why do you talk so? I shall certainly be at home again in a fortnight, but if I had thought you would feel so badly, I would have made arrangements to take you with me. It is too late now, however, and you must let me go, dearest. Be a good girl while I am gone, and when I return I will bring you some handsome presents."

So saying, he embraced her once more, then putting her gently from him, sprang into the carriage and was driven rapidly away.

Elsie stood watching until it was out of sight, and then ran away to her own room to put her arms round her nurse's neck and hide her tears on her bosom.

"Dere, dere darlin'! Dat will do now. Massa Horace he be back 'fore long, and ole Chloe don' like to see her chile 'stressin' herself so," and the large, dusky hand was passed lovingly over the bright curls, and tenderly wiped away the falling tears.

"But, oh, mammy! I'm afraid he will never come back. I'm afraid the steamboat boiler will burst, or the cars will run off the track, or—"

"Hush, hush, darlin'! Dat's wicked. You must jes' trust de Lord to take care of Massa Horace. He's jes as able to do it in one place as in tudder, an you an' your ole mammy keep prayin' for Massa, I'se sure he'll come back safe, kase don't you remember what de good book says, 'If any two of you agree—'"

"Oh my, yes, Dear mammy! Thank you so for remembering it," exclaimed the little girl, lifting her head and smiling through her tears. "I won't cry any more now, but will just try to keep thinking how glad I will be when papa comes home again."

"A very sensible resolution, my dear," said Adelaide, putting her head in at the door, "so come, dry your eyes, and let mammy put on your bonnet and cloak as fast as possible. I have begged a holiday for you, and am going to carry you off to the city to do some shopping, et cetera."

"Ah! I think I know what that et cetera means, auntie, don't I?" laughed Elsie, as she hastened to obey.

"Dear me! How very wise some people are," said her aunt, smiling and nodding good-naturedly. "But make haste, my dear, for the carriage is at the door."

When Elsie laid her head upon her pillow that night she acknowledged to herself, that in spite of her father's absence—and she had, at times, missed him sadly—the day had been a very short and pleasant one to her, owing to her Aunt Adelaide's thoughtful kindness in taking her out into new scenes, and giving agreeable occupation to her thoughts.

She rose at her usual early hour the next morning, and though feeling lonely, comforted herself with the hope of receiving the promised letter, and her face was full of eager expectation, as her grandfather, in his usual leisurely manner, opened the bag and distributed its contents.

"Two letters, Elsie!" he said, in a tone of surprise, just as she was beginning to despair of her turn coming at all. "Ah! One is from Horace, I see, and the other from Miss Allison, no doubt."

Elsie could hardly restrain her eagerness while he held them in his hand, examining and commenting upon the address and postmark.

But at length he tossed them to her, remarking, "There! If you are done your breakfast, you had better run away and read them."

"Oh, thank you, grandpa!" she said, gladly availing herself of the permission.

"Elsie is fortunate today," observed Lora, looking after her. "I wonder which she'll read first."

"Her father's, of course," replied Adelaide. "He is more to her than all the rest of the world put together."

"A matter of small concern to the rest of the world, I think," remarked Mrs. Dinsmore, dryly.

"Perhaps so, mamma," said Adelaide, quietly, "yet I think there are some who prize Elsie's affection."

Yes, Adelaide was right. Miss Rose's letter was neglected and almost forgotten, while Elsie read and reread her papa's with the greatest delight.

It gave an amusing account of the day's journey, but what constituted its chief charm for the little girl was that it was filled with expressions of the tenderest affection of her.

Then came the pleasant task of answering, which occupied almost all her spare time, for letter-writing was still, to her, a rather new and difficult business, Miss Allison having hitherto been her only correspondent. And this was a pleasure which was renewed every day, for her papa faithfully kept his promise, each morning bringing her a letter, until at length one came announcing the speedy return of the writer.

Elsie was almost wild with delight.

"Aunt Adelaide," she cried, running to her to communicate the glad tidings, "papa says he will be here this very afternoon."

"Well, my dear, as we have already attended to all the business that needed to be kept secret from him, I am very glad to hear it, especially for your sake," replied Adelaide, looking up for a moment from the book she was reading. She then returned to it again, while her little niece danced out of the room, with her papa's letter still in her hand, and a face beaming with happiness.

She met Mrs. Dinsmore in the hall.

"Why are you skipping about in that fashion, Elsie?" she asked, severely. "I believe you will never learn to move and act like a lady."

"I will try, madam, indeed," Elsie answered, subsiding into a slow and steady gait which would not have disgraced a woman of any age, "but I was so glad that papa is coming home today, that I could not help skipping."

"Indeed!" and with a scornful toss of the head, Mrs. Dinsmore sailed past her and entered the drawing room.

Elsie had once, on her first arrival at Roselands, addressed Mrs. Dinsmore, in the innocence of her heart, as "grandma," but that lady's horrified look, and indignant repudiation of the ancient title, had made a deep impression on the little girl's memory, and effectually prevented any restoration of the relationship.

As the hour drew near when her father might reasonably be expected, Elsie took her station at one of the drawing room windows overlooking the avenue, and the moment the carriage appeared in sight, she ran out and stood waiting for him on the steps of the portico.

Mr. Dinsmore put out his head as they drove up the avenue, and the first object that caught his eye was the fairy-like form of his little daughter, in her blue merino dress, the golden brown curls waving in the wind. He sprang out and caught her in his arms the instant the carriage stopped.

"My darling, darling child," he cried, kissing her over and over again, and pressing her fondly to his heart, "how glad I am to have you in my arms again!"

"Papa, papa, my own dear, dear papa!" she exclaimed, throwing her arms around his neck. "I'm so happy, now that you have come home safe and well."

"Are you, darling? But I must not keep you out in this wind, for it is quite chilly."

He set her down, and leaving the servant to attend to his baggage, led her into the hall.

"Will you come into the drawing room, papa?" she said. "There is a bright, warm fire there."

"Is there not one in my dressing room?" he asked.

"Yes, papa, a very good one."

"Then we will go there. I dare say the rest of the family are in no great hurry to see me, and I want my little girl to myself for half an hour," he said, leading the way upstairs as he spoke.

They found, as Elsie had reported, a very bright fire in the dressing room. A large easy chair was drawn up near it, and a handsome dressing gown and slippers were placed ready for use, all the work of Elsie's loving little hands.

He saw it all at a glance, and with a pleased smile, stooped and kissed her again, saying, "My dear little daughter is very thoughtful for her papa's comfort."

Then exchanging his warm outdoor apparel and heavy boots for the dressing gown and slippers, he seated himself in the chair and took her on his knee.

"Well, daughter," he said, passing his hand caressingly over her curls, "papa has brought you a present. Will you have it now, or shall it be kept for Christmas?"

"Keep it for Christmas, papa," she answered gaily, "Christmas is almost here, and besides, I don't want to look at anything but you tonight."

"Very well, look at me as much as you like," was his laughing rejoinder. "And now tell me, have you been a good girl in my absence?"

"As good as I ever am, I believe, papa. I tried very hard; but you can ask Miss Day."

"No, I am entirely satisfied with your report, for I know my little girl is quite truthful."

Elsie colored with pleasure, then calling to mind the time when he had for a moment suspected her of falsehood, she heaved a deep sigh, dropping her head upon his chest.

He seemed to understand her thoughts, for, pressing his lips to her forehead, he said gently and kindly, "I think I shall never again doubt my little daughter's truth."

She looked up with a grateful smile.

"Miss Day has gone away to stay until after New Year's day, papa," she said, "and so our holidays have begun."

"Ah! I am very well satisfied," said he. "I think you have earned a holiday, and I hope you will enjoy it. But I don't know that I shall let you play all the time," he added with a smile. "I have some notion of giving you a lesson now and then, myself."

"Dear papa, how pleasant!" she exclaimed delightedly. "I do so love to say lessons to you."

"Well, then, we will spend an hour together every morning. But are you not to have some company?"

"Oh, yes, papa! Quite a house full," she said with a slight sigh. "The Percys, and the Howards, and all the Carringtons, and some others too, I believe."

"Why do you sigh, daughter?" he asked. "Do you not expect to enjoy their company?"

"Yes, sir, I hope so," she answered, rather dubiously, "but when there are so many, and they stay so long, they are apt to disagree, and that, you know, is not pleasant. I am sure I shall enjoy the hour with you better than anything else. It is so sweet to be quite alone with my own darling papa," and the little arm stole softly round his neck again, and the rosy lips touched his cheek.

"Well, when are the little plagues coming?" he asked, returning her caress.

"Some of them tomorrow, papa—no, Monday— tomorrow is the Sabbath day."

"Shall I bring in de trunks now, massa?" asked Mr. Dinsmore's servant, putting his head in at the door.

"Yes, John, certainly."

"Why, you brought back a new one, papa, didn't you?" asked Elsie, as John carried in one she was sure she had never seen before, and in obedience to a motion of her father's hand, set it down quite near them.

"Yes, my dear, it is yours. There, John, unlock it," tossing him the key. "And now daughter, get down and see what you can find in it worth having."

Elsie needed no second bidding, but in an instant was on her knees beside the trunk, eager to examine its contents.

"Take the lid off the band-box first, and see what is there," said her father.

"Oh, papa, how very pretty!" she cried, as she lifted out a beautiful little velvet hat adorned with a couple of ostrich feathers.

"I am very glad it pleases you, my darling," he said, putting it on her head, and gazing at her with proud delight in her rare beauty. "There! It fits exactly, and is very becoming."

Then taking it off, he returned it to the box, and bade her look further.

"I am reserving the present for Christmas," he said, in answer to an inquiring look.

Elsie turned to the trunk again.

"Dear papa, how good you are to me!" she said looking up at him, almost with tears of pleasure in her eyes. She lifted out, one after another, a number of costly toys, which she examined with exclamations of delight. And then came several handsome dresses, some of the finest, softest merino, and others of thick, rich silk, all ready-made in fashionable style, and doing credit to his taste and judgment. And lastly there was a beautiful velvet pelisse, trimmed with costly fur, just the thing to wear with her pretty new hat.

He laughed and patted her cheek.

"We must have these dresses tried on," he said, "at least one of them, for as they were all cut by the same pattern — one of your old dresses which I took with me — I presume they will all fit alike. There, take this one to mammy, and tell her to put it on you, and then come back to me."

"Oh! I wondered how you could get them the right size, papa," Elsie answered, as she skipped merrily out of the room.

She was back again in a very few moments, arrayed in the pretty silk he had selected.

"Ah! It seems to be a perfect fit," said he, turning her round and round, with a very gratified look. "Mammy must dress you tomorrow in one of these new frocks, and your pretty hat and pelisse."

Elsie looked troubled.

"Well, what is it?" he asked.

"I am afraid I shall be thinking of them in church, papa, if I wear them then for the first time."

"Pooh! Nonsense! What harm if you do? This squeamishness, Elsie, is the one thing about you that displeases me very much. But there! Don't look so distressed, my love. I dare say you will get over it by-and-by, and be all I wish. Indeed, I some-times think you have improved a little already, in that respect."

Oh, what a pang these words sent to her heart! Was it indeed true that she was losing her tenderness of conscience? That she was becoming less afraid of displeasing and dishonoring her Saviour than in former days? The very thought was anguish.

Her head drooped upon her bosom, and the small white hands were clasped convulsively together, while a bitter, repenting cry, a silent earnest prayer for pardon and help went up to Him whose ear is ever open to the cry of His children.

Her father looked at her in astonishment.

"What is it darling?" he asked, drawing her tenderly toward him, and pushing back the curls from her face. "Why do you looked so pained? What did I say that could have hurt you so? I did not mean to be harsh and severe, for it was a very trifling fault."

She hid her face on his shoulder and burst into an agony of tears.

"It was not that papa, but—but—"

"But what, my darling? Don't be afraid to tell me," he answered, soothingly.

"Oh, papa! I—I am afraid I don't—love Jesus—as much as I did," she faltered out between her sobs.

"Ah! That is it, eh? Well, well, you needn't cry any more. I think you are a very good little girl, though rather a silly one, I am afraid, and quite too morbidly conscientious."

He took her on his knee as he spoke, wiped away her tears, and then began talking in a lively strain of something else.

Elsie listened, and answered him cheerfully, but all the evening he noticed that whenever she was quiet, an unusual expression of sadness would steal over her face.

"What a strange child she is!" he said to himself, as he sat musing over the fire, after sending her to bed. "I cannot understand her. It is very odd how often I wound, when I intend to please her."

As for Elsie, she scarcely thought of her new finery, so troubled was her tender conscience, so pained her little heart to think that she had been wandering from her dear Saviour.

But Elsie had learned that "If any man sin, we have an advocate with the Father, Jesus Christ the righteous," and to Him she went with her sin and sorrow. She applied anew to the pardoning, peace-speaking blood of Christ—that "blood of sprinkling that speaketh better things than that of Abel," and thus the sting of conscience was taken away and her peace restored. She was soon resting quietly on her pillow, for, "so He giveth His beloved sleep."

Even her father's keen, searching glance, when she came to him in the morning, could discover no trace of sadness in her face; very quiet and sober it was, but entirely peaceful and happy, and so it remained all through the day. Her new clothes did not trouble her; she was hardly conscious of wearing them, and quite able to give her usual solemn and fixed attention to the services of the sanctuary.

"Where are you going, daughter?" Mr. Dinsmore asked, as Elsie gently withdrew her hand from his on leaving the dining room.

"To my room, papa," she replied.

"Come with me," he said. "I want you."

"What do you want me for, papa?" she asked, as he sat down and took her on his knee.

"What for? Why to keep, to love, and to look at," he said laughing. "I have been away from my little girl so long, that now I want her close by my side, or on my knee all the time. Do you not like to be with me?"

"Dearly well, my own darling papa," she answered, flinging her little arms round his neck, and laying her head on his chest.

He cuddled her, and chatted with her for some time, then, still keeping her on his knee, took up a book and began to read.

Elsie saw with pain that it was a novel. She longed to beg him to put it away, and spend the precious hours of the holy Sabbath in the study of God's word, or some of the lesser helps to Zion's pilgrims which the saints of our own or other ages have prepared. But she knew that it would be quite out of place for a little child like her to attempt to counsel or reprove her father, and that, tenderly as he loved and cherished her, he would never for a moment allow her to forget their relative positions.

At length she ventured to ask softly, "Papa, may I go to my own room now?"

"What for?" he asked. "Are you tired of my company?"

"No, sir, oh, no! But I want—" she hesitated and hung her head for an instant, while the rich color mounted to cheek and brow. Then raising it again, she said fearlessly, "I always want to spend a little while with my best Friend, on Sabbath afternoon, papa."

He looked puzzled, and also somewhat displeased.

"I don't understand you, Elsie," he said. "You surely can have no better friend than your own father, and can it be possible that you love anyone else better than you love me?"

Again the little arms were round his neck, and hugging him close and closer, she whispered, "It was Jesus I meant, papa. You know He loves me even better than you do, and I must love Him best of all, but there is no one else that I love half so much as I love you, my own dear, dear, precious father."

"Well, you may go, but only for a little while, mind," he answered, giving her a kiss, and setting her down. "Nay," he added hastily, "stay as long as you like. If you feel it a punishment to be kept here with me, I would rather do without you."

"Oh, no, no, papa!" she said beseechingly, and with tears in her eyes. "I do so love to be with you. Please don't be angry. Please let me come back soon."

"No, darling, I am not angry," he answered, smoothing her hair and smiling kindly on her. "Come back just when you like, and the sooner the better."

Elsie did not stay away very long. In less than an hour she returned, bringing her Bible and *Pilgrim's Progress* with her.

Her father welcomed her with a smile, and then turned to his novel again, while she drew a stool to his side. Sitting down, she leaned her head against his knee, and read until the short winter day began to close in, and Mr. Dinsmore, whose hand had been every now and then laid caressingly upon her curls, said, "Put away your book now, daughter. It is growing too dark for you to read without straining your eyes."

"Please, papa, let me finish the paragraph first. May I?" she asked.

"No, you must always obey the instant I speak to you."

Elsie rose at once, and without another word laid her books upon the table, then coming back, claimed her accustomed place upon his knee, with her head resting on his shoulder.

He put his arm round her, and they sat silently thus for some moments. At length Elsie asked, "Papa, did you ever read *Pilgrim's Progress*?"

"Yes—a good while ago, when I was quite a boy."

"And did you not like it, papa?"

"Yes, very much, though I have nearly forgotten the story now. Do you like it?"

"Very much, indeed, papa. I think it comes next to the Bible."

"Next to the Bible, eh? Well, I believe you are the only little girl of my acquaintance who thinks that the most beautiful and interesting book in the world. But, let me see, what is this *Pilgrim's Progress* about? Some foolish story of a man with a great load on his back, is it not?"

"Foolish, papa! Oh, I am sure you don't mean it! You couldn't think it foolish. Ah, I know by your smile that you are only saying it to tease me. It is a beautiful story, papa, about Christian—how he lived in the City of Destruction, and had a great burden on his back, which he tried in every way to get rid of, but all in vain, until he came to the Cross. But then it seemed suddenly to loosen of itself, and dropped from his back, and rolled away, and fell into the sepulcher, where it could not be seen any more."

"Well, and is not that a foolish story? Can you see any sense or meaning in it?" he asked, with a slight smile, and a keen glance into the eager little face upturned to his.

"Ah, papa! I know what it means," she answered, in a half-sorrowful tone. "Christian, with the load on his back, is a person who has been convicted of sin by God's Holy Spirit, and feels his sins a heavy burden—too heavy for him to bear. He tries to get rid of them by leaving off his wicked ways, and by doing good deeds. But he soon finds he can't get rid of his load that way, for it only grows heavier and heavier, until at last he gives up trying to save himself, and just goes to the cross of Jesus Christ. And the moment he looks to Jesus and trusts in Him, his load of sins is all gone."

Mr. Dinsmore was surprised, as indeed he had often been at Elsie's knowledge of spiritual things.

"Who told you all that?" he asked.

"I read it in the Bible, papa, and besides, I know, because I have felt it."

He did not speak again for some moments, and then he said very gravely, "I am afraid you read too many of those dull books. I don't want you to read things that fill you with sad and gloomy thoughts, and make you unhappy. I want my little girl to be merry and happy as the day is long."

"Please don't forbid me to read them, papa," she pleaded with a look of apprehension, "for indeed they don't make me unhappy, and I love them so dearly."

"You need not be alarmed. I shall not do so unless I see that they do affect your spirits," he answered in a reassuring tone, and she thanked him with her own bright, sweet smile.

She was silent for a few moments, then asked suddenly, "Papa, may I say some verses to you?"

"Sometime," he said, "but not now, for there is the tea bell." And taking her hand, he led her down to the dining room.

They went to the drawing room after tea, but did not stay long. There were no visitors, and it was very dull and quiet, no one seeming inclined for conversation. Old Mr. Dinsmore sat nodding in his chair, Louise was drumming on the piano, and the rest were reading or sitting listlessly, saying nothing, and Elsie and her papa soon slipped away to their old seat by his dressing room fire.

"Sing something for me, my love, some of those little hymns I often hear you singing to yourself," he said, as he took her on his knee, and Elsie gladly obeyed.

Some of the pieces she sang alone, but in others, which were familiar to him, her father joined his deep bass notes to her sweet treble, at which she was greatly delighted. Then they read several chapters of the Bible together, and thus the evening passed so quickly and pleasantly that she was very much surprised when her papa, taking out his watch, told her it was her bedtime.

"Oh, papa! It has been such a nice, nice evening!" she said, as she bade him goodnight, "so like the dear old times I used to have with Miss Rose, only—"

She paused and colored deeply.

"Only what, darling?" he asked, drawing her caressingly to him.

"Only, papa, if you would pray with me, like she did," she whispered, winding her arms about his neck, and hiding her face on his shoulder.

"That I cannot do, my love. I have never learned how, and so I fear you will have to do all the praying for yourself and me too," he said, with a vain effort to speak lightly, for both heart and conscience were touched.

The only reply was a tightening of the clasp of the little arms about his neck, and a half-suppressed sob. Then two trembling lips touched his, a warm tear fell on his cheek, and she turned away and ran quickly from the room.

Oh, how earnest and importunate were Elsie's pleadings at a throne of grace that night, that her "dear, dear papa might soon be taught to love Jesus, and how to pray to Him." Tears fell fast while she prayed, but she rose from her knees feeling a joyful assurance that her petitions had been heard, and would be granted in God's own good time.

She had hardly laid her head upon her pillow, when her father came in. He said, "I have come to sit beside my little girl till she falls asleep," placed himself in a chair close by her side, taking her hand in his and holding it, as she loved so to have him do.

"I am so glad you have come, papa," she said, her whole face lighting up with pleased surprise.

"Are you?" he answered with a smile. "I'm afraid I am spoiling you; but I can't help it tonight. I think you forgot your wish to repeat some verses to me?"

"Oh, yes, papa!" she said. "But may I say them now?"

He nodded assent, and she went on. "They are some Miss Rose sent me in one of her letters. She cut them out of a newspaper, she said, and sent them to me because she liked them so much, and I too think they are very sweet. The piece is headed:

"'I want a sweet sense of Thy pardoning love,
That my manifold sins are forgiven;
That Christ, as my Advocate, pleadeth above,
That my name is recorded in Heaven.
'I want every moment to feel
That thy Spirit resides in my heart—
That His power is present to cleanse and to heal,
And newness of life to impart.
'I want—Oh! I want to attain
Some likeness, my Saviour, to thee!
That longed-for resemblance once more to regain,
Thy comeliness put upon me.
'I want to be marked for thine own—
Thy seal on my forehead to wear;
To receive that new name on the mystic white stone
Which none but thyself can declare.
'I want so in thee to abide
As to bring forth some fruit to thy praise;
The branch which thou prunest, though
feeble and dried,
May, languish, but never decays.
'I want thine own hand to unbind
Each tie to terrestrial things,
Too tenderly cherished, too closely entwined,
Where my heart so tenaciously clings.
'I want, by my aspect serene,
My actions and words, to declare
That my treasure is placed in a country unseen,
That my heart's best affections are there.
'I want as a trav'ller to haste
Straight onward, nor pause on my way;
Nor fore thought in anxious contrivance to waste
On the tent only pitched for a day.

'I want— and this sums up my prayer—
To glorify thee till I die;
Then calmly to yield up my soul to thy care,
And breathe out in faith my last sigh.'"

He was silent for a moment after she had repeated the last verse, then laying his hand softly on her head, and looking searchingly into her eyes, he asked, "And does my little one really wish all that those words express?"

"Yes, papa, for myself and you too," she answered. "Oh, papa! I do want to be all that Jesus would have me! Just like Him, so like Him that everybody who knows me will see the likeness and know that I belong to Him."

"Nay, you belong to me," he said, leaning over her and patting her cheek. "Hush! Not a syllable from your lips! I will have no gainsaying of my words," he added, with a mixture of authority and playfulness, as she seemed about to reply. "Now shut your eyes and go to sleep. I will have no more talking tonight."

She obeyed at once. The white lids gently closed over the sweet eyes, the long, dark lashes rested quietly on the fair, round cheek, and soon her soft regular breathing told that she had passed into the land of dreams.

Her father sat, still holding the little hand, and still gazing tenderly upon the sweet young face, till, something in its expression reminding him of words she had just repeated,

"I want to be marked for thine own—
Thy seal on my forehead to wear,"

he laid the little hand gently down, rose, and bent over her with a troubled look.

"Ah, my darling, that prayer is granted already!" he murmured. "For, ah me! You seem almost too good and pure for earth. But oh! God forbid that you should be taken from me to that place where I can see that your heart is even now. How desolate should I be!" and he turned away with a shiver and a heavy sigh, and hastily left the room.

*These beautiful words are not mine, nor do I know either the name of the author or where they were originally published. —M.F.

CHAPTER THIRTEENTH

But then her face,
So lovely, yet so arch, so full of mirth,
The overflowings of an innocent heart.

——Roger's Italy

An angel face! its sunny wealth of hair,
In radiant ripples bathed the graceful throat
And dimpled shoulders.

——Mrs. Osgood

THE COLD GREY LIGHT OF A WINTER morning stole in through the half-closed blinds as Elsie awoke. She started up in bed, with the thought that this was the day on which several of her young guests were expected, and that her papa had promised her a walk with him before breakfast, if she were ready in time.

Aunt Chloe had already risen, and a bright fire was blazing and crackling on the hearth, which she was carefully sweeping up.

"Good morning, mammy," said the little girl. "Are you ready to dress me now?"

"What, you 'wake, darlin'?" cried the fond old creature, turning quickly round at the sound of her nursling's voice. "Better lie still, honey, till de room gets warm."

"I'll wait a little while, mammy," Elsie said, lying down again, "but I must get up soon, for I wouldn't miss my walk with papa for a great deal. Please throw the shutters wide open, and let the daylight in. I'm so glad it has come."

"Why my bressed lamb, you didn't lie awake lookin' for de mornin,' did you? You ain't sick, nor sufferin' any way?" exclaimed Chloe, in a tone of mingled concern and inquiry, as she hastily set down her broom, and came toward the bed, with a look of loving anxiety on her dark face.

"Oh, no mammy! I slept nicely, and feel as well as can be," replied the little girl, "but I am glad to see this new day, because I hope it is going to be a very happy one. Carry, Howard, and a good many of my little friends are coming, you know, and I think we will have a very pleasant time together."

"Your ole mammy hopes you will, darlin'," replied Chloe, heartily, "an' I'se glad 'nough to see you lookin' so bright an' well. But jes you lie still till it gets warm here. I'll open de shutters, and fotch some more wood for de fire, an' clar up de room, an' by dat time I reckon you can get up."

Elsie waited patiently till Chloe pronounced the room warm enough, then sprang up with an eager haste, asking to be dressed as quickly as possible, that she might go to her papa.

"Don't you go for to worry yourself, darlin', dere's plenty ob time," said Chloe, beginning her work with all speed, however. "De mistress hab ordered de breakfast at nine, dese holiday times, to let de ladies an' gentlemen take a mornin' nap if dey likes it."

"Oh, yes, mammy! And that reminds me that papa said I must eat a cracker or something before I take my walk, because he thinks it isn't good for people to exercise much on an entirely empty stomach," said Elsie. "Will you get me one when you have done my curls?"

"Yes, honey, dere's a paper full in de drawer yonder," replied Chloe, "an' I reckon you better eat two or three, or you'll be mighty hungry 'fore you gits your breakfast."

It still wanted a few minutes of eight o'clock when Elsie's gentle rap was heard at her papa's dressing-room door. He opened it, and stooping to give her a good-morning kiss, said, with a pleased smile, "How bright and well my darling looks! Had you a good night's rest?"

"Oh, yes, papa! I never awoke once till it began to be light," she replied, "and now I'm all ready for our walk."

"In good season, too," he said. "Well, we will start presently, but take off your hat and come and sit on my knee a little while first. Breakfast will be late this morning, and we need not hurry. Did you get something to eat?" he asked, as he seated himself by the fire and drew her to his side.

"Yes, papa, I ate a cracker, and I think I will not get very hungry before nine o' clock, and I'm very glad we have so much time for our walk," she replied, as she took her place on his knees. "Shall we not start soon?"

"Presently," he said, stroking her hair, "but it will not hurt you to get well warmed first, for it is a sharp morning."

"You are very careful of me, dear papa," she said laying her head on his chest, "and oh, it is so nice to have a papa to love me and take care of me!"

"And it is so nice to have a dear little daughter to love and to take care of," he answered, pressing her closer to him.

The house was still very quiet, no one seeming to be astir but the servants, as Mr. Dinsmore and Elsie went down the stairs and passed out through the hall.

"Oh, papa! It is going to be such a nice day, and I feel so happy!" Elsie gaily exclaimed, as they started down the avenue.

"Do you, daughter?" he said, regarding her with an expression of intense yearning affection. "I wish I could make you always as merry and happy as you are at this moment. But alas! It cannot be, my darling," he added with a sigh.

"I know that, papa," she said with sudden gravity, "'for man that is born of woman is of few days, and full of trouble,' the Bible says. But I don't feel frightened at that, because it tells me, besides, that Jesus loves me, oh, so dearly! And will never leave nor forsake me. And that He has all power in heaven and earth, and will never let anything happen to me but what shall do me good. Oh, papa, it is such a happy thing to have the dear Lord Jesus for your friend!"

"It is strange how everything seems to lead your thoughts to Him," he said, giving her a wondering look.

"Yes, papa, it is because I love Him so," she answered, simply. And the father sighed as the thought arose, "Better than she loves me, even as she told me herself. Ah! I would I could be all—

everything to her, as she is fast becoming to me. I cannot feel satisfied, and yet I believe few daughters love their fathers as well as she loves me." And fondly pressing the little hand he held, he looked down upon her with beaming eyes.

She raised hers to his face with an expression of confiding affection, and, as though she had read his thoughts, "Yes, papa," she said. "I love you dearly, dearly, too—better than all the world besides."

Breakfast—always a plentiful and inviting meal at Roselands—was already upon the table when they returned, and they brought to it appetites sufficiently keen to make it very enjoyable.

Elsie spent the first hour after breakfast at the piano, practicing, and the second in her papa's dressing room, studying and reciting to him. Then they took a long ride on horseback, and when they returned she found that quite a number of the expected guests had already arrived.

Among them was Caroline Howard, a favorite friend of Elsie's, a pretty, sweet-tempered little girl, about a year older than herself.

Caroline had been away paying a long visit to some friends in the north, and so the two little girls had not met for nearly a year, and of course they had a great deal to say to each other.

They chatted a few moments in the drawing room, and then Elsie carried her friend off with her to her own room, that they might go on with their talk while she was getting dressed for dinner. Caroline had much to tell of her northern relatives, and of all she had seen and heard, and Elsie of her new-found parent, and her happiness in being so loved and cared for. And so the little tongues ran very fast, neither of them feeling Chloe's presence any restraint. But she soon completed her task and went out, leaving the two sitting on the sofa together, laughing and talking merrily while awaiting the summons to dinner, which they were to take that day along with their elders.

"How pretty your hair is, Elsie," said Caroline, winding the glossy ringlets around her finger. "I wish you'd give me one of these curls. I want to get a bracelet made for mamma, and she thinks so much of you, and your hair is such lovely color, that I am sure she would be delighted with one made of it."

"A Christmas gift is it to be?" asked Elsie. "But how will you get it done in time? For you know day after tomorrow is Christmas."

"Yes, I know, but if I could get into the city this afternoon, I think I might get them to promise it by tomorrow night."

"Well, yon shall have the curl, at any rate, if you will just take the scissors and help yourself, and poor mammy will have the fewer to curl the next time," Elsie answered, laughingly. "But mind," she added, as Caroline prepared to avail herself of the permission, "that you take it where it will not be missed."

"Of course I will. I don't want to spoil your beauty, though you are so much prettier than I," was Caroline's laughing rejoinder. "There," she cried, holding up the severed ringlet, "isn't it a beauty? But don't look scared, it will never be missed among so many. I don't even miss it myself, although I know it is gone."

"Well," Elsie said, shaking back her curls, "suppose we go down to the drawing room now, and I will ask papa to take us to the city this afternoon, or, if he is too busy to go himself, to let Pomp or Ajax drive us in."

"I think it would be better fun to go alone, Elsie— don't you?" asked Caroline, with some hesitation; adding quickly, "Don't be vexed, but I must confess I am more than half afraid of your father."

"Oh, you wouldn't be, Carry, if you knew him," Elsie answered, in her eager way. "I was a little myself, at first, but now I love him so dearly, I never want to go anywhere without him."

They found Mr. Dinsmore in the drawing room, where most of the guests and the older members of the family were assembled. He was conversing with a strange gentleman, and his little girl stood quietly at his side, patiently waiting until he should be ready to give her his attention. She had to wait some moments, for the gentlemen were discussing some political question, and were too much engaged to notice her.

But at length her father put his arm around her, and with a kind smile asked, "What is it, daughter?"

"Carry and I want to go to the city, this afternoon. Won't you take us, papa?"

"I wish I could, my dear, but I have an engagement, which makes it quite impossible."

"Ah, I'm sorry! But then, papa, we may have one of the carriages, and Pomp or Ajax to drive us, may we not?"

"No, daughter. I am sorry to disappoint you, but I am afraid you are too young to be trusted on such an expedition with only a servant. You must wait until tomorrow, when I can take you myself."

"But, papa, we want to go today. Oh, please do say yes! We want to go so very much, and I am sure we could do very nicely by ourselves.

Her arm was around his neck, and both tone and look were very coaxing.

"My little daughter forgets that when papa says no, she is never to ask again."

Elsie blushed and hung her head. His manner was quite too grave and decided for her to venture another word.

"What is the matter? What does Elsie want?" asked Adelaide, who was standing near, and had overheard enough to have some idea of the trouble.

Mr. Dinsmore explained, and Adelaide at once offered to take charge of the little girls, saying that she intended shopping a little in the city herself that very afternoon.

"Thank you," said her brother, looking very much pleased. "That obviates the difficulty entirely. Elsie, you may go, if Mrs. Howard gives Caroline permission."

"Thank you, dear papa, thank you so very much," she answered gratefully, and then ran away to tell Carry of her success, and secure Mrs. Howard's permission, which was easily obtained.

Elsie had intended buying some little present for each of the house-servants, and had taken a great deal of pleasure in making out a list of such articles as she thought would be suitable. But, on examining her purse, she found to her dismay that she had already spent so much on the miniature, and various gifts intended for other members of the family, that there was very little left. It was with a very sober, almost sorrowful face, that she came down to take her place in the carriage. It brightened instantly, though, as she caught sight of her father waiting to see her off.

"All ready, my darling?" he said, holding out his hand. "I think you will have a pleasant ride."

"Ah, yes, if you were only going too, papa," she answered regretfully.

"Quite impossible, love, but here is something to help you in your shopping. Use it wisely." And he put a twenty-dollar gold piece in her hand.

"Oh, thank you, papa! How good and kind you are to me!" she exclaimed, her whole face lighting up with pleasure. "Now I can buy some things I wanted to get for mammy and the rest. But how could you know I wanted more money?"

He only smiled, lifted her up in his arms, and kissed her fondly, and then, placing her in the carriage, said to the coachman, "Drive carefully, Ajax. You are carrying my greatest treasure."

"Nebber fear, marster, dese ole horses nebber tink ob running away," replied the Negro, with a bow and a grin, as he touched his horse with the whip, and drove off.

It was growing quite dark when the carriage again drove up the avenue, and Mr. Horace Dinsmore, who was beginning to feel a little anxious, came out to receive them, and ask what had detained them so long.

"Long!" said Adelaide, in a tone of surprise. "You gentlemen really have no idea what an undertaking it is to shop. Why I thought we got through in a wonderfully short time."

"Oh, papa, I have bought such quantities of nice things," cried Elsie, springing into his arms.

"Such as tobacco-pipes, red flannel, and—," remarked Adelaide, laughing.

"Indeed, Miss Adelaide!" exclaimed Carry, somewhat indignantly. "You forget the—"

But Elsie's little hand was suddenly placed over her mouth, and Carry laughed pleasantly, saying, "Ah! I forgot, I mustn't tell."

"Papa, papa!" cried Elsie, catching hold of his hand. "Do come with me to my room, and let me show you my purchases."

"I will, darling," he answered, pinching her cheek. "Here, Bill"—to a servant—"carry these bundles to Miss Elsie's room."

Then picking her up, he tossed her over his shoulder, and carried her upstairs as easily as though she had been a baby, she clinging to him and laughing merrily.

"Why, papa, how strong you are," she said, as he set her down. "I believe you can carry me as easily as I can my doll."

"To be sure. You are my doll," said he, "and a light burden for a man of my size and strength. But here come the bundles! What a number! No wonder you were late in getting home."

"Oh, yes, papa, see! I want to show you!" and catching up one of them, she hastily tore it open, displaying a very bright handkerchief. "This is a turban for Aunt Phillis, and this is a pound of tobacco for old Uncle Jack, and a nice pipe, too. Look, mammy! Won't he be pleased? And there's some flannel for poor old Aunt Dinah, who has the rheumatism; and that—oh, no, no, mammy! Don't you open that! It's a nice shawl for her, papa," she whispered in his ear.

"Ah!" he said, smiling. "And which is my present? You had better point it out lest I stumble upon it and learn the secret too soon."

"There is none here for you, sir," she replied, looking up into his face with an arch smile. "I would give you the bundle you carried upstairs, just now, but I'm afraid you would say that was not mine to give, because it belongs to you already."

"Indeed it does, and I feel richer in that possession than all the gold of California could make me," he said, pressing her to his heart.

She looked surpassingly lovely at that moment, her cheeks burning, and her eyes sparkling with excitement, the dark, fur-trimmed pelisse, and the velvet hat and plumes, setting off to advantage the whiteness of her pure complexion, and the glossy ringlets falling in rich masses on her shoulders.

"My own papa! I'm so glad I do belong to you," she said, throwing her arms around his neck, and laying her cheek to his for an instant. Then springing away, she added: "But I must show you the rest of the things. There are a good many more."

And she went on opening bundle after bundle, displaying their contents, and telling him for whom she intended them, until at last they had all been examined, and then she said, a little wearily, "Now mammy, please put them all away until tomorrow. But first take off my things, and get me ready to go downstairs."

"No, daughter," Mr. Dinsmore said in a gentle but firm tone, "you are not ready to have them put away until the price of each has been set down in your book."

"Oh, papa!" she pleaded. "Won't tomorrow do? I'm tired now, and isn't it almost teatime?"

"No, never put off till tomorrow what may as well be done today. There is nearly an hour yet before tea, and I do not think it need fatigue you much."

Elsie's face clouded, and the slightest approach to a pout might have been perceived.

"I hope my little girl is not going to be naughty," he said, very gravely.

Her face brightened in an instant. "No, papa," she answered cheerfully, "I will be good, and do whatever you bid me."

"That is my own darling," said he, "and I will help you, and it will not take long."

He opened her writing desk as he spoke, and took out her account-book.

"Oh, papa!" she cried in a startled tone, springing forward and taking hold of his hand. "Please, please don't look! You know you said I need not show you until after Christmas."

"No, I will not," he replied, smiling at her eagerness, "you shall put down the items in the book while I write the labels, and Aunt Chloe pins them on. Will that do?"

"Oh, that's a nice plan, papa!" she said merrily, as she threw off her hat and pelisse, and seating herself before the desk, took out her pen and ink.

Chloe put the hat and pelisse carefully away, brought a comb and brush, and smoothed her nursling's hair, and then began her share of the business on hand.

Half an hour's work finished it all, and Elsie wiped her pen, and laid it away, saying joyously, "Oh, I'm so glad it is all done!"

"Papa knew best, after all, did he not?" asked her father, drawing her to him, and patting her cheek.

"Yes, papa," she said softly. "You always know best, and I am very sorry I was naughty."

He answered with a kiss, and taking her hand, led her down to the drawing room.

After tea the young people adjourned to the nursery, where they amused themselves with a variety of innocent games. Quite early in the evening, and greatly to Elsie's delight, her father joined them. Though some of the young strangers were at first rather shy of him, they soon found that he could enter heartily into their sports, and before the time came to separate for the night, he had made himself very popular with nearly all.

Time flew fast, and Elsie was very much surprised when the clock struck eight. Half-past was her bed-time, and, as she now and then glanced up at the dial-plate, she thought the hands had never moved so fast. As it struck the half hour she drew near her father's side.

"Papa," she asked, "is the clock right?"

"Yes, my dear, it is," he replied, comparing it with his watch.

"And must I go to bed now?" she asked, half hoping for permission to stay up a little longer.

"Yes, daughter, keep to rules."

Elsie looked disappointed, and several little voices urged, "Oh, do let her stay up another hour, or at least till nine o'clock."

"No, I cannot often allow a departure from rules," he said kindly, but firmly, "and tomorrow night Elsie will find it harder to go to bed in season than tonight. Bid your little friends goodnight, my dear, and go at once."

Elsie obeyed, readily and cheerfully. "You, too, papa," she said, coming to him at last.

"No, darling," he answered, laying his hand caressingly on her head, and smiling approvingly on her. "I will come for my goodnight kiss before you are asleep."

Elsie looked very glad and went away feeling herself the happiest little girl in the land, in spite of the annoyance of being forced to leave the merry group in the nursery. She was just ready for bed when her papa came in, and, taking her in his arms, folded her to his heart, saying, "My own darling! My good obedient little daughter!"

"Dear papa, I love you so much!" she replied, twining her arms around his neck. "I love you all the better for never letting me have my own way, but always making me obey and keep to rules."

"I don't doubt it, daughter," he said, "for I have often noticed that spoiled, coddled children, usually have very little love for their parents, or indeed for anyone but themselves. But I must put you in your bed, or you will be in danger of taking cold."

He laid her down, tucked the clothes snugly about her, and pressing one more kiss on the round, rosy cheek, left her to her slumbers.

CHAPTER
FOURTEENTH

You play the spaniel,
And think with wagging of your
tongue to win me.

—*Shakespeare's Henry viii*

These delights, if thou canst give,
Mirth, with thee I mean to live.

—*Milton's L'Allegro*

THE YOUNG PARTY AT ROSELANDS had now grown so large—several additions having been made to it on Monday afternoon and evening—that a separate table was spread for them in the nursery, where they took their meals together. Mrs. Brown, the housekeeper, took the head of the table, for the double purpose of keeping them in order, and seeing that their wants were well supplied.

Elsie came in to breakfast, from a brisk walk with her papa, looking fresh and rosy, and bright as the morning. That was quite different from some of the little guests, who had been up far beyond their usual hours the night before. Having just left their beds, they had come down pale and languid in looks, and in some instances showing peevish and fretful tempers, very trying to the patience of their attendants.

"Oh, Elsie!" exclaimed Carry Howard, as the little girl took her place at the table. "We were all so sorry that you had to leave us so soon last night. We had lots of fun after you left. I think your papa might have let you stay up a little longer, but he has promised that tonight—as we are to have the Christmas tree, and ever so much will be going on—you shall stay up till half-past nine, if you like. Aren't you glad? I'm sure I am."

"Yes, papa is very kind, and I know I feel much better for going to bed early last night," said Elsie, cheerfully.

"Yes, indeed," remarked Mrs. Brown, "late hours and rich food are very bad for little folks, and I notice that Miss Elsie has grown a deal stronger and healthier-looking since her papa came home. He takes such good care of her."

"Indeed he does," said Elsie heartily, thanking Mrs. Brown with one of her sweetest smiles.

"What are we going to do today, Elsie?" asked Caroline.

"Whatever you all prefer," said Elsie. "If you like I will practice that duet with you the first hour after breakfast, or do anything else you wish, but the second hour I must spend with papa, and after that I have nothing to do but entertain my company all day."

"Do you do lessons in holidays?" asked Mary Leslie, a merry, fun-loving child, about Elsie's own age, who considered lessons an intolerable bore, and had some vague idea that they must have been invented for the sole purpose of tormenting children. Her blue eyes opened wide with astonishment when Elsie quietly replied that her papa had kindly arranged to give her an hour every morning because he knew it would be so much pleasanter for her than spending the whole day in play.

Elsie did keenly enjoy the quiet hour spent in studying and reciting to her father, sitting on a low stool at his feet, or perhaps oftener on his knee, with his arm around her waist.

She had an eager and growing thirst for knowledge, and was an apt scholar, whom anyone with the least love for the profession might have delighted in teaching. Mr. Dinsmore, a thorough scholar himself, and loving knowledge for its own sake—loving also his little pupil with all a father's fond, yearning affection—delighted in his task.

When Elsie left her father she found that the Carringtons had just arrived. She and Lucy had not seen each other since the week the latter had spent at Roselands early in the summer, and both felt pleased to meet.

Mrs. Carrington gave Elsie a warm embrace, remarking that she had grown, and was looking extremely well, better than she had ever seen her. But no one was more delighted to meet Elsie than Herbert, and she was very glad to learn that his health was gradually improving. He was not, however, at all strong, even yet, and his mother thought it best for him to lie down and rest a little after his ride. She promised to sit by him and the two little girls went in search of the rest of the young folks.

Several of the older boys had gone out walking or riding, but the younger ones, and all the little girls, were gathered in a little back parlor, where, by Adelaide's care and forethought, a variety of storybooks, toys, and games had been provided for their amusement. Elsie's entrance was hailed with delight, for she was a general favorite.

"Oh, Elsie! Can't you tell us what to play?" cried Mary Leslie. "I'm so tired," and she yawned wearily.

"Here are some dissected maps, Mary," replied Elsie, opening a drawer. "Would you not like them?"

"No, indeed, thank you. They are too much like lessons."

"Here are blocks. Will you build houses?"

"Oh, I am too big for that! They are very nice for little children."

"Will you play jack-stones? Here are some smooth pebbles."

"Yes, if you, Carry, and Lucy will play with me."

"Agreed!" said the others. "Let's have a game."

So, Elsie having first set the little ones to building block houses, supplied Harry Carrington—an older brother of Lucy's—with a book, and two younger boys with dissected maps to arrange, the four girls sat down in a circle on the carpet and began their game.

For a few moments all went on smoothly, but soon angry and complaining words were heard coming from the corner where the house building was going on. Elsie left her game to try to make peace.

"What is the matter, Flora, dear?" she asked soothingly of a little curly-headed girl, who was sobbing, and wiping her eyes with her apron.

"Enna took my blocks," sobbed the child.

"Oh, Enna! Won't you give them back?" asked Elsie, coaxingly. "You know Flora is a visitor, and we must be very polite to her."

"No, I won't," returned Enna, flatly. "She's got enough now."

"No, I haven't. I can't build a house with those," Flora said, with another sob.

Elsie stood a moment looking much perplexed, then, with a brightening face, exclaimed in her cheerful, pleasant way, "Well, never mind, Flora, dear, I will get you my doll. Will not that do quite as well?"

"Oh, yes! I'd rather have the doll, Elsie," the little weeper answered eagerly, smiling through her tears.

Elsie ran out of the room, and was back again almost in a moment, with the doll in her arms.

"There, dear little Flora," she said, laying it gently on the child's lap, "please be careful of it, for I have had it a long while, and prize it very much, because my guardian gave it to me when I was a very little girl, and he is dead now."

"I won't break it, Elsie, indeed I won't," replied Flora, confidently, and Elsie sat down to her game again.

A few moments afterward Mr. Horace Dinsmore passed through the room.

"Elsie," he said, as he caught sight of his little daughter, "go up to my dressing-room."

There was evidently displeasure and reproof in his tone, and, entirely unconscious of wrongdoing, Elsie looked up in surprise, asking, "Why, papa?"

"Because I bid you," he replied, and she silently obeyed, wondering greatly what she had done to displease her father.

Mr. Dinsmore passed out of one door while Elsie left by the another.

The three little girls looked inquiringly into each other's faces.

"What is the matter? What has Elsie done?" asked Carry in a whisper.

"I don't know. Nothing, I guess," replied Lucy indignantly. "I do believe he's just the crossest man alive! When I was here last summer he was all the time scolding and punishing poor Elsie for just nothing at all."

"I think he must be very strict," said Carry, "but Elsie seems to love him very much."

"Strict! I guess he is!" exclaimed Mary. "Why, only think, girls, he makes her do her lessons in the holidays!"

"I suspect she did not know her lesson, and has to learn it over," said Carry, shaking her head wisely, and that was the conclusion they all came to.

In the meantime, Elsie sat down alone in her banishment, and tried to think what she could have done to deserve it.

It was some time before she could form any idea of its cause, but at length it suddenly came to her recollection. Once several months before this, her father had found her sitting on the carpet, and had bade her get up immediately and sit on a chair or stool: "Never let me see you sitting on the floor, Elsie, when there are plenty of seats at hand. I consider it a very unladylike and slovenly trick."

She covered her face with her hands, and sat thus for some moments, feeling very sorry for her forgetfulness and disobedience, very penitent on account of it. And then, kneeling down, she asked forgiveness of God.

A full hour she had been there alone, and the time had seemed very long, when at last the door opened and her father came in.

Elsie rose and came forward to meet him with the air of one who had offended and knew she was in disgrace. But putting one of her little hands in his, she looked up pleadingly into his face, asking, in a slightly tremulous tone, "Dear papa, are you angry with me?"

"I am always displeased when you disobey me, Elsie," he replied, very gravely, laying his other hand on her head.

"I am very sorry I was naughty, papa," she said humbly, and casting down her eyes, "but I had quite forgotten that you had told me not to sit on the floor, and I could not think for a good while what it was that I had done wrong."

"Is that an excuse for disobedience, Elsie?" he asked in a tone of grave displeasure.

"No, sir, I did not mean it so, and I am very, very sorry. Dear papa, please forgive me, and I will try never to forget again."

"I think you disobeyed in another matter," he said.

"Yes, sir, I know it was very naughty to ask why, but I think I will remember not to do it again. Dear papa, won't you forgive me?"

He sat down and took her on his knee.

"Yes, daughter, I will," he said, in his usual kind, affectionate tone. "I am always ready to forgive my little girl when I see that she is sorry for a fault."

She held up her face for a kiss, which he gave.

"I wish I could always be good, papa," she said, "but I am naughty so often."

"No, I think you have been a very good girl for quite a long time. If you were so naughty as Arthur and Enna, I don't know what I should with you — whip you every day, I suspect, until I made a better girl out of you. Now you may go down to your mates, but remember, you are not allowed to play jack-stones again."

It was now lunchtime, and Elsie found the children in the nursery engaged in eating.

Flora turned to her as she entered.

"Please, Elsie, don't be cross," she said coaxingly. "I am really sorry your doll's broken, but it wasn't my fault. Enna would try to snatch it, and that made it fall and break its head."

Poor Elsie! This was quite a trial, and she could scarcely keep back the tears as, following Flora's glance, she saw her valued doll lying on the window-seat with its head broken entirely off. She said not a word, but, hastily crossing the room, took it up and gazed mournfully at it.

Kind Mrs. Brown, who had just finished helping her young charge all round, followed her to the window.

"Never mind, dear," she said in her pleasant, cheery tone, patting Elsie's cheek and smoothing her hair, "I've got some excellent glue, and I think I can stick it on again and make it almost as good as ever. So come, sit down and eat your lunch, and don't fret any more."

"Thank you, ma'am, you are very kind," Elsie said, trying to smile, as the kind-hearted old lady led her to the table and filled her plate with fruit and cakes.

"These cakes are very simple, not at all rich, my dear, but quite what your papa would approve of," she said, seeing the little girl look doubtfully at them."

"Doesn't your papa let you eat anything good, Elsie?" asked Mary Leslie across the table. "He must be cross."

"No, indeed, he is not, Mary, and he lets me eat everything that he thinks is good for me," Elsie answered with some warmth.

She was seated between Caroline Howard and Lucy Carrington.

"What did your papa send you away for, Elsie?" whispered the latter.

"Please don't ask me, Lucy," replied the little girl, blushing deeply. "Papa always has a good reason for what he does, and he is just the dearest, kindest, and best father that ever anybody had."

Elsie spoke in an eager, excited, almost angry manner, quite unusual with her, while the hot tears came into her eyes. She knew very well what was Lucy's opinion of her father, and more than half suspected that she had been making some unkind remark about him to the others, and she was eager to remove any unfavorable impression they might have received.

"I am sure that he must love you very dearly, Elsie," remarked Caroline, soothingly. "No one could help seeing that just by the way he looks at you."

Elsie answered her with a pleased and grateful look, and then changed the subject by proposing that they should all walk as soon as they had finished eating, as the day was fine, and there would be plenty of time before dinner.

The motion was carried without a dissenting voice, and in a few moments they all set out, a very merry party, full of fun and frolic. They had a very pleasant time, and returned barely in season to be dressed for dinner.

They dined by themselves in the nursery, but were afterward taken down to the drawing room. Here Elsie found herself immediately seized upon by a young lady, dressed in a very bright and fashionable style, whom she did not remember ever to have seen before. But she insisted on seating the little girl on the sofa by her side, and keeping her there a long while, loading her with caresses and flattery.

"My dear child," she said, "what lovely hair you have! So fine, and soft, and glossy. Such a beautiful color, too, and it curls so splendidly! Natural ringlets, I'm sure, are they not?"

"Yes, ma'am," Elsie answered, simply, wishing from the bottom of her heart that the lady would release her, and talk to someone else.

But the lady had no such intention.

"You are a very sweet little girl, I am sure, and I shall love you dearly," she said, kissing her several times. "Ah! I would give anything if I had such a clear fair complexion and such rosy cheeks. That makes you blush. Well, I like to see it. Blushes are very becoming. Oh, you needn't pretend you don't know you're handsome! You're a perfect little beauty. Do tell me, where did you get such splendid eyes? But I needn't ask, for I have only to look at your father to see where they came from. Mr. Dinsmore"—to Elsie's papa, who just then came toward them— "you ought to be very proud of this child. She is the very image of yourself, and a perfect little beauty, too."

"Miss Stevens is pleased to flatter me," he said, bowing low, "but flattery is not good for either grown-up children or younger ones, and I must beg leave to decline the compliment, as I cannot see that Elsie bears the slightest resemblance to me or any of my family. She is very like her mother, though," he added with a half sigh and a tender, loving glance at his little girl, "and that is just what I would have her. But I am forgetting my errand, Miss Stevens. I came to ask if you will ride this afternoon, as we are getting up a small party."

"Yes, thank you, I should like it dearly. It is such a lovely day. But how soon do you start?"

"As soon as the ladies can be ready. The horses will be at the door in a very few moments."

"Ah! Then I must go and prepare," she said, rising and sailing out of the room.

Mr. Dinsmore took the seat she had vacated, and, passing his arm round the little girl, said to her in an undertone, "My little daughter must not be so foolish as to believe that people mean all they say to her. Some persons talk in a very thoughtless way, and, without perhaps intending to be exactly untruthful say a great deal that they really do not mean. And I should be sorry, indeed, to see my little girl so spoiled by all this silly flattery as to grow up conceited and vain."

She looked at him with her own sweet, innocent smile, free from the slightest touch of vanity.

"No, papa," she said, "I do not mind, when people say such things, because I know the Bible says, 'Favor is deceitful, and beauty is vain,' and in another place, 'He that flattereth his neighbor spreadeth a net for his feet.' So I will try to keep away from that lady. Shall I not, papa?"

"Whenever you can do so without rudeness, daughter," and he moved away, thinking to himself, "How strangely the teachings of that Book seem to preserve my child from every evil influence."

A sigh escaped him. There was lurking within him a vague consciousness that her father needed such a safeguard, but had it not.

Lucy, who was standing at the window, turned quickly round.

"Come, girls," she said, "let us run out and see them off. They're bringing up the horses. And see! There's Miss Adelaide in her riding dress and cap. How pretty she looks! And there's that Miss Stevens coming out now, hateful thing! I can't bear her! Come, Elsie and Carry!"

And she ran out, Caroline and Elsie following. Elsie, however, went no further than the hall, where she stood still at the foot of the stairs.

"Come, Elsie," called the other two from the portico, "come out here."

"No," replied the little girl, "I cannot come without something round me. Papa says it is too cold for me to be out in the wind today with my neck and arms bare."

"Pooh! Nonsense!" said Lucy. "'Tain't a bit cold. Do come now."

"No, Lucy, I must obey my father," Elsie answered in the most pleasant but no less decided tone.

Someone caught her round the waist and lifted her up.

"Oh, papa!" she exclaimed. "I did not know you were there! I wish I was going too. I don't like to have you go without me."

"I wish you were, my love. I always love to have you with me, but you know it wouldn't do. You have your little guests to entertain. Goodbye, darling. Don't go out in the cold."

He kissed her, as he always did now, when leaving her even an hour or two, and set her down.

The little girls watched until the last of the party had disappeared down the avenue, and then ran merrily upstairs to Elsie's room. There they busied themselves until teatime in various little preparations for the evening, such as dressing dolls, and tying up bundles of confectionery, etc., to be hung upon the Christmas tree.

The children had all noticed that the doors of a parlor opening into the drawing room had been closed since morning to all but a favored few, who passed in and out, with an air of mystery and importance. They were generally laden with some odd-looking bundle when going in, which they invariably left behind on coming out again, and many a whispered consultation had been held as to what was probably going on in there. Elsie and Carry seemed to be in on the secret, but only smiled and shook their heads wisely when questioned.

But at length tea being over, and all, both old and young, assembled as if by common consent in the drawing room, it began to be whispered about that their curiosity was now on the point of being gratified.

All were immediately on the qui vive, and every face brightened with mirth and expectation, and when, a moment after, the doors were thrown open, there was a universal burst of applause.

A large Christmas tree had been set up at the further end of the room, and, with its myriad of lighted tapers, and its load of toys and bonbons, interspersed with many a richer and more costly gift, made quite a display.

"Beautiful! Beautiful!" cried the children, clapping their hands and dancing about with delight, while their elders, perhaps equally pleased, expressed their admiration after a more staid and sober fashion. When they thought their handiwork had been sufficiently admired, Mrs. Dinsmore and Adelaide approached the tree and began the pleasant task of distributing the gifts.

Everything was labeled, and each, as his or her name was called out, stepped forward to receive the present.

No one had been forgotten; each had something, and almost everyone had several pretty presents. Mary Leslie and little Flora Arnott were made perfectly happy with wax dolls that could open and shut their eyes; Caroline Howard received a gold chain from her mamma, and a pretty pin from Elsie; Lucy, a set of coral ornaments, besides several smaller presents; and others were equally fortunate. All was mirth and hilarity, only one clouded face to be seen, and that belonged to Enna, who was pouting in a corner because Mary Leslie's doll was a little larger than hers.

Elsie had already received a pretty bracelet from her Aunt Adelaide, a needle-case from Lora, and several little gifts from her young guests. She was just beginning to wonder what had become of her papa's promised present, when she heard her name again, and Adelaide, turning to her with a pleased look, slipped a most beautiful diamond ring on her finger.

"From your papa," she said. "Go and thank him. It is well worth it."

Elsie sought him out where he stood alone in a corner, an amused spectator of the merry scene.

"See, papa," she said, holding up her hand. "I think it is very beautiful. Thank you, dear papa, thank you very much."

"Does it please you, my darling?" he asked, stooping to press a kiss on the little upturned face, so bright and happy.

"Yes, papa, I think it is lovely! The very prettiest ring I ever saw."

"Yet I think there is something else you would have liked better, is there not?" he asked looking searchingly into her face.

"Dear papa, I like it very much. I would rather have it than anything else on the tree."

"Still you have not answered my question," he said, with a smile, as he sat down and drew her to his side, adding in a playful tone, "Come, I am not going to put up with any evasion. Tell me truly if you would have preferred something else, and if so, what it is."

Elsie blushed and looked down, then raising her eyes, and seeing with what a tender, loving glance he was regarding her, she took courage to say, "Yes, papa, there is one thing I would have liked better, and that is your miniature."

To her surprise he looked highly pleased at her reply, and giving her another kiss, said, "Well, darling, someday you shall have it."

"Mr. Horace Dinsmore," called Adelaide, taking some small, glittering object from the tree.

"Another present for me?" he asked, as Walter came running with it.

He had already received several, from his father and sisters, but none had seemed to give him half the pleasure that this did when he saw that it was labeled, "From his little daughter."

It was only a gold pencil. The miniature—with which the artist had succeeded so well that nothing could have been prettier except the original herself—she had reserved to be given in another way.

"Do you like it, papa?" she asked, her face glowing with delight to see how pleased he was.

"Yes, darling, very much, and I shall always think of my little girl when I use it."

"Keep it in your pocket, and use it every day, won't you, papa?"

"Yes, my love, I will, but I thought you said you had no present for me?"

"Oh, no, no, papa! I said there was none for you amongst those bundles. I had bought this, but had given it to Aunt Adelaide to take care of, for fear you might happen to see it."

"Ah! That was it, eh?" and he laughed and stroked her hair.

"Here, Elsie, here is your bundle of candy," said Walter, running up to them again. "Everybody has one, and that is yours, Adelaide says."

He put it in her hand, and ran away again. Elsie looked up in her father's face inquiringly.

"No, darling," he said, taking the paper from her hand and examining its contents, "not tonight. Tomorrow, after breakfast, you may eat the cream-candy and the rock, but none of the others—they are colored, and very unwholesome."

"Won't you eat some, papa?" she asked with winning sweetness.

"No, dearest," he said, "for though I, too, am fond of sweet things, I will not eat them while I refuse them to you."

"Do, papa," she urged, "it would give me pleasure to see you enjoying it."

"No, darling, I will wait until tomorrow too."

"Then please keep it for me until tomorrow, papa, will you?"

"Yes," he said, putting it in his pocket. And then, as the gifts had all been distributed, and the little folks were in high glee, a variety of sports were commenced by them, in which some of their elders also took a part. And thus the hours sped away so rapidly that Elsie was very much surprised when her father called her to go to bed.

"It is half-past nine already, papa?" she asked.

"It is ten, my dear child, and high time you were in bed," he said, smiling at her look of astonishment. "I hope you have enjoyed yourself."

"Oh, so much, papa! Goodnight, and thank you for letting me stay up so long."

CHAPTER FIFTEENTH

Ask me not why I should love her;—
Look upon those soulful eyes!
Look while mirth of feeling move her,
And see there how sweetly rise
Thoughts gay and gentle from a breast
Which is of innocence the nest—
Which, though each joy were from it shred,
By truth would still be tenanted!

IT WAS YET DARK WHEN ELSIE awoke, but, hearing the clock strike five, she knew it was morning. She lay still a little while, and then, slipping softly out of bed, put her feet into her slippers, threw her warm dressing gown around her, and feeling for a little package she had left on her dressing table, she secured it and stole noiselessly from the room.

All was darkness and silence in the house, but she had no thought of fear, and, gliding gently down the hall to her papa's door, she turned the handle very cautiously, when, to her great delight, she found it had been left unfastened, and yielded readily to her touch.

She entered as quietly as a little mouse, listened a moment until satisfied from his breathing that her father was still sound asleep. Then, stepping softly across the room, she laid her package down where he could not fail to see it as soon as daylight came and his eyes were opened. This accomplished, she stole back again as noiselessly as she had come.

"Who dat?" demanded Chloe, starting up in bed as Elsie reentered her own apartment.

"It is only I. Did I frighten you, mammy?" answered the little girl with a merry laugh.

"Ki? Chile, dat you? What are you doin' runnin' 'bout de house all in de dark, cold night?"

"It isn't night, mammy. I heard it strike five some time ago."

"Well, den, dis chile gwine get right up an' make de fire. But jes you creep back into de bed, darlin', 'fore you cotch your death ob cold."

"I will, mammy," Elsie said, doing as she was desired, "but please dress me as soon as the room is warm enough, won't you?"

"Yes, darlin', kase ob course I knows you want to be up early o' Christmas mornin'. Ki! Miss Elsie, dat's a beautiful shawl you gave your ole mammy. I shan't feel de cold at all dis winter."

"I hope not, mammy. And were Aunt Phillis, and Uncle Jack, and all the rest pleased with their presents?"

"I reckon dey was, darlin', mos' ready to go off de handle, 'tirely."

Chloe had soon built up her fire and coaxed it into a bright blaze, and in a few moments more she pronounced the room sufficiently warm for her nursling to get up and be dressed.

Elsie was impatient to go to her father, but, even after she had been carefully dressed and all her morning duties attended to, it was still so early that Chloe advised her to wait a little longer. She assured her that it was only a very short time since

John had gone in to make his master's fire and supply him with hot water for shaving.

So the little girl sat down and tried to drown her impatience in the pages of a new book—one of her Christmas presents. But Chloe presently stole softly behind her chair, and, holding up high above her head some glittering object attached to a pretty gold chain, let it gradually descend until it rested upon the open book.

Elsie started and jumped up with an exclamation of surprise.

"Wonder if you knows dat gen'lman, darlin'?" laughed Chloe.

"Oh, it is papa!" cried the little girl, catching it in her hand. "My own dear, darling papa! Oh, how good of him to give it to me!" and she danced about the room in her delight. "It is just himself, so exactly like him! Isn't it a good likeness, mammy?" she asked, drawing near the light to examine it more closely. "Dear, dear, darling papa!" and she kissed it again and again.

Then gently drawing her mother's miniature from her bosom, she laid them side by side.

"My papa and mamma, are they not beautiful, mammy? Both of them?" she asked, raising her swimming eyes to the dusky face leaning over her, and gazing with such mournful fondness at the sweet girlish countenance, so life-like and beautiful, yet calling up thoughts of sorrow and bereavement.

"My darling young missus!" murmured the old nurse. "My own precious chile dat dese arms hab carried so many years, dis ole heart like to break wheneber I tinks ob you, an' 'members how your bright young face done gone away foreber."

The big tears were rolling fast down the sable cheeks, and dropping like rain on Elsie's curls, while the broad bosom heaved with sobs. "But your ole mammy's been good to your little chile dat you lef' behind, darlin', 'deed she has," she went on.

"Yes, mammy, indeed, indeed you have," Elsie said, twining her arms lovingly around her. "But don't let us cry any more, for we know that dear mamma is very happy in heaven, and does not wish us to grieve for her now. I shall not show you the picture any more if it makes you cry like that," she added half playfully.

"Not always, chile," Chloe said, wiping away her tears, "but jes dis here mornin'—Christmas mornin', when she was always so bright and merry. It seems only yesterday she went dancin' about jes like you."

"Yes, mammy dear, but she is with the angels now—my sweet, pretty mamma!" Elsie whispered softly, with another tender, loving look at the picture ere she returned it to its accustomed resting-place in her bosom.

"And now I must go to papa," she said more cheerfully, "for it is almost breakfast time."

"Is my darling satisfied now?" he asked, as she ran into his arms and was folded in a close embrace.

"Yes, papa, indeed I am. Thank you a thousand times. It is all I wanted."

"And you have given me the most acceptable present you could have found. It is a most excellent likeness, and I am delighted with it."

"I am so glad, papa, but it was Aunt Adelaide who thought of it."

"Ah! That was very kind of her. But how does my little girl feel this morning, after all her dissipation?"

"Oh, very well, thank you, papa."

"You will not want to say any lesson today, I suppose?"

"Oh, yes, if you please, papa, and it does not give you too much trouble," she said. "It is the very pleasantest hour in the day, except—"

"Well, except what? Ah, yes, I understand. Well, my, love, it shall be as you wish, but, come to me directly after breakfast, as I am going out early."

Elsie had had her hour with her father, but, though he had left her and gone out, she still lingered in his dressing room, looking over the next day's lesson. At length, however, she closed the book and left the room, intending to seek her young guests, who were in the lower part of the house.

Miss Stevens' door was open as she passed, and that lady called to her, "Elsie dear, you sweet little creature, come here, and see what I have for you."

Elsie obeyed, though rather reluctantly, and Miss Stevens, bidding her sit down, went to a drawer, and took out a large paper of mixed candy, all of the best and most expensive kinds, which she put into the little girl's hands with one of her sweetest smiles.

It was a strong temptation to a child who had a great fondness for such things, but Elsie had prayed from her heart that morning for strength to resist temptation, and it was given her.

"Thank you ma'am, you are very kind," she said gratefully, "but I cannot take it, because papa does not approve of my eating such things. He gave me a little this morning, but said I must not have any more for a long time."

"Now, that is quite too bad," exclaimed Miss Stevens, "but at least take one or two, child. That much couldn't possibly hurt you, and your papa need never know."

Elsie gave her a look of grieved surprise.

"Oh! Could you think I would do that?" she said. "But God would know, Miss Stevens, and I should know it myself, and how could I ever look my papa in the face again after deceiving him so?"

"Really, my dear, you are making a very serious matter of a mere trifle," laughed the lady. "Why, I have deceived my father more than fifty times, and never thought it any harm. But here is something I am sure you can take, and indeed you must, for I bought both it and the candy expressly for you."

She replaced the candy in the drawer as she spoke and took from another a splendidly-bound book which she laid in Elsie's lap, saying, with a triumphant air, "There, my dear, what do you think of that? Is it not handsome?"

Elsie's eyes sparkled—books were her greatest treasures. But feeling an instinctive repugnance to taking a gift from one whom she could neither respect nor love, she made an effort to decline it, though at the same time thanking the lady warmly for her kind intentions.

But Miss Stevens would hear of no refusal, and fairly forced it upon her acceptance, declaring that, as she had bought it expressly for her, she should feel extremely hurt if she did not take it.

"Then I will, Miss Stevens," said the little girl, "and I am sure you are very kind. I love books and pictures, too, and these are lovely engravings," she added, turning over the leaves with undisguised pleasure.

"Yes, and the stories are right pretty, too," remarked Miss Stevens.

"Yes, ma'am, they look as if they were, and I should like dearly to read them."

"Well, dear, just sit down and read, there's nothing to hinder. I'm sure your little friends can do without you for an hour or two. Or, if you prefer it, take the book and enjoy it with them. It is your own, you know, to use as you like."

"Thank you, ma'am, but, though I can look at the pictures, I must not read the stories until I have asked papa, because he does not allow me to read anything now without first showing it to him."

"Dear me! How very, very strict he is!" exclaimed Miss Stevens.

"I wonder," she thought to herself, "if he would expect to domineer over his wife in that style?"

Elsie was slowly turning over the leaves of the book, enjoying the pictures very much, studying them intently, but resolutely refraining from even glancing over the printed pages. But at length she closed it, and, looking out of the window, said, with a slight sigh, "Oh, I wish papa would come! But I'm afraid he won't for a long while, and I do so want to read these stories."

"Suppose you let me read one to you," suggested Miss Stevens. "That would not be your reading it, you know."

Elsie looked shocked at the proposal. "Oh, no, ma'am! Thank you, I know you mean to be kind, but I could not do it. It would be so very wrong — quite the same, I am sure, as if I read it with my own eyes," she answered hurriedly. And then, fearing to be tempted further, she excused herself and went in search of her young companions.

She found them in the drawing room.

"Wasn't it too provoking, Elsie, that those people didn't send home my bracelet last night?" exclaimed Caroline Howard. "I have just been telling Lucy about it. I think that it was such a shame for them to disappoint me, for I wanted to have it on the tree."

"I am sorry you were disappointed, Carry, but perhaps it will come today," Elsie answered in a sympathizing tone. And then she showed the new book, which she still held in her hand.

They spent some time in examining it, talking about it, and admiring the pictures, and then went out for a walk.

"Has papa come in yet, mammy?" was Elsie's first question on returning.

"Yes, darlin', I tink he's in the drawin' room dis berry minute," Chloe answered, as she took off the little girl's hat, and carefully smoothed her hair.

"There, there, mammy! Won't that do now? I'm in a little bit of a hurry," Elsie said with a merry little laugh, as she slipped playfully from under her nurse's hand, and ran downstairs.

But she was doomed to disappointment for the present, for her papa was seated on the sofa, beside Miss Stevens, talking to her, and so she must wait a little longer. At last, however, he rose, went to the other side of the room, and stood a moment looking out of the window.

Then Elsie hastened to take her book from a table, where she had laid it, and going up to him, said, "Papa!"

He turned round instantly, asking in a pleasant tone, "Well, daughter; what is it?"

She put the book into his hand, saying eagerly, "It is a Christmas gift from Miss Stevens, papa. Will you let me read it?"

He did not answer immediately, but turned over the leaves, glancing rapidly over page after page, but not too rapidly to be able to form a pretty correct idea of the contents.

"No, daughter," he said, handing it back to her, "you must content yourself with looking at the pictures. They are by far the best part. The stories are very unsuitable for a little girl of your age, and would, indeed, be unprofitable reading for anyone."

She looked a little disappointed.

"I am glad I can trust my little daughter, and feel certain that she will not disobey me," he said, smiling kindly on her, and patting her check.

She answered him with a bright, happy look, full of confiding affection, laid the book away without a murmur, and left the room—her father's eyes following her with a fond, loving glance.

Miss Stevens, who had watched them both closely during this little scene, bit her lips with vexation at the result of her maneuver.

She had come to Roselands with the fixed determination to lay siege to Mr. Dinsmore's heart, and flattering and spoiling his little daughter was one of her modes of attack, but his decided disapproval of her present, she perceived, did not augur well for the success of her schemes. She was by no means in despair, however, for she had great confidence in the power of her own personal attractions, being really tolerably pretty, and considering herself a great beauty, as well as very highly accomplished.

As Elsie ran out into the hall, she found herself suddenly caught in Mr. Travilla's arms.

"A merry Christmas and a happy New Year! little Elsie," he said, kissing her on both cheeks. "Now I have caught you figuratively and literally, my little lady, so what are you going to give me, eh?"

"Indeed, sir, I think you've helped yourself to the only thing I have to give at present," she answered with a merry silvery laugh.

"Nay, give me one, little lady," said he, "one such hug and kiss as I dare say your father gets half-a-dozen times in a day."

She gave it very heartily.

"Ah! I wish you were ten years older," he said as he set her down.

"If I had been, you wouldn't have got the kiss," she replied, smiling archly.

"Now, its my turn," he said, taking something from his pocket. "I expected you'd catch me, and so thought it best to come prepared."

He took her hand, as he spoke, and placed a beautiful little gold thimble on her finger. "There, that's to encourage you in industry."

"Thank you, sir. Oh, it's a little beauty! I must run and show it to papa. But I must not forget my politeness," she added, hastily throwing open the drawing room door. "Come in, Mr. Travilla."

She waited quietly until the usual greetings were exchanged, then went up to her father and showed her new gift.

He quite entered into her pleasure, and remarked, with a glance at Miss Stevens, that her "friends were very kind."

The lady's hopes rose. He was then pleased with her attention to his child, even though he did not altogether approve her choice of a gift.

There was a large party to dinner that day, and the children came down to the dessert. Miss Stevens, who had contrived to be seated next to Mr. Dinsmore, made an effort, on the entrance of the juveniles, to have Elsie placed on her other side. But Mr. Travilla was too quick for her, and had his young favorite on his knee before she could gain her attention.

The lady was disappointed, and Elsie herself only half satisfied, but the two gentlemen, who thoroughly understood Miss Stevens and saw through all her maneuvers, exchanged glances of amusement and satisfaction.

After dinner Mr. Travilla invited Elsie, Carry, Lucy, and Mary, to take a ride in his carriage, which invitation was joyfully accepted by all—Mr. Dinsmore giving a ready consent to Elsie's request to be permitted to go.

They had a very merry time, for Mr. Travilla quite laid himself out for their entertainment, and no one knew better than he how to amuse ladies of their age.

It was nearly dark when they returned, and Elsie went at once to her room to be dressed for the evening. But she found it unoccupied—Aunt Chloe, as it afterward appeared, having gone down to the quarter to carry some of the little girl's gifts to one or two who were too old and feeble to come up to the house to receive them.

Elsie rang the bell, waited a little, and then, feeling impatient to be dressed, ran down to the kitchen to see what had become of her nurse.

A very animated discussion was going on there, just at that moment, between the cook and two or three of her sable companions, and the first words that reached the child's ears, as she stood on the threshold, were, "I tell you, you old darkie, you dunno nuffin' 'bout it! Massa Horace gwine marry dat bit ob paint an' finery!" "No such ting! Massa's got more sense."

The words were spoken in a most scornful tone, and Elsie, into whose childish mind the possibility of her father's marrying again had never entered, stood spellbound with astonishment.

But the conversation went on, the speakers quite unconscious of her vicinity.

It was Pompey's voice that replied.

"Ef Marse Horace don't like her, what for they been gwine ridin' ebery afternoon? Will you tell me dat, darkies? An' don't dis chile see him sit beside her mornin', noon, an' night, laughin' an' talkin' at de table an' in de parlor? An' don't she keep a kissin' little Miss Elsie, an' callin' her pretty critter, sweet critter, an' de like?"

"She ma to our sweet little Miss Elsie! Bah! I tell you, Pomp, Marse Horace got more sense," returned the cook, indignantly.

"Aunt Chloe don't b'lieve no such stuff," put in another voice. "She says Marse Horace couldn't put such trash in her sweet young mistis's place."

"Aunt Chloe's a berry fine woman, no doubt," observed Pomp disdainfully, "but I reckon Marse

Horace ain't gwine to infide his matermonical intentions to her, and I consider it quite consequential on Marster's being young and handsome that he will take another wife."

The next speaker said something about his having lived a good while without, and though Miss Stevens was setting her cap, maybe he wouldn't be caught. But Elsie only gathered the sense of it, hardly heard the words, and, bounding away like a frightened deer to her own room, her little heart beating wildly with a confused sense of suffering, she threw herself on the bed. She shed no tears, but there was, oh, such a weight on her heart, such a terrible though vague sense of the instability of all earthly happiness.

There Chloe found her, and wondered much what ailed her darling, what made her so silent, and yet so restless, and caused such a deep flush on her cheek. She feared she was feverish, her little hand was so hot and dry, but Elsie insisted that she was quite well, and so Chloe tried to think it was only fatigue.

She would feign have persuaded the little girl to lie still upon her bed and rest, and let her tea be brought to her there, but Elsie answered that she would much rather be dressed, and join her young companions in the nursery. They, too, wondered what ailed her, she was so very quiet and ate almost nothing at all. They asked if she was sick. She only shook her head. Was she tired, then? Yes, she believed she was, and she leaned her head wearily on her hand.

But, indeed, most of the party seemed dull. They had gone through such a round of pleasure and excitement, for the last two or three days, that now a reaction was beginning, and they wanted rest, especially the very little ones, who all retired quite early, when Elsie and her mates joined their parents in the drawing room.

Elsie looked eagerly around for her father, the moment she entered the room. He was beside Miss Stevens, who was at the piano, performing a very difficult piece of music. He was leaning over her, turning the leaves, and apparently listening with a great deal of pleasure, for she was really a fine musician.

Elsie felt sick at heart at the sight — although a few hours before it would have given her no concern — and she found it very difficult to listen to and answer the remarks Mrs. Carrington was making to her about her Christmas presents, and the nice ride they had had that afternoon.

Mr. Travilla was watching her. He had noticed, as soon as she came in, the sad and troubled look which had come over her face, and, following the glance of her eyes, he guessed at the cause.

He knew there was no danger of the trial that she feared, and would have been glad to tell her so, but he felt that it was too delicate a subject for him to venture on — it might seem too much like meddling in Mr. Dinsmore's affairs. But he did the next best thing — got the four little girls into a corner, and tried to entertain them with stories and charades.

Elsie seemed interested for a time, but every now and then her eyes would wander to the other side of the room, where her father still stood listening to Miss Stevens' music.

At length Mr. Travilla was called away to give his opinion about some tableaux the young ladies were arranging. And Elsie, knowing it was her usual time for retiring, and not caring to avail herself of her father's permission to stay up until nine o'clock, stole quietly away to her room unobserved by anyone, and feeling as if Miss Stevens had already robbed her of her father.

She wiped away a few quiet tears, as she went, and was very silent and sad, while her mammy was preparing her for bed. She hardly knew how to do without her goodnight kiss, but feeling as she did, it had seemed quite impossible to ask for it while Miss Stevens was so near him.

When she knelt down to pray, she became painfully conscious that a feeling of positive dislike to that lady had been creeping into her heart, and she asked earnestly to be enabled to put it away. But she prayed, also, that she might be spared the trial that she feared, if God's will were so, and she thought surely it was because she had found out that Miss Stevens was not good, not truthful, nor sincere.

"Perhaps dear papa will come to say goodnight before I am asleep," she murmured to herself as, calmed and soothed by thus casting her burden on the Lord, she laid her head upon her pillow.

He, however, had become interested in the subject of the tableaux, and did not miss his little girl until the sound of the clock striking ten reminded him of her. He looked around expecting to see her still in the room, but, not seeing her, he asked Lucy Carrington where she was.

"Oh!" said Lucy. "She's been gone these two hours, I should think! I guess she must have gone to bed."

"Strange that she did not come to bid me goodnight," he exclaimed in a low tone, more as if thinking aloud than speaking to Lucy.

He hastily left the room.

Mr. Travilla followed.

"Dinsmore," said he.

Mr. Dinsmore stopped, and Travilla, drawing him to one side, said in an undertone, "I think my little friend is in trouble tonight."

"Ah!" he exclaimed, with a startled look. "What can it be? I did not hear of any accident — she has not been hurt? Is not sick? Tell me, Travilla, quickly, if anything ails my child."

"Nothing, nothing, Dinsmore, only you know servants will talk, and children have ears, and eyes, too, sometimes, and I saw her watching you tonight with a very sad expression."

"Nonsense!" exclaimed Mr. Dinsmore, growing very red and looking extremely vexed. "I wouldn't have had such thoughts put into the child's head for any money. Are you sure of it, Travilla?"

"I am sure she was watching you very closely tonight, and looking very miserable."

"Poor darling!" murmured the father. "Thank you, Travilla," shaking his friend heartily by the hand. "Good night. I shall not be down again if you will be so good as to excuse me to the others."

And he went up the stairs almost at a bound, and the next moment was standing beside his sleeping child, looking anxiously down at the little flushed cheeks and tear-swollen eyes, for, disappointed that he did not come to bid her good night, she had cried herself to sleep.

"Poor darling!" he murmured again, as he stooped over her and kissed away a tear that still trembled on her eyelash.

He longed to tell her that all her fears were groundless, and that none other could ever fill her place in his heart, but he did not like to wake her, and so, pressing another light kiss on her cheek, he left her to dream on unconscious of his visit.

The End